For Andrew Briggs and Roger Wagner

Contents

"The l   ind the vivid
descri   his amid the
excitei...   ... ... on the loose. A truly
wonderful read, and of course I could not escape thinking
about our own museum in London, albeit, that is, on a smaller
scale. I encourage readers to enjoy the novel and to savour the
interview at the culmination of the book."
SHAIN FITZGERALD, DIRECTOR, THE ROYAL INSTITUTION

"A r rder, a dodo, a fantastical scientific setting all wrapped up
      : mystery. A fabulous read."

      EW BRIGGS, AUTHOR AND PROFESSOR OF
      MATERIALS AT THE UNIVERSITY OF OXFORD

      Golding has a great storytelling gift; she writes with
      iveness and brio, telling a tale packed with incident but
      imping on detail and atmosphere."

      NEWBERY, AUTHOR OF *THE KEY TO FLAMBARDS*

      strange, vast and wonderfully imagined museum, an
      ntice sculptor and student scientist must solve a murder.
      Golding has written a gripping helter-skelter story that
      ep you guessing and start you thinking."

      WAGNER, ARTIST AND PAINTER

      mythical alternative history where girls are forbidden
          Ree and her trusty dodo solve a murder in the science
museum. Action-packed with themes from across the history of
science, th : book is sure to delight young and older readers alike."
PROFESS   . A. LOUIS, RUDOLPH PEIERLS CENTRE FOR
THEORETICAL PHYSICS

"Julia Golding has created a truly wonderful exploration of what it means to be human. From the outset we are invited to consider the realities of life in times gone by in a world that draws on our own history.

But the mysterious world of the museum also introduces a fascinating distinction, prompting us to imagine a place where asking certain types of question is praised, while other questions are scorned or even forbidden. Through the enquiring eyes of Ree and Henri we discover how asking all kinds of questions is not only necessary for investigating a crime, but fundamental to being human.

The fascinating characters we meet in *The Curious Crime* show us how all human endeavours, including art, music, poetry, science, engineering, and religion are connected by creativity, imagination, and an insatiable quest for better understanding of the world around us.

This extraordinary book encourages us to consider the mysteries of humanity from the bonds of friendship and family to the wonders of our world and the universe of which we are a part. This story will inspire and empower readers to ask questions, explore their world and take their place in the irresistible search for answers handed down from one generation of humans to the next."

STEPH BRYANT AND LIZZIE HENDERSON, THE FARADAY INSTITUTE FOR SCIENCE AND RELIGION

The Curious Crime

by
Julia Golding

LION
CHILDREN'S

Published by
Lion Hudson Limited
Wilkinson House, Jordan Hill Business Park
Banbury Road, Oxford OX2 8DR, England
www.lionhudson.com

ISBN 9780 7459 7787 4
e-ISBN 9780 7459 7788 1

First edition 2018

A catalogue record for this book is available from the British Library

Printed and bound in the UK, August 2018, LH 26

Part III: Cenozoic   187

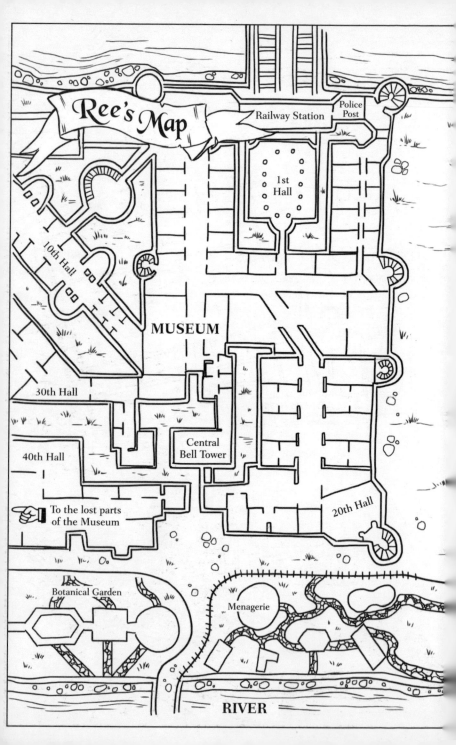

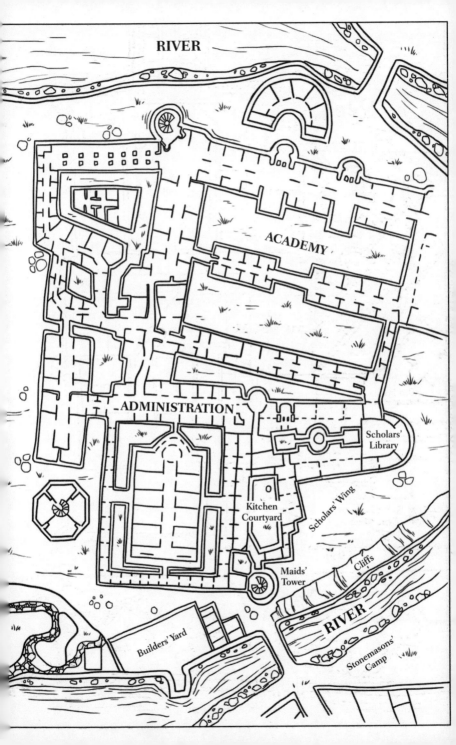

RIVER

ACADEMY

ADMINISTRATION

Scholars'
Library

Kitchen
Courtyard

Scholars' Wing

Cliffs

Maids'
Tower

RIVER

Builders' Yard

Stonemasons'
Camp

Part I

Palaeozoic

Palaeozoic era: from the Greek *palaios*, meaning "old", and *zoe*, meaning "life".

Extract from Henri's notebooks

Chapter 1

Of Dodos and Men

There was a creature trapped in the rock.

Ree ran her fingers over the capital stone, feeling for the shape that lay just under the surface. A fin like a shark. Spindly hind legs like a frog. A beast that inhabited two worlds, walking out of the water to colonize land. The desire to release it burned in her chest as she took up her chisel. She loved this moment just before she began to carve her picture.

But what were the eyes like? The museum fossils gave no clues. Perched on the scaffolding, Ree looked beneath her at the display case covered with a sheet. Scuffing at a corner with the toe of her boot, she pushed the cotton aside. Exactly as she remembered, the stuffed turtle gazed mournfully up at her. Eyes like that would be perfect for the creature she was carving, she thought, imagining it leaving the tropical sea for the last time.

The dodo perched on the scaffold next to Ree croaked and

deposited a dropping on the planks.

"Philoponus, behave," murmured Ree, picking up her mallet, "or do I have to put you back in your pen?"

Her friend, the last known survivor of the species, made a deep grumble before he pecked up a fragment of stone she had already chiselled off. He hated it when she stopped paying full attention to him and concentrated on her craft.

"Are you sure you should be eating that?" she asked absent-mindedly.

Phil stretched his neck, his long broad beak with its hooked end pointing at the vaulted glass ceiling. He shook himself. Downy grey feathers flew.

Ree sneezed. "Idiotic overgrown pigeon. Look, I've got to work and you know it." Settling the wooden handle of the chisel in her palm, she raised the mallet and gave a tap to the well-worn end. The blade cut into the sandstone, releasing a trickle of dust. Her fingertips caressed the gritty surface, wiping it clean. Her father had taught her that each block she worked already had its own ideas about what it should become. She had to ease the picture out, not force it against its will.

The boards creaked as her father, the foreman of the works, approached. A stocky man, nose bent on the bridge, he moved with the even pace of one who knew things should not be rushed. His knees clicked as he crouched beside his daughter.

"How is your project coming along, Ree?"

She took a swig from her water bottle to clear her throat. "Good, Da. I've decided to do the animals moving out of the water onto land – you know, like the guides tell the visitors?"

"That's grand." James Altamira scratched Philoponus's neck, causing the bird to shiver with delight and lean heavily on the chief stonemason. The dodo really was the most affectionate, if attention-seeking, creature. "But keep your hat on right and tight, darlin'. Lord John and the trustees are making a surprise inspection some time this week."

With a sigh, Ree picked up her cap and pulled it down over her ears, tucking her plaits inside. She wanted to cut her hair short but her father insisted she keep it long, ready for the day when she would have to go back to wearing women's clothes. It was a dickens of a pain though because the dodo thought it funny to pluck off the cap when she least expected. The dangerous joke had grown very tired. She had given up wearing the cap this morning, trusting that her high position would keep her hidden.

"Don't even think about it," she warned Phil, recognizing the look in his pale eyes, black pupils dilated. Most people would mistake the expression as wide-eyed innocence. She knew it to be mischief. "You'll get me into hot water."

Ree took a few more taps, feeling a little self-conscious with her father observing, even though she was used to playing "Reece", his gifted "son" and apprentice. Girls were not allowed to work as stonemasons. Thanks to their professional bond, none of her fellow craftsmen would give her away, but the museum authorities would be horrified to know that some of the best carvings had been done by a female of the species. This, as Ree told Phil many times, was a cork-brained prejudice that should be popped out of people's heads so her skill could flow freely.

Ree's thoughts branched off in another direction. "What if Lord John wants to speak to me, Da? You know how Lord Hoity-toity loves to talk to us, pretending he can do what we do."

"Well, he tries hard." Her father grimaced, tugging on one end of his rust-brown moustache.

"You had to redo that stonework he slapped together for the central column as soon as he went back to his mansion for the evening. And he was so pleased with himself, thinking he'd done a good job."

"Darlin', you have to learn that the masters must be kept happy if we're to have a job. What harm does it do anyone if he feels he's one of us?"

"He's not really though, is he?"

Her father shrugged, refusing to debate the issue. "And if he does quiz you during the inspection, then I'll say you're shy." Father and daughter exchanged a grin. Ree was many things but shy was not one of them.

"Bloomin' high-ups."

"I know you don't like Lord John, Ree, but he's a good man. He allows us to let loose our imagination and invent our own designs. He says he wants this to be a cathedral to man's creativity."

"Just man's though." Ree raised her chisel to the uncut surface but then lowered it. It was never a good idea to work when angry.

Her father squeezed her shoulder. "It won't always be like this. In fact, it wasn't like this when I was young. Girls went to school. Some entered the professions. There was even a lady doctor in the museum, they say."

She had heard him say such things before. It sounded like a fairy tale to her. "And now a lady doctor would be even rarer than the dodo."

James Altamira frowned. "I'm optimistic. Good sense will prevail. You just have to be patient."

"I know, Da." She shouldn't burden him with her frustrations. But how much longer would she have to wait for things to change? At thirteen, she could just about get away with hiding her plaits under her cap, but in a few years she'd no longer be able to hide; she'd have to wear skirts and leave behind the job she loved. Still, that wasn't Da's fault. She touched a fingertip to one side of his frown, hoping to make him cheer up.

He rewarded her with a genuine smile and kissed the tip of her finger. "Good lass. Remember the danger. Keep your ears and eyes open." With a final tug on her cap, he headed for the ladder, descended to the museum floor, and crossed to his own column. Ree waved at him as he settled to work and received a salute in reply. They sat above the heads of the visitors like monkeys in the treetops, other stonemasons hidden away in far corners working on their own carvings. Visitors wouldn't even know the workers were there, high in the roped-off sections of the vast entrance hall. It was the most perfect feeling she knew.

Time passed swiftly as Ree lost herself in her project, creating magic in taps and scrapes. School parties came and went, boys with scrubbed faces and dirty knees, fingering marbles in their pockets with the click-click of the desperate to play. They twittered like flocks of parrots over the fossilized dinosaur bones and yawned like lions through the descriptions of how one species came from another in a vast tree of life.

The sun climbed, hot on the back of Ree's neck through the glass ceiling. Phil went to sleep, his head tucked under one stubby wing.

"Where did it all begin?" The question floated up to Ree in her treehouse. She peeked over the edge to see an earnest little boy with straw-coloured hair standing by a museum guide. The guides had to keep their charges close as it was easy to get lost in the labyrinthine building. The authorities had introduced strict protocols after one overseas guest had gone astray and only been found a week later trapped in an underground storage room. He died that same night in hospital, having consumed poisonous mushroom specimens in his hunger.

"All what begin, young man?" asked the guide.

"Life," said the boy.

"We don't know."

The boy looked hopefully up at him. "Then do you know why are we alive, sir? What does it all mean?"

Ree heard the harsh intake of breath; the balding crown of the guide's head reddened. He summoned the accompanying schoolmaster with a toot on his silver whistle. "We do not ask 'why', only 'how'. You should be aware of this by now, boy."

The teacher hurried over. "Yes, sir?"

"How old is this child?"

"Seven, sir."

"Old enough. What are you teaching your students? This child asked a forbidden question."

The schoolmaster cuffed the boy on the ear. "Please accept my humblest apologies, Mr Shelley. Maxwell will be punished when we return to school."

"I'm not sure that is good enough," huffed the offended guide.

The schoolmaster seized hold of Maxwell's ear and twisted the lobe. "Tell the gentleman what I taught you."

Maxwell squeaked with pain.

"Go on!"

"That we only study ev-dence. We do not theorize or specky-late about things that cannot be tested in a lab-rattery." The little boy stumbled over the words in his alarm. "We will not fall into the errors of the p…past."

The schoolmaster released the boy's ear. "They repeat that every morning, as instructed by the government."

"It is not enough to chant words; they must understand them too." Shelley frowned down at the child. "I expect you to learn your lesson properly. I will send guardians to your school to test you next week on the museum-approved curriculum. Understand, boy? You will lose your place in your class if you fail. No crying now. Crying is for girls, not young scholars."

Ree "specky-lated" about the chances of getting away with throwing one of Phil's droppings at the guide but decided it was too risky.

"Run along now and mind your teacher." The guide made a note in his pocket book of the boy's name and school. "Nip such curiosity in the bud, sir, that's what you have to do."

"I will," said the schoolmaster. "Maxwell will pass the examination, I promise you."

"He had better or it might not only be his school career on the line." The guide stalked away, his rolled umbrella brandished over his head like a captain's cutlass ordering his sailors to swing into battle. "Follow me, scholars."

"Did you hear that blinkin' dust-sucker?" Ree asked the dodo. *"Crying is for girls."* She mimicked his nasal voice. Her father had warned her to steer clear of Simplicius Shelley, the guide who had torn a strip off boy and teacher. Shelley was ambitious, hungry for promotion from the assistant curator level of guide. He had his sights set on being a full curator and maybe one distant day even museum chancellor, answerable only to the trustees. To prove his worth he came down hard on the least infraction of the rules. A girl sitting with a chisel in her hand was as clear a contravention of the laws as you could get.

So her revenge would be to carry on working. Ree blew on the surface of her carving to loosen any dust that stuck to the emerging shape. She had finished the creature and was now working on the curve of the wave where it met the beach. A starfish would look perfect in a rock pool. She had never seen one by the sea, being city bred, but she had looked at the live specimens in one of the rooms dedicated to the seashore: a beautiful pink creature, splayed like a baby's hand reaching out to its mother's breast.

A blast of cold air swirled the dust and feathers of her platform into a little twister.

"Snakes and ladders, some pea-brain has opened the main doors!" muttered Ree, grabbing the jacket she had taken off earlier and making it into a tent to shelter Phil. The scaffolding rattled and swayed. Everyone who worked here knew that the grand entrance should only be opened when all the other doors to the entrance hall were carefully closed and bolted. Through-draughts slammed doors and windows, shattered glass, brought exhibits down off the walls. Just last month an open door had resulted in one schoolboy being skewered by an iron-age spear in the prehistoric weapons room. It fell from its rusted wires and went through his foot, pinning him like a beetle to a board. There was a good reason why parents had to sign danger waivers when their sons came on a visit to Museum Island.

A burble of angry voices grew in strength, competing with the banging of doors and shattering of glass in distant parts of the building. Guides were piping on their silver whistles like a flock of distressed widgeons.

"You cannot keep out the truth!" a man shouted.

An invasion! Ree lay on her stomach and peeked over the edge, eyes scrunched against the swirling dust, hand clapped to her hat to keep it in place. A crowd of men and women dressed in white surged through the main doors and linked hands around the skeleton of the diplodocus. Their loose clothing flapped, the women's long hair getting loose and streaming in the wind. The spokesman, memorable for his red sideburns and moustache, stood by the dinosaur's bony snout. The guides gathered ineffectually by the entrance, braced against the wind that whipped their black robes, but they were outnumbered. Not for long, though: the whistles would summon the museum police.

A pellet of stone hit her forearm. Rubbing the spot, Ree looked up. Her father was waving at her from his platform, telling her to scoot back out of sight, plainly worried that she would draw attention to herself. She retreated an inch but she wasn't going to miss out on witnessing the battle.

The leader lifted the hands linked to his, almost as if he was about to start playing the child's game "In and Out the Dusty Bluebells", but his intention was far from playful.

"Listen, friends! The authorities are leading you astray, making this once great institution into a place of dry bones. We children of Theophilus demand it be returned to its true purpose. A belief in God is not incompatible with the work done here. Rather, we must look for the finger of God in the laws of nature themselves!"

Newton's apple! thought Ree. She was hearing an actual member of the Theophilus movement preach! She thought all religious types went extinct when the scientific authorities had dismissed the idea of gods and goddesses. These were treasonous words!

Panic struck the other visitors. They knew they could be judged guilty even for listening to such talk. Teachers herded boys out of the emergency exits so they would not have their ears polluted.

"Do not be afraid to look for meaning in the signs left for us to read," bellowed the man, straining to make his voice rise above the commotion. "To ask 'why?' is to be human."

A thudding on the steps leading up to the main entrance sounded like the outbreak of a spring storm. The police were coming. The scaffolding juddered and a plank fell away. Ree drew further back, clinging on to one of the corner posts, concerned now for her own safety. As police clashed with protestors, a ragged scrum formed; it barged into the base of her work platform. The scaffolding lurched one way, then another, buffeted by the struggle below. Then a concerted push by the police forced the protestors hard against it and the scaffolding started to topple.

"Philoponus!" cried Ree.

Hanging on to the post for dear life, she was flung through the air. The top of the tower landed with a splintering crash on the tiles of the floor many feet below. The case containing the turtle exploded in a shower of glass, the stuffed creature thrown on its back in a sea of shards. Philoponus made use of his stubby wings and managed to flutter clear at the last moment, making a better landing than Ree. Lying among the splinters, she heard the whacks as the police wielded truncheons to break up the protestors. Screams of women and yells of men rang through the hall as the members of the Theophilus movement were hauled away to the lockups beneath. Four officers were required to subdue the leader, who was still shouting his protests. Close to Ree, an unconscious woman was dragged away by the arms, tumbled hair brushing across the tiles.

Phil prodded Ree with his beak, crooning in distress.

"I'm… all right," she managed.

20

"Ree!" Her father was at her side, making a quick check for broken bones. "Oh Darwin's beard, are you hurt?"

Mr Shelley ran up, black cloak streaked with stone dust. "Is the boy dead? Injured?"

"No, no." Ree could hear the catch in her father's voice and the frantic fumbling as he pulled her cap straight. "He's... he's just stunned, is all."

"Let me summon the doctor. He might have a head injury – those can be very dangerous."

"Thank you, sir, but I'll make sure sh... he gets the right attention. I think I'd better carry Reece clear of this mess. I'll get my men to tidy up at once so you can resume your schedule for visits."

This suggestion cleverly turned the guide from his intention of calling the doctor. "Yes, indeed; the march of scientific progress must not be slowed by the interference of those rebels."

Ow, thought Ree, flexing her fingers, preparing for the painful moment when she would have to get up.

Her da waited for Shelley to retreat before issuing his orders. "Jan, can you see that this scaffolding is cleared? I'm taking Ree home for the day."

"Of course, James," said Jan Simplon, her da's second-in-command of the stonemasons.

"Is Ree all right?" asked Jan's son, Paul, Ree's fellow apprentice and friend.

"Will be, I'd say," said her father.

"I'm fine, Da," Ree protested, trying to sit up.

"No, lass, *lad*, after a near miss like that, my heart can't take seeing you carry on as if nothing's happened. You take the rest of the day off – and that's an order."

Ree knew he was referring as much to the near miss of exposure as to her fall. "All right. But can I sit somewhere with Phil rather than go home?"

"You and that daft bird." Her da smiled, colour returning to

21

his ashen face. "Take him somewhere quiet – and keep out of the way!" He brushed dust from her nose. "You're a mess, son."

"So what's new?"

He smiled and turned to supervise the stonemasons, asking Paul to collect up her scattered tools. Hobbling, Ree retreated to one of the less-visited balconies and watched as the planks and poles were cleared. Her body felt bruised and her palms had a few new cuts, but clinging on to the pole had saved her the worst of the impact. She was still a little shaky, however, and so was Phil. She stroked his soft chest as he huddled against her.

"It's all right, Phil."

He huffed.

"The protestors? The museum authorities won't kill them, only sentence them to transportation to the other side of the world."

Phil poked her in her sore ribs, trying to get as close as possible.

"Hey, need to breathe here." She turned his beak to a less painful position. "Those Theophilus people – I wonder why they do it? They're fighting for a lost cause, aren't they?"

Phil gave one of his low grumbles.

"Do you want me to take you back to your pen?"

He nudged her in the armpit. She took that as a sign that he wanted to stay and be hugged.

"All right then, you soppy old bird." Ree took comfort from the sensation of the warm bundle resting in the cradle made by her crossed legs. The dodo wasn't that old really. Rescued as a chick five years ago by a collector on a scientific voyage to Mauritius, Philoponus had been hand-reared until he was donated to the museum. He now lived in the menagerie of rare creatures but had never quite adjusted to the idea that he was a zoo animal rather than a person. When given the choice, he elected to be with humans rather than the ostrich and rhea who shared his enclosure. Ree suspected he looked down on the other two flightless birds as being decidedly below his intelligence.

She patted her pockets and came across a slice of dried apple that Phil hadn't yet found. She fed it to him, careful not to get nipped by the hooked end of his beak. He didn't mean to hurt her, but he really didn't know exactly how powerful his beak was when he snapped up a treat. Scars from their earliest encounters joined the callouses left by chisels. Examining them now, Ree saw that hers were unmistakably a working girl's hands.

Ree looked back at her carving, on the pillar just across from her position in the balcony. A new shape was emerging from the stone. *We must look for the finger of God in the laws of nature themselves*, the man had said. Even if there were no gods anymore, she couldn't help but see a hand reaching down, nudging the creature onto the shore. It was buried in the rock and it wanted out.

She was creating this decoration, wasn't she? Summoning something from stony nothing. It always felt a little like performing magic. Why not leave a tribute to the maker like an artist's signature on a portrait? Ree hummed to herself, holding up her right hand in the gap between the balcony and her carving. Oh yes, that was exactly what the stone wanted to say. The creator's hand would be female.

Chapter 2
Lord John Interrupts

Henri Volp was running late, but he couldn't tear himself away until he had worked out what had gone wrong with his experiment. Detection was his passion, and he had been working on a kit to identify materials left behind at crime scenes. He'd successfully come up with a test for differentiating between human and animal bloodstains, and a promising method for identifying some poisons, but this last substance that he had on his workbench was defeating him. Why had he included it in the samples? He had been so busy revising for his end of term exams that he'd rather lost track of things. Laboratory tidiness wasn't his strong point: Henri would be the first to admit that. He scratched at it with a fingernail. What was it? To the touch it didn't give anything away, remaining just a greyish white lump. Bone? No, that wasn't right.

"Hey, *amigo*, you'll miss the start of the exam!" called Ramon, a Spanish scholar in his year. He thumped on the door as he thundered down the stairs outside Henri's room. "Hurry up!"

Crouched on the desk with her tail wrapped around her feet, Henri's crab-eating macaque stared at him with her solemn hazel eyes. On permanent loan from the menagerie, Zena had become his best friend since Henri arrived at the academy. The two white patches on the monkey's brows and pensive expression gave her an air of wisdom, but Henri knew that Zena was just waiting for him to entertain her.

"What do you think this is?" he asked her.

Chattering away in her own language, she reached out and picked a piece of fluff off his scholar's robes – one of her own gingery hairs, he guessed. Zena took her grooming duties seriously.

Henri glanced up at the academy clock tower. Three minutes until he had to be in the examinations hall. He hated leaving any mystery unsolved. "I'll never be able to concentrate if I don't get to the bottom of this. I'll just run a quick test. Let's see how it reacts to good old H_2O."

Something was nagging at the back of Henri's mind, some early experience of chemistry. With a geometry exam to attend, he didn't have time to follow that inkling to its end. Settling protective glasses over his eyes, he picked up the white rock with tweezers and dropped it into a beaker of water.

Bang! Flames shot up eyebrow high from the beaker. Zena screeched and jumped to the mantlepiece. Henri nearly squawked and jumped too, but stopped himself as the flames were spreading. His notes! They'd caught fire. Smoke filled his illegal laboratory. He dashed for the bucket of water, thought better of it, and went for the tub of sand. He tipped it over the smouldering remains of his test. He'd be roasted by his tutors for setting up an experiment outside the academy laboratories and in his rooms, no less. He had to get this under control before anyone smelled the smoke. Finally, he succeeded, with the loss of several pieces of equipment, a week's worth of careful notes, and a scorched desktop.

"Well, that went well." Heart pounding, Henri patted himself to extinguish the embers burning holes in his clothing. "I am an idiot! What a beginner's mistake. A piece of pure sodium – how could I not recognize it?" He scrubbed at his short curly hair, checking it wasn't burning. "But it's not found naturally – wasn't on my samples list. How on earth did it get there?"

Zena chattered away, agitatedly shredding one of Henri's candle spills in nimble fingers.

Realization dawned as to who was the saboteur. "Zena?"

The monkey leaped up on top of the wardrobe and hid. She was a notorious thief. Henri could have kicked himself for not suspecting her meddling in his chemistry kit, mixing up his various experiments. She could've seriously injured them both.

"Don't blame the monkey," Henri muttered, making a final check that nothing was still on fire and there was no more mischief for Zena to do in his absence. "Blame the monkey owner." He grabbed his satchel and sprinted for the examinations hall.

Last to arrive, Henri was stopped at the door by one of the junior students.

"Henri?" Hans Orsted, a Danish student with a gift for physics, had clearly been waiting for him.

Henri looked anxiously over the boy's head. Everyone else was seated and the exam paper had already been handed out. "What is it, Hans? I'm supposed to be in there, you know?"

"Yes, but it's Rainbow. Someone killed my mouse."

"What? You mean, like a cat?" Hans never went anywhere without his mouse in a pocket so it was hard to imagine when a cat could have had the opportunity to get to it.

"No, as in *murdered* – by a person." Hans gulped. "Someone cut her head off."

Master Ricardo, the teacher overseeing the exam, stamped his wooden rod on the floor, causing all the candidates in the examinations hall to jump.

"Volp!" He lingered over the "v" sound of Henri's surname with vicious pleasure. "Are you going to join us for this little matter of a test of your grasp of Euclidean geometry, or do you insist on gossiping like an old woman over the garden fence?"

Henri gave Hans an apologetic look. "I'll come and find you as soon as I've finished here. Keep the... er... evidence to show me, all right?"

Hans nodded miserably. "I will."

"Sorry, I have to go." Henri hurried into the room and took his place near the back.

"Now, if our senior scholar will allow, let us begin our examination," sneered Ricardo. "You may turn your papers over now."

An hour into the ninety-minute exam, Henri had already finished. He'd always found geometry logical and therefore simple stuff. His brain had turned to wondering what had happened to Hans's mouse. *Decapitation?* Hardly something that could be put down to an accident. He itched to get to the crime scene before it was disturbed. *Where had it happened? When? Why?*

The door at the side of the teacher's platform opened and Lord John strode in, followed by a procession of men in academic gowns and black mortar boards. A flutter like a stiff breeze ran through the room. The trustees. Lord John, instantly recognizable from his glossy reddish brown hair and even bushier sideburns, was already speaking, completely ignoring the signs for "Silence!"

"As you see, gentlemen, the top class of fourth year scholars are taking their end of term examinations. A good crop this year. Very talented."

Master Ricardo shot to his feet. "Boys, all stand!"

Henri and his fellow students stood in a rumble of chair legs on floorboards.

Lord John, the only one in the party dressed in ordinary clothes of tailed jacket, grey trousers, and gold satin waistcoat, waved off the gesture with unconvincing humility. "Please, please, I did not mean to disturb the boys' concentration. Carry on, chaps, carry on."

At a gesture from Ricardo, the exam candidates resumed their seats.

"How are they doing, Ricardo, with…" Lord John picked up a question paper from the desk of the nearest boy just as the unfortunate student was making a measurement with his ruler. "Geometry? By Newton, that was my nightmare when I was sitting in their seats! All those lines and angles quite made my head spin. There's no such thing as a straight line in nature, of course." He put the paper down on the wrong desk and turned away, not seeing the frantic exchange behind his back to put matters to rights.

"They are managing very well, my lord." Ricardo offered Henri as evidence. "If I'm not mistaken, our senior scholar has already finished."

"Has he indeed? Excellent, excellent. Where is this prodigy?" Lord John didn't wait for Ricardo to point him out but strode down the aisle, settling correctly on the boy who had put down his pen. "Ah, the North African boy. Remind me of your name, young man?"

Henri stood up. "Henri Volp, sir."

"Your father is a French diplomat and your mother is from Algiers, isn't she?"

"Yes, sir."

"Quite right, quite right. Selected in our first international competition for youthful talent, if I remember, and awarded the senior scholarship?"

"Correct, sir." It was just as well the entries had been

anonymous; Henri doubted a student from Algeria would have been chosen otherwise.

"Good, good. So you're quite a top chap when it comes to this geometrical business?"

"Sir?"

"Do you have any other talents?"

Henri formed his mouth to say forensic science but Ricardo got there first. "Volp is an all-rounder, sir. I am yet to find an area in which he does not excel."

"Marvellous, marvellous."

Henri wondered why Lord John felt he had to repeat his exclamations twice. Was he working on some mirroring principle, the verbal equivalent of butterfly's wings?

"You must send him to the trustees' tea at four o'clock," said Lord John. "Such scholarship should be rewarded."

"It would be a great honour for him." Ricardo was fairly bursting with pride.

"And you should come along too, Ricardo. The student is only as good as his master, after all."

Well, that demonstrably wasn't true, thought Henri, else there would be no progress in science. As the great Newton said, we stand on the shoulders of giants. And in that company, Ricardo would only qualify as a dwarf.

"Oh, thank you, my lord." The teacher bowed.

With a genial smile at the boys who were still valiantly trying to complete their task like swimmers battling a strong counter-current, Lord John swept from the room, taking the trustees with him.

Ricardo walked back to the front of the room, a new bounce in his step. "In view of the interruption, scholars, I will allow you another ten minutes to complete the paper."

But mouse murder! Annoyed by the delay to the start of his investigation, Henri groaned and began setting out on rough paper his theories as to what might have killed Hans's pet.

Ree decided to come late to the entrance hall, as her father and his fellow stonemasons were moving the scaffolding now they had finished their carvings. She had been told she would only be in the way. She took the opportunity to do a long overdue wash and string their shirts between their hut and a handy tree. Early spring sunshine took the chill from the air as she pegged the snapping damp cloth to the line. Primroses bloomed around the trunk of the birch. She loved those flowers. Her mother had planted them and they came back each year like a little greeting sent from beyond the grave.

Ree had never known any other home than this camp. Years ago, the builders had been allowed a piece of scrubland just across the bridge from Museum Island. Their settlement was supposed to be temporary but the work never seemed to cease. The original tents had become huts and the camp now resembled an army barracks crammed on an unwanted piece of steep riverbank.

Shading her eyes, she stood for a moment to appreciate the magnificent view across the river. She might live on a muddy slope with no piped water or proper roads, but she had the best outlook. There was nowhere else on earth quite like this. Museum Island was the undisputed centre of world science and learning – the jewel in her little nation's crown. In fact, the museum was worth more than the country's armies and navy put together as a source of wealth and influence, thanks to the quality of the work done there. Other nations squabbled and fought, but all agreed to leave Ree's land untouched so that the museum's work, so beneficial to mankind, could continue. Where the museum led, the world followed. The museum chancellor was as powerful today as any pope or Holy Roman Emperor in the Middle Ages had ever been.

An early mist lingered, smudging the buildings to shades of grey, blue, and violet. The bulk of the island dominated the city, with six bridge-legs reaching it from different points, making it appear like a water monster sculling on the river. The island had once housed a temple, then a cathedral, and finally the curators had taken over and dedicated it to science. With many towers and pinnacles, the museum had no regularity for the eye to trace. It had become too big for any one person to know. Ree was only familiar with the first few rooms and their antechambers by the entrance hall where the stonemasons worked. The rest remained a mystery.

Checking with a tug that the washing was firmly fixed, Ree returned inside to pack a tin box of sandwiches for her father and herself. She packed it in her canvas satchel with some crusts for Phil, then tucked her plaits under her blue cap and started the walk to work. The journey began with a climb up the wooden steps leading to the main thoroughfare. The drains didn't work well here so she had to watch her step, skirting a puddle that glistened with oily rainbow colours. She exchanged greetings with the stallholders along her route, bought some wrinkled apples off a greengrocer for a penny, and a bottle of ginger beer for sixpence. Careful to avoid the carriages and carts clattering over the narrow bridge, she kept near the parapet, jostling with the other pedestrians crossing to the island. On this bridge from the poor end of the city, they were mainly workers and suppliers for the kitchens. The museum had a huge staff as well as an academy of scholars that needed feeding three times a day. The privileged visitors didn't see this side as they usually came across the central bridge from the north bank, travelling by private carriage or steam train.

Reaching the barrier that separated the builders' yard from the kitchen courtyard, Ree touched her cap brim to the guard on the gate. Knowing her well by sight, he let her through with no challenge, merely puffing on his pipe like a mild-tempered dragon guarding a not-very-treasured hoard. Weaving between the stacks of timber and buttery blocks of sandstone, Ree took a diversion to the menagerie. This lay on the south side of the island, so that the smell of the animals and their dung would be swept from the richer parts of town. An iron railing curved in shapes of trees and flowers ringed the enclosure. Ree had a year ago borrowed a key to the supply gate from the head keeper and conveniently forgotten to return it so she had free entrance whenever she wished. It was one of her favourite places in the museum, always with some new creatures to admire and old friends to greet. She nodded to the red colobus monkeys sitting in their trees, poked a lettuce leaf through the wire to the giant tortoises, called a greeting to the Asian elephants and zebra-like quagga in their pen in the middle of the menagerie, and finally reached her destination: the cage for the flightless birds. First she checked that visitors hadn't yet been allowed in; then she scrambled over the eight-foot wall. The lesser rhea and the North African ostrich darted over to the far side like startled duchesses running in ballgowns from an unwanted suitor. Ree had tried to make friends, but they never got beyond their surprise that she should take an interest in them. With the long-term aim of changing their minds, Ree dropped a few of the crusts she had saved in their trough.

"Good morning, Lady Emma, Lady Rachael," she called.

The birds fluttered their plumes.

It was clear that Phil had already left the pen for the day. Theoretically he shouldn't do this, but everyone turned a blind eye as he hopped up the stack of crates his keeper had left strategically placed by the wall. Mr Billibellary didn't believe in cages. The rhea and the ostrich had never shown Phil's exploratory spirit so no one had challenged the arrangement.

Ree used the crates to climb out and drop to the ground. Phil managed this with a kind of controlled plummet, stubby wings outstretched, and it was a shame she had missed this today as it always made her laugh. But where was he now? She found Mr Billibellary feeding rats to the Indian python. The snake lay like languid strung bunting along the branch of the dead tree, the only ornament in its cage. Two unfortunate rats sniffed nervously below. Ree quickly resolved she would not be here when the python decided it was dinnertime.

"Good morning, sir. Where's Philoponus got to?"

"Gone walkabout, mate," said Mr Billibellary, giving her an easy smile that deepened the lines on his much-wrinkled face. Originally from an Aboriginal settlement in Australia, he had the darkest skin of anyone Ree had yet met, contrasting starkly with his halo of white hair and beard. On the rare occasions when Ree got him talking, he was full of stories of his people and his own long walkabout around the world. "That cheeky bird got wind that the first kitchen is laying out a bonzer tea for the trustees."

"Uh-oh."

"No worries. Whatever Phil's got planned, he'll get away with it. That bird is everyone's pet."

Ree smiled and shook her head. "I've always thought he regarded us all as his."

"You may be right about that, mate."

A bell rang and the gates to the menagerie opened. The school parties poured in, eager for their reward after the museum tour. This was why the authorities had decided the zoo would only open in the afternoon: the antics of the animals had proved too much of a distraction from the sober science inside.

"I'd best get to work," Ree said.

"See you tomorrow, Reece." Billibellary stowed the empty rat sack in his barrow and wheeled it in the opposite direction to the visitors.

As the python began to unspool from its branch, Ree hurried off through the crowds, keeping her head down. Taking a back door into the museum, she cut through a series of complex interlinking quadrangles and emerged in the entrance hall, which was built on the far side of the island to the menagerie. She slipped in a side entrance wedged between two glass cases of dinosaur footprints only to find her father still overseeing the erection of a scaffolding tower. From the sharpness of his orders, Ree sensed that his mood had turned sour since breakfast.

"I've done the wash, Da, and brought your sandwiches."

Hearing her voice, he turned, grabbed her arm, and marched her away from the other stonemasons.

"Maria, what have you done?"

She gaped. He never used her proper name in public, not unless he had really lost his temper. What could she possibly have done to upset him since breakfast? "What's happened, Da?"

"Your capital stone."

"What's wrong with it?"

"You've carved a hand on it!"

She bit the inside of her lip, trying to work out what was so bad about that. "Don't you like it? I used my own hand as a model."

"It's a very good hand but it can't stay. You'll have to change it at once into the sun or a cloud." He gestured to her pillar and she saw that the scaffold had not been moved. The capital stone she had been working on was now shrouded in cloth.

"But it was just a little joke – I was creating the creatures out of the rock. It was a playful signature: *I did this*."

He stared at her in disbelief. "A joke?"

She nodded slowly. "Yes? Don't those dull old crow guides ever laugh?" They flocked around the museum all day looking so serious. Surely the scientists would welcome some light relief?

Her father took her by the shoulders and gave her a little shake. "Wake up, child. You can't afford to joke about such things! Have you been asleep for the last thirteen years?"

"Da, I don't understand."

"It is forbidden to suggest that any process other than one within nature creates anything: don't you know that?"

Ree wanted to argue that she hadn't suggested that, and she *was* within nature, but his expression warned her that this was not the time for a debate. "I'm sorry."

"They've done away with gods and myths. The guides say that science explains everything – or will do. The museum is dedicated to only what science can prove. Haven't you listened to their speeches?"

"Some. But they're very boring." She remembered the wild energy of the Theophilus protestors. They were the ones to blame for setting her off on this path, though she had not been thinking about God or any myth like that with her picture. She'd been thinking about being a craftswoman, bringing something out of nothing.

"You get up there now and start undoing the damage. And hope that no one notices before it's too late."

"I'll go right now." Ashamed by her stupidity, she handed him the satchel. "Your sandwiches."

He looked down at the bag and then at her. His shoulders sagged. "Oh, darlin', I know you didn't mean any harm." He hugged her to his chest. "It's my fault. I should've kept a closer eye on you."

"The carving will be spoiled if I change it."

"Better spoiled than spotted. Hurry up now." He pushed her in the direction of her scaffold.

Ree quickly scaled the ladder, aware that the other stonemasons were already treating her differently since her mistake came to light. Her fellow apprentice, Paul, wouldn't meet her eye. Until today, he had always regarded her with amused tolerance. That hammered home even more than her father's words that she had done something truly terrible, something that risked them all. Swallowing against the lump in her throat, Ree kneeled before the capital. It was one of her best-ever designs, as good as the squirrel in the oak leaves she had carved on the other side of the hall. She took up the chisel and mallet and began to chip away at the wrist, hastily deciding to refashion the hand into a rough-shaped sun. It was going to be awful – she already knew that.

"Gentlemen, I thought you'd enjoy seeing how the works are progressing." Lord John entered the entrance hall with his flock of scarlet- and black-robed men behind him.

"Oh no," muttered Ree. The inspection her da had told her about a few days ago: of all the bad luck! She began to chisel recklessly at her carving. But stone was not like clay. It could not be hurried. Sweat crept down her spine.

The dodo flutter-hopped off the glass case where he had been observing the visitors like a seagull following the fishing fleet. He landed with a flump beside her.

"Not now, Phil, please!"

The bird nudged her pockets, expectant she would have treats for him.

"Leave me alone!"

He squawked indignantly, not understanding that his friend was in a terrible fix.

"Ah, look up, gentlemen: there's the dodo I told you about," said Lord John, coming to a stop under her platform. "The zookeeper says he's formed an attachment to the stonemasons. Apparently the species requires small pebbles to help digest their diet of fruit, nuts, and shellfish."

"Good gracious! Extraordinary!" murmured the trustees.

Aware he had an audience, Phil puffed his ash-grey feathers and shook his beak.

"A splendid fellow. We have to hope that a female dodo has survived in the wild or you are looking at the last one. Expeditions have been dispatched to discover if we can rescue the species from extinction. Until we get word back, we must make sure no harm comes to this chap."

Lord John was mounting the ladder.

Please, no.

"My lord," called Ree's father. "There's a new design here I'd like you to approve. Your suggestions will make all the difference."

"In a moment, Altamira. Gentlemen, if two or three of you

would like to come up and meet our dodo? I'm afraid we can't accommodate more on this platform." Lord John reached Ree's level and gave her an absent nod. She stood, body hiding her carving, shaking hands linked behind her. "Now, Master Dodo, I expect you to be on your best behaviour. These are important men who want to be introduced to you."

Uncertain of this stranger, Phil shuffled to sit on Ree's feet.

"Ah, I see he has adopted you, boy. Do you have any tips how to make friends?" Lord John's smile was genial. Two more men joined them on the platform, one with a monocle, the other sporting a bristling black beard like a chimney sweep's brush.

"Cat got your tongue, boy?" asked Monocle, frowning at her.

Ree gave a rough bow, not dipping too low in case they glimpsed what was behind her. Feeling in her pocket, she held out the crust to Lord John. Phil tried to snap at it but she passed it over his head.

"Manners maketh man and dodo, Philoponus," said Lord John with a chuckle. "Bribery? I see that all animals are essentially the same."

Ree wanted to warn him to mind the hook on the beak but was scared her voice would give her away.

Her father, fortunately, arrived in the nick of time, head and shoulders appearing at the top of the ladder. "Beware of the beak, sir!"

Lord John lifted his fingers clear just before he gained a scar on his smooth skin. "Gracious me! The dodo might not have retained flight but it was certainly given other evolutionary advantages. I wouldn't like to meet an angry one." He dropped the crust, chuckling as Phil caught it deftly from the air with a clack of his beak. "Wonderful, wonderful." He looked across at the trustees, who were taking in the view of the entrance hall from this vantage point. "One asks how it got up here? Do you know, boy?"

"He hops," said Ree in a low voice.

"Yes, sir, he has worked out some clever routes using the glass cases as stairways. We never know where he's going to crop up next." James edged so that he was standing beside his daughter, a barrier of two before the carving. "I think perhaps we might be exceeding the safety limits on this scaffold, sir, what with five of us up here. Shall we go down?"

"Six. You forget the dodo. He looks like he may weigh as much as your apprentice." Lord John laughed happily.

James joined in the laughter with a strained chuckle. "Not quite, sir."

"It would be a shame to waste this opportunity to look at what you've been doing. Gentlemen, shall we inspect the progress on the capital decoration? I've been encouraging the workmen to let their imaginations run as wild as the old carvers did on medieval cathedrals and colleges."

"I hope you're not letting them put in those ghastly gargoyles? Next thing you know it'll be your face up here, grimacing at the visitors," said Black Beard.

Lord John didn't look too distressed by the suggestion. "It would be my own fault if that happens. Now, boy, stand aside. Let's see what you're carving."

"I'm sorry, sir, but I've made a mess of this one. I was just redoing it," said Ree in as deep a voice as she could manage. "My father's work is far superior and much more worthy of inspection." She was going to be sick if the lord and the trustees didn't leave immediately.

"Reece is right, sir. This isn't a good example of our work," said her father quickly, "and he's very shy."

"Nonsense." Lord John pushed between them. "I can see a very nice starfish by your elbow, Altamira. Don't be ashamed, lad. We'll know that it's only a beginner's piece."

There was silence apart from the scratching of Phil's claws on the planks as he scavenged for crumbs.

"Ah." Lord John was lost for words.

"Good heavens, is that what I think it is?" The monocle dropped from the trustee's eye but he quickly stuffed it back in again before Phil snapped it from its ribbon.

"Altamira, what is the meaning of this?" demanded Lord John.

Ree's nails dug into her palms. "Don't blame my father, sir. I made a mistake."

"You've put the hand of a… a *deity* in one of the museum's supporting columns?" Black Beard looks at Ree as if she had vomited on his polished toecaps. "How dare you?"

"I didn't mean it as a god. I meant it to be me, creating the picture out of the stone."

"Creating!"

Her father squeezed her arm in warning. Somehow she had said the wrong thing. Ree dropped to one knee, head bent in supplication. "Please, sirs, I'm heartily sorry and beg your pardon. Da has explained it was wrong and I was already correcting it when you came. Look at the chisel marks if you don't believe me."

"Likely story," muttered Monocle.

Lord John bent closer. "The boy does appear to be telling the truth. It will be gone before the end of the day, I trust?" he asked her father.

"Yes, sir." James picked up the mallet Ree had dropped. "We'll both work on it. You'll never see it again."

Phil didn't like being ignored. He hopped between Ree and Lord John, shoving his beak in her ear with snapping sounds.

"Well, I suppose there's no harm done, is there? The public haven't seen it, so we can forget about it. Errors of youth and all that."

"Forget? I think not, Lord John. There must at least be an enquiry," said Black Beard.

Getting insufficient response from Ree, Phil grabbed the brim of her cap and pulled it off. Two braids flopped down and swung like bell ropes as she knelt with bent head. He croaked with triumph.

"What on earth!" exclaimed Monocle.

"It's a girl!" squawked Black Beard.

Lord John went very quiet, completely unlike his usual self. "Altamira," he said sadly, "I think you have some explaining to do."

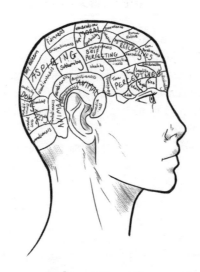

Chapter 3

Never Take a Dodo to a Tea Party

Henri took out his most powerful magnifying glass and examined the junior common room. This was the place from which Rainbow had been taken when Hans let her out for a run the night before. A billiards competition had distracted him and he had lost track of her. Hans said he had assumed she would find her way back as she always did and had not been too worried until it was time for bed. Even then, he had only been anxious she had got lost under the floorboards and had been certain he could tempt her out the next morning. When he came to renew his search before breakfast, he had found her torso lying on a handkerchief in the middle of the billiards table. Blood had soaked through, leaving a nasty stain on the cloth. There was no sign of the head.

"And you're sure it's her?" asked Henri. Sadly there was

little doubt as the mouse had had distinctive caramel and white patches. It had been an engaging little creature.

"Yes, completely. But who would do such a thing?" asked Hans.

"I'm not sure. We all know that the laboratory technicians breed mice for experiments. There's no need to take someone's pet, if that's what this is about." Henri saw that the head had been cut off with a sharp implement, a scalpel most likely, so that ruled out a bite from a cat or some other more natural explanation. "Hans, I think it looks like someone wanted to hurt you. Have you fallen out with anyone recently?"

Hans shook his head.

"Got into trouble?"

Hans sighed. "Nothing out of the ordinary. I got lines from Master Ricardo and a detention from Professor Gall for talking in class."

"Hardly motive for mouse murder," agreed Henri. "But whoever did this made a mistake, keeping the head. Don't tell anyone that and I'll do my best to find the one responsible."

"Thanks, Henri."

"And I'll run some tests on the handkerchief – see if that can tell us anything." Putting the handkerchief inside the leather wallet of his detective kit, Henri checked the clock on the wall of the common room. "But it'll have to wait, unfortunately, as I'm invited to tea with the trustees."

"There's nothing unfortunate about that," said Hans. "It's an honour, Henri!"

"Not to me. I'm hopeless at talking to adults – you know, all that small talk you're supposed to do at parties? Scares me to death."

"But think of the cakes – and the sweets!"

Henri grinned and clapped Hans on the back. "True. Thanks, Hans, you've just managed to persuade me. Tell your friends they can use the billiards table again. I've seen all I need here."

Henri stood alone by the tea table in a corner of the trustees' dining room. He wondered what he was doing there amidst the intricately carved oak furniture, blue and gold drapes decorated with garden birds stealing strawberries, and a painted ceiling showing the constellations. After extending the invitation, Lord John seemed to have forgotten him, making no effort to introduce Henri to the guests. Henri's teacher was experiencing a similar difficulty, hanging on the edges of conversations of people far more important than him.

At least, thought Henri, unlike Master Ricardo, he had no desire to impress the trustees and was perfectly happy working his way through the cream-filled pastries, anchovy toast triangles, chocolate-dipped apricots, and stuffed dates. Hans had been right: this was much superior to the fare served in the scholars' hall. He piled his choices on his bone china plate with the gold rim, working out the mathematically best way to achieve maximum load.

An elderly trustee glanced his way and scowled. Dr Erasmus, a once famous botanist but now overlooked by the new generation of scientists, had probably already forgotten the scene where Lord John had invited the scholarship boy to tea. Working on the "out of sight, out of mind" principle, Henri moved behind a pillar, taking his plate of food with him. He had every right to enjoy this tea undisturbed. He could hear a scuffling from under the table and suspected the orange-clawed foot that peeped out belonged to the dodo. The wretched creature got everywhere it shouldn't. Leaning against a carved oak panel, Henri chewed on a date, possibly one from his own home. Moments like this when he felt acutely out of place made him miss Algeria.

It was by an odd chance that he got to be here at all. He had always assumed he would stay in his home country and join his father in the civil service. His thoughts went back to the morning he sat the entrance test in a French government building in Algiers. It had been held in a white-balconied villa belonging to the Ministry of Education, right on the seafront, palm trees waving outside the windows. How he missed the heat! The museum was usually so cold. Twenty other boys had also taken the exam that day, handpicked from schools across the country. Henri had been in a particularly brilliant mood, his thoughts sparking and combining like the aeronautical display from a flock of starlings. It must have shown in his work because he alone had been selected to have the full scholarship in the museum academy. And now he was here, at the heart of the world's scientific knowledge, occupying a prime position that in a few years' time would allow him to carry out the research he longed to do into the mysteries of forensic science. Not bad for a boy from North Africa.

"Too shocking for words!" The exclamation dragged Henri's thoughts away from his own bright future to the others in the room. He realized his earlier observation had not been accurate: Dr Erasmus hadn't been frowning at him in particular; all the trustees were scowling at everyone in general. Professor André, zoologist, was so upset his monocle was swinging free on his chest like a fast-ticking pendulum. "I can't believe, Lord John, you've let it come to this!"

"I know, Professor, I know. I have to admit I'm deeply shaken. I had always thought the foreman was a trustworthy individual." Lord John waved off the offer of a cup from a waiter. "I couldn't possibly drink tea, not at a time like this.'

His flutterings and fussing turned the complainer to carer as a seat was fetched for his lordship and a glass of water pressed into his hand.

"The man will be tried, of course?" The chairman of the trustees, Professor Gall, stroked his bristling black beard.

"Can't avoid it. I have some pity for the man. He lost his wife and infant son two years ago to the typhoid that summer so I suppose he was at his wits' end about how to look after the surviving child."

"Your pity is misplaced, my lord." Professor André exchanged an exasperated look with Gall. "There was always service in the kitchens. He has indubitably led his daughter astray from her rightful destiny."

Henri wiped his fingers on his handkerchief and quietly disposed of his plate on a side table. *A girl had got into trouble in the museum? How had that happened?*

"Or she could have stayed at home and looked after his house," continued Professor Gall. "He was doing her no favours encouraging her to believe she could match a man in her work."

"Exactly," said André. "Evolutionary biology teaches us our roles: man to protect and provide for his family, woman to have children and nurture them."

Henri rolled his eyes. Biologists had departed from logic some decades ago when Darwin's ideas first shook up the scientific establishment. They had confused their opinions and prejudices about men and women with the idea of a "natural" way of behaving, leaving far behind the message that Darwin had intended. They totally ignored facts from other cultures and species that showed how roles varied in nature. Look at the emperor penguin and the seahorse. Nurturing babies was not only for females for many species. Henri didn't have a very high opinion of the reasoning processes of men like Professors André and Gall.

"Her desire to make something should have been directed at knitting stockings, or sewing shirts," added Dr Erasmus, seconding his colleague's view. Henri sighed, though he didn't expect anything else from the crusty older generation.

"But surely we should allow for the possibility that there may be exceptions to the rules?" suggested Lord John. "Evolution is about change, is it not?"

Bravo, Lord John, thought Henri, surprised at the nobleman's insight.

"You don't understand, Lord John, not like we men of science do," said Professor Gall. "In my subject of phrenology you can tell everything you need to know about gender from the bumps on the head."

"But there have been outstanding female artists, surely you can allow that? The girl's carvings showed true talent."

"But her outrageous choice of subject proves the female brain is just not capable of adopting the new manly rigour of science."

What had the girl done? Henri wondered. How had she managed to upset everyone so badly? It was quite an accomplishment. He pictured her, a giantess wielding a chisel in protest, carving her objections on the walls of the museum...

"I fear the responsibility rests with the father, not the daughter. He says as much himself." Lord John fanned himself with his napkin.

"You'll convene a hearing?" asked Professor Gall.

"Yes, of course. Tomorrow morning."

Professor Gall clicked his fingers to summon a waiter to fetch him a fresh cup. "I can be there."

Lord John sat up straight, his swooning stance forgotten. "Oh, but I thought I would deal with this on the Committee of Works."

"Nothing but a full hearing in front of the Museum Tribunal will do, Lord John. This is not a question of the museum's fixtures and fittings, to be settled by the dismissal of a shoddy workman; it is a matter concerning the very foundations of knowledge to which our society is dedicated. Our laws have been broken and someone must pay."

The museum pest appeared from under the tea table, white cloth caught on a hind claw, disaster a second away.

"Mind the dodo!" called Henri as he made a dive to catch the teetering cake stand. Waiters rushed to rescue the cloth and the bird was shooed out of the room with many indignant squawks from both pecked man and cake-deprived beast.

Henri lay on his back holding the silver stand, most of the cakes still intact. Among the casualties was an éclair, wedged under his chin, and an almond torte upside down on his stomach. The head waiter relieved him of the burden and the debris. He offered a clean napkin for Henri to wipe himself down.

The interruption cleared the air of the antagonism the rebellious carver had provoked. There were several chuckles and mutters of "Whatever next?".

"Dashed good save!" exclaimed Lord John, applauding Henri. "Here, gentlemen, you remember our senior scholar? He's years ahead of his peers, taught with the older boys. It appears we should encourage him to try out for the museum cricket team too!"

"A very promising youth, despite... well, anyway," agreed Professor André. "Tell me, young sir, what branch of science most interests you?"

They were inviting him, the outsider, to talk about himself? Henri felt an agreeable swell of pride and pleasure.

"Well, sir, I do find myself drawn to applying science to the detection of crime."

"Interesting. Quite an up-and-coming area, thanks to Dr Bell's pioneering work. Tell us more." Professor André took a seat by Henri so he could pay attention and eat sandwiches at the same time. Professor Gall turned away in disgust, muttering darkly.

Henri looked around with amazement at the group of attentive adults who remained to listen to a cream-stained boy as if he might have something worth saying. "I have been wondering how we might come up with a method of identifying criminals by their fingerprints. I understand a chief magistrate in India has been using ink prints to identify his workers to prevent fraud at the pay office."

"Go on," said Professor André.

"It struck me this might have a use for the police force if we can find a way of lifting fingerprint traces from the scenes of crime. That's the hard part – oh, and making a classification system so we can access the information, of course."

"Excellent point," agreed the trustee librarian.

As the sun set over the river to the west of the island, flooding the windows with an oblique light as orange as dodo claws, Henri discovered the delight of being taken seriously as a man of science.

Ree sat alone in the cabin she shared with her father. Her fingers ran over the base of the stone stool, feeling the familiar carvings without needing to see them. These had been her practice pieces, offcuts from the museum works. Her father had teased her by keeping them as the family footstools, even though the running horse looked more like a pregnant donkey and the flower did not resemble any that could be found in a greenhouse or garden.

What had she done? She would gladly trade her right arm to turn time back to last week and stop herself at the moment when she began to carve the hand. She wanted to beg someone, some higher power, to intervene, but people were no longer allowed to pray and it didn't do any good in any case because all that was over. But it was so tempting to try it when there was nothing left.

O God-who-was-no-longer-there, what could she do to make this right?

That was stupid. Weak. She thumped her knees. No supernatural power was going to help her; she would have to do everything herself.

Her father was now in the museum lockups and she wasn't allowed to see him before his trial. She had expected to be the one in prison, but somehow everyone had blamed him. That wasn't fair. Hers was the hand that had made the carving, hers was the brain that had conjured up the shape from the stone. Ree rocked in silent agony, afraid to let out a sound in case she couldn't bring herself to stop.

Please, help me, someone.

Another hour passed and it grew completely dark. A brisk knock came on the door and her neighbour, Mrs Simplon, entered, accompanied by her son, Paul, Ree's friend and fellow apprentice. Ree only then wondered why she had been left alone so long. Normally after a disaster all the workers clustered around the stricken family.

"I've taken in your washing, Maria." Mrs Simplon, a tidy woman with curly blonde hair pulled back from her face by two tortoiseshell combs, put the neat stack down on the plank table. "No point letting it get damp in the night dew after such a good drying day." She bustled about the room, lit the fire Ree had left set that morning, and put a kettle on the hotplate. "You won't have eaten, I expect. You mustn't give your poor father more trouble by starving yourself. He would hate you to punish yourself like this."

Ree tried to speak but couldn't. She was very conscious of Paul standing with his back to the door. They were usually good friends – or had been while they both pretended she was a boy. All that would change too now.

"We'd better look out some suitable clothes for the hearing tomorrow. If you make a good impression, then maybe your father will have an easier time." Mrs Simplon sniffed at the stale loaf. "It'll do for toast. Paul, make yourself useful while Maria and I look through her things." She thrust the toasting fork in her son's direction.

"Yes, Ma." Paul crouched by the fire and fitted a piece of bread to the end. He still hadn't spoken to her.

"Now where are your gowns, pet?" Mrs Simplon looked around the room, seeing only the caps and jackets on the pegs.

Come on, Ree, pull yourself together. "I only have boy's clothes. I've grown out of all my dresses."

Mrs Simplon clicked her tongue. "Well, that won't do. What about your mother's things? Do you still have them?"

"Some." Galvanized by the thought of doing something that might help her father, Ree stood up, rubbing the circulation back into her numb limbs. They were screaming with pins-and-needles. She crouched by her father's bed and pulled out a chest. "He kept some for me for when I'm older."

Mrs Simplon lifted the lid and took out the lavender sachet. "They've been kept properly at least." She pawed through the layers, rejecting the brighter garments. She settled on a white blouse and dark brown skirt and shook them out. Holding them against Ree, she tutted again. "You'll be swamped in these, lamb. Not that your mother was a big woman, but you're nothing more than a minnow. Time to get out the needle and thread."

"Here you are, er, Maria." Paul handed her a singed piece of toast spread with a little butter. He had never called her by her full name before. It made everything between them even more awkward.

"Thank you." Ree tried a bite but couldn't seem to swallow. Tears pricked her eyes but she wasn't going to – she *refused* to – cry.

"You'll need some tea to wash that down," Mrs Simplon said astutely.

Taking the hint, Paul moved to the kettle, which had started to boil. "Where's your tea?"

Ree pushed a strand of hair off her face, weary beyond anything she could remember. "We've run out. I was going to get some on my way back from work."

Mrs Simplon dropped the skirt she had been pinning up on the table. "Stay here. I'll just nip next door and fetch some of ours. I'll need my good scissors too. Yours are so blunt they won't cut a cobweb, let alone this hem."

When the door banged behind her, Ree felt very conscious that she had been left alone with Paul. But what could she say to him? It had been easy when she was the cheeky little boy-girl in the troop of apprentices but now that pretence was no longer possible.

"Is your father all right?" Paul asked, starting on a second slice of toast.

"I don't know. They won't let me see him."

Paul danced the bread as close to the flames as he dared, the light flickering on his reddened face and short blond hair. He had once confessed to her that, if he let it grow, it curled like his mother's and made him look too pretty, so he got it cropped regularly at the ruthless barber's on Bridge Street. "I have to ask, Maria: how could you have been so stupid?"

Ree picked at a loose piece of skin by her fingernail. "I didn't mean it the way they took it."

"But any fool would know not to do that. It's the first thing they teach you at school."

"I've not been to school, have I?" Ree retorted. Paul had received a basic education at the workers' academy in reading and writing until he was eleven. He had also been taught the new science.

"But you must've at least heard what the guides tell visitors? I thought you were clever." He put the toast on the breadboard and spread a generous amount of butter before biting into it himself.

"I'm sorry to disappoint you." Irritated by his tone, Ree tried to work out what was going on in Paul's head. She had expected some sympathy from him but instead he seemed more angry than anything. "As I tried to explain, it was about our craft, not about God making things."

"My da says he tried to talk your father out of letting you work but he never listened. He said your talent was too good to waste." Paul waved the butter knife. "How could you not be better than us when he always gave you the soft inside jobs and left the rest of us chipping away on the outside, whatever the weather?"

"I didn't know you minded."

Paul pulled off a crust. "Never saw the point in making a fuss. Your father was the boss."

Ree wanted to correct him, insist that her da was *still* the boss, but it seemed a silly thing to quarrel over.

"According to my ma, your only hope is to say you never knew what you were doing was wrong." Paul rummaged through the shelves of their little food cupboard and came up with a small jar of apple and blackberry jam Ree had made last autumn. "Mind if I…?"

Ree shrugged. It hardly mattered what he did.

Paul spread the jam on his last half of toast. "Do you want some?"

She shook her head. She couldn't eat jam while her father was sitting in jail.

He took a bite and crunched in appreciation. "Hmm, this is very good. Did you make it?"

Ree nodded.

"I didn't know you did such 'female' things. And you always beat me at marbles. It's not fair." Ree realized that, after having aired his complaint, Paul was now extending his version of an olive branch.

"And you always beat me at hopscotch." She managed to swallow a little of her toast.

"That's because I've got longer legs." He smiled, cheered up by the thought that in one area at least he was a champion. "I'm sorry this has happened this way, Ree, but maybe it was always going to end like this? Maybe your da took too many risks?"

"It's my fault, not his."

"Whatever happens tomorrow, Ma, Da, and I will be here for you. We won't run for cover like the others are doing."

"Run for cover?" Ree asked, putting down her toast.

"Didn't you notice that no one else has come near? They think the trustees are going to get rid of all of us as a bunch of Theophilus lovers. Da doesn't believe that. He says they can't afford to lose the best stonemasons in the country at this point in the building. They'll never get it finished if they do that."

"That's ridiculous! It was nothing to do with those protestors."

"How do you think they got rid of all Theophilus ideas in such a short time?" Paul paused, a steely glint in his eye. "I'll tell you: by stamping out any suggestion that religion might come back. You're not the first to have something you've said or done taken the wrong way. What you meant doesn't matter. They judge it on how it is seen by others."

Mrs Simplon returned at that point with a tea caddy and a large pair of scissors. "Run along now, Paul. Stop scaring her. Your supper is on the table. Maria and I are going to get her dressed for tomorrow."

Paul polished off the last slice of toast. "Hope it goes well, Ree." He banged the door behind him, footsteps crunching as he went down the path.

"Now up you get. I need to measure this on you." Mrs Simplon guided Ree to stand on the table, fed the skirt over Ree's head like a python swallowing a rat, and then pinned the hem to just above Ree's ankle. "There's a good six inches to come off and that will still leave you with some spare length when you grow." She whipped the skirt off again and wielded her scissors with expert assurance. "We can't do much about the blouse. You'll just have to roll up the cuffs and tuck it into the waistband of the skirt. Now let's have a look at your hair."

"My hair?" Ree touched her plaits nervously, wondering if Mrs Simplon had yet more plans for her wicked-looking scissors.

"This is all about creating the right impression. You need to wear it loose to make you look less" – she scrutinized Ree's face – "determined." She pushed a finger gently into the end of Ree's chin. "You have a little dent there that makes your expression the opposite of soft and silly."

"I don't want to look soft and silly!" Ree said defensively.

"Yes, you do. We live in a man's world and the only way for clever women to survive the absurdities of the male of the species is to pretend to be what they expect." Mrs Simplon gestured to Ree to undo her plaits.

Ree had never heard Mrs Simplon talk so freely before. "You don't agree with them then? You think my da was right to let me work?" Ree felt her scalp protesting as the tight braids unwound, straight black hair hanging heavy around her shoulders like a cape.

"Look at that: not even a kink to it after being in a plait all day. You have your mother's hair. Heavy as the thickest silk thread and never took a curl no matter how long she spent over it with curling papers and tongs." Mrs Simplon lifted a hank. "Could do with a wash. Matted with stone dust. I'll heat some water and help you with that." Putting her sewing aside, she refilled the kettle from the tub of water kept by the door. The hot metal hissed as it was submerged. "As to whether your da was right, I can't say, pet."

"Why not?" asked Ree.

"He acts the way he wants the world to be. Most of us act the way we think will do best for our families. If they changed to saying we all have to be Theophilus followers tomorrow, then likely I'd be first in the queue to take the oath."

"So what do you *really* think?"

Mrs Simplon shook her head, pouring the water over Ree's head. "That's between me and my own conscience, lamb, and I'm certainly not going to start telling you that, not when you're up for questioning tomorrow. You've got to concentrate on getting your own story straight. Say what you think they want to hear. Whether or not it is what you really believe is irrelevant."

"Isn't that lying?" said Ree, hanging upside down over the basin.

"You've been pretending that you're a boy for years now." Mrs Simplon said, giving Ree's hair a final wring with a towel. "I would say you have plenty of practice."

Mrs Simplon only left when she was satisfied that Ree was scrubbed clean of any trace of her scandalous profession. The skirt and blouse hung on the peg that normally held her father's jacket, symbol of the new life that Ree would have to put on from the following day. Sitting in bed in a nightshirt, her hair still too damp to lie down, Ree watched the fire die to embers in the grate. She ran through her answers to the questions she expected to face. She tried to picture herself like one of those portraits of idealized girls that came as collectible cards in matchboxes. Pretty, wide-eyed, decorative, without a single interesting thing to say. She rubbed the dent in her chin, trying to smooth it away. She knew how to act the boy, but could she work out how to be a convincing girl in time to save her father?

Chapter 4

Coal Dust and Tiger Cubs

Mrs Simplon returned at dawn to accompany Ree to the hearing.

"We'd best make an early start," she said, pushing a warm buttered roll into Ree's hand. "There's enough curiosity about you in the newspapers. We don't want journalists hounding you all the way over the bridge." She took Ree's brush and began dealing with the night-tangles in her hair.

The mouthful of bread that Ree had been eating turned to ash. She swallowed. "Newspapers?"

The brush tugged at her scalp. "Stars, child, didn't you realize that anything that happens in the museum is immediately international news? That's why people go there to protest: they're bound to get publicity for their cause even if they pay a heavy price. Most newspapers send reporters when they get the tip that a story is about to break. You're front page news."

Ree gulped down a cup of water but the lump in her throat wouldn't go. "What are they saying?"

The brush paused. Mrs Simplon pursed her lips, evidently regretting now that she had spoken.

"Please, I need to know what they are writing about me."

The strokes began again, this time gentler. "That your father was secretly an agent for the Theophilus movement and put you up to it."

"But that's a lie!" She wanted to escape, to shake some sense into the journalists, but instead was pinned to the chair.

Mrs Simplon took two strands from Ree's temples and tied them back with a black ribbon. "Of course it is, but that doesn't matter to the press. They're after a story and this fits the facts of the one they want to tell." She patted Ree's shoulder, a signal that it was time to go. "You can't worry about that. You just worry about making a good impression on the trustees."

Holding Ree's hand, Mrs Simplon hurried her over the bridge in the thin flow of workers on the early shift. It was a cold morning and the river sparkled with diamond-bright glints, cutting everything into jagged shapes and shadows. A dead animal – a dog maybe, or a large cat, horribly headless – snagged briefly on one of the bridge supports before being washed away, giving a flash of white belly as it rolled over. Ree bit the inside of her cheek. People didn't seem to care what they threw in the river, thinking it gone, when all they really did was make it into someone else's problem. The dead creature bothered her, revolving in her mind, ugly, sickening, like the thought of the trial. The two thoughts became meshed. How could she be the sweet and soft little girl Mrs Simplon said they wanted when her brain was stuck on drowned carcasses?

"We'll go in by a back entrance and wait in the kitchens until it's time," said Mrs Simplon. "The press won't find us in there." She turned the opposite way to the builders' yard into the kitchen courtyard. On three sides were the kitchens that served the whole museum, on the fourth the maids' tower, where the female servants slept. They had to squeeze past the coal man heaving his knobbled sacks and a grocer's cart laden with cabbages, which gleamed like the pile of skulls in the anatomy chamber. "This is the Lesser Kitchen Number Three. My sister is cook here. She'll let us wait with her if we keep out of the way."

A skinny woman, tall as an afternoon shadow, presided over the fireplace. "Reubens, take the bacon to the scholars' hall before it spoils. Joachim, there's another basket of bread. Hurry now!" She waved them off with a metal spoon.

"Ingrid, we're here." Mrs Simplon kissed her sister's cheek, expertly dodging the utensil.

"Margaret." Ingrid the cook gave her a cool nod. She reminded Ree of the peppermint plant she kept on a windowsill. It had become too long and leggy as it struggled to catch enough light, but retained all its sharpness and bite. Ree had always thought museum cooks would be fat jolly creatures, and wondered what that said about the richness of the diet served from the Lesser Kitchen Number Three. "So this is the rebel?" Ingrid sniffed as if testing yesterday's milk jug for freshness.

"Hardly a rebel. Foolish, lost in her imagination. She's a little bit of nothing really. Sit down, Maria."

Better to be thought nothing than to be regarded as an enemy of the state, decided Ree, taking the low stool.

Mrs Simplon sat down on a chair near the cook and examined a rack of cooling buns with a nod of approval. They looked like a little family of golden hedgehogs, nose to nose. "You always had a gift with bread. I don't suppose you can rustle up a cup of tea for your big sister, Ingrid?"

With another sniff, this one saying "of course there's tea", Ingrid poured two cups of tar-black Darjeeling and put them in front of her guests. Ree took a cautious sip, finding the bitterness of the brew clung to her teeth and tongue like a punishment. A white cat stalked across the mantlepiece and dislodged a pottery candlestick without reproof. It leaped down and circled on Mrs Simplon's lap. The two women settled down to exchange family news while the servants came and went, Ingrid pausing only occasionally to rap out an order. "Not in the vegetable sink, you simpleton. Empty it in the scullery." This was to a tired-looking maid carrying a mop and bucket. "What? More bacon?" she scowled at a boy. "Their high-mightinesses must be joking. Scholars get one rasher each and I don't care if they didn't divide it fairly. That's their problem. They're the ones studying mathematics." The boy scurried back with the bad news to the students in the academy's dining hall.

By nine o'clock the breakfast had been cleared and a lull came to the workings of the kitchen. The boys who had been serving took their own meal away to the servants' hall. The maids had all vanished.

"Where have the girls gone?" Ree asked in a break in the conversation.

"What's that?" Ingrid turned her grey eyes on her guest. They seemed to slice and dice her like the vegetable knife she wielded. "Can't just sit, can you? You have to watch." She made that sound like a sin.

"The girls do the cleaning at night," explained Mrs Simplon. "They aren't supposed to be seen by the public or the scholars. Too distracting."

"And then they're supposed to go to their dormitories. Fat chance of that." Ingrid folded her arms, sharp elbows jutting. "Some go off to work a second job on the south bank, help their mothers, or laze around in my kitchens begging scraps off my boys. They know better than to let me catch sight of them. Speaking of scraps, would you like to feed the tiger?"

This question was so unexpected, Ree's mouth dropped open. "A tiger?"

"In the basket over there. That keeper from the zoo asked me to give it somewhere warm to sleep. He knows I like cats."

Ree kneeled beside the log basket and discovered that there was indeed a tiger cub curled up on a blanket, long whiskers twitching as it dreamed. The wonder of it was like opening an ordinary oyster and finding a pearl as big as your thumb.

"What's its name?"

"I was going to call it Maggie as it reminded me of a fierce older sister of mine." Ingrid smiled at her sister, for the first time giving Ree a hint of how she might have been as a young girl playing with Mrs Simplon.

"Oh you!" laughed Mrs Simplon. "Just you wait until it grows up and takes a swipe at you for that piece of impertinence. Where's it from?"

"Some place called Java, where the coffee grows. Mr Billibellary says it'll be smaller than most breeds, with extra-long whiskers. The mother died on the journey over so she needs to be hand-reared. Got my boys on to it but I think it's about time for another feed and I don't see any of them in sight, do you? There's some minced meat on the table, Maria. Try it on that."

Ree nudged the little dish under the tiger's nose. It yawned, revealing small white teeth and a pink tongue. Yellow eyes opened, blinked, then focused on the food. Getting to its feet, it fell on the meal, eating it in gulps, black tip to the tail twitching.

"You'd better let her out when she's finished. Take her to the yard to do her business then bring her back here. I don't want the coal man running her over."

Scooping the creature up under its warm belly, Ree carried the tiger to the kitchen courtyard and put it down. The tiger immediately ran to a sand box in one corner but then got distracted and started chasing after a loose cabbage leaf. Laughing at its antics, so like a very large kitten, Ree let it play. The coal man watched from his perch on the back of his empty cart, smoking his pipe, face striped with dust a little like a tiger-man himself.

The clocks in the museum started striking ten – first Old Saul in the central bell tower where the chancellor lived, then others all over the island, some quick as if to get the whole thing over with as soon as possible, others dragging their beats so that they finished long after Saul. With a heavy feeling, Ree chased the cub into a corner, tripping over her skirts as she tried to recapture it. But it was too quick and she was too slow in her stupid clothes. The coal man had to get down and help her, stopping the cub in its game of tag by throwing an empty sack over its head. Ree took the now dusty creature back to the kitchen.

"Look at you!" Mrs Simplon grabbed a linen towel and began brushing at Ree's blouse. "You're covered in coal dust. Have you no sense at all, girl?"

Ree looked down. "Covered" was an exaggeration, but there was a grey smudge on her chest and her hands were black. She quickly washed in the basin Ingrid produced, using a nailbrush to clean off every speck.

"If she pulls her hair forward, that should hide the worst," observed Ingrid. "I'm sorry, Margaret. I thought the cub would distract her."

"It certainly did that. Ah well, no time to go back and change. She'll have to do. Hurry up now. We mustn't be late."

Ree muttered her thanks to the cook and followed Mrs Simplon through the kitchens and down several long corridors, up two flights of stairs, and down a spiral one embedded with curling ammonite fossils, to emerge by the entrance hall. She was surprised her neighbour knew the way but she didn't put a foot wrong.

"How do you know where we're going, Mrs Simplon?" asked Ree.

"I used to work here myself," her neighbour replied. "That was how I met Paul's father."

It was a relief to have someone who knew where they were

going. Ree feared she would've been wandering lost if left to herself. "Where are we heading?"

"They always hold the trials in the lecture theatres in the academy. They should have a list up on the main noticeboard." Mrs Simplon took a turn through an archway carved with owls and pelicans, one of Ree's father's pieces. "Let's see." Standing in front of a green felt-covered board, she ran her finger down the list and drew in a sharp breath.

"What?" The sick feeling was back, like a muddy drowned creature squirming in Ree's stomach.

"We were hoping for one of the minor rooms in front of the Committee of Works. However, they've decided to hold it in the Grand Theatre before the museum chancellor and trustees."

Hopelessness settled on Ree's shoulders like a yoke weighed down with heavy buckets. "This isn't right. This isn't fair. I'm the one who should be on trial – not Da."

Mrs Simplon gave her a pitying look. "That's not how the world works, pet. Remember what I told you. You can best help your father by looking as innocent as the day you were born."

Inside Ree, fury twirled with the guilt in what felt like a sodden mat of wet fur and river water.

"Now none of that. You can't go in there looking like you'd like to take a mallet to them all."

Ree took a deep breath and tried to smooth her face out into a calm expression.

"Hmm. Those who know you wouldn't be fooled, but it will do for now." Mrs Simplon tapped the dent in her chin. "Lower that and do your best to pretend for your father."

After passing through a series of deserted quadrangles so quickly Ree did not have time to notice much beyond green lawns and covered walkways, they entered a much busier part of the academy. They worked their way through the mass of students gathering for the trial.

"They want the youngsters to witness them dispensing their

justice – or at least what passes for justice in here," Mrs Simplon said with a dismissive wave at the oak beamed ceiling of the corridor. They were carved with Greek letters that no doubt spelt out something wise. Hurrying Ree by some reporters, Mrs Simplon passed the doors leading into the semicircular lecture room. With its raked seating, it had been modelled on an ancient Greek theatre, capable of seating thousands. Normally, Ree would have enjoyed the craftmanship involved, but now it looked more like a mouth waiting to swallow her.

"Don't dwell on it," said Mrs Simplon, walking on until they came to a small door at the end of the corridor. A clerk sat at a desk outside, making notes in a heavy ledger.

"Oh, I hope we're in the right place, curator?" The man wasn't a curator, merely a clerk, but he swelled at the compliment. "I have brought a witness for today's trial, sir," said Mrs Simplon in a humble tone. Ree shot her a quick glance, then remembered why it was necessary.

"There she is! There's the girl!" called one of the reporters. Footsteps pattered in the corridor, heading in their direction.

As if he had all the time in the world, the man ran his nib down the list of names in front of him, though Ree doubted that there were any other females on it.

"Oh, I'm sorry, I should've said. She's Maria Altamira, the daughter of the accused." Mrs Simplon looked anxiously behind her, hoping to fend off the reporters with a glare.

"Why did you do it?" shouted a man wearing a squashy brown hat, but he was unable to get past Mrs Simplon's protective skirts that had shifted to envelop Ree.

"Ignore them," murmured Mrs Simplon.

"Do you believe in a creator?" called another.

The clerk raised a brow and made a flamboyant tick next to Ree's name. "Miss Altamira, you are to wait in there." He gestured to the room behind him. "Stay there until we call you."

"Thank you, sir." Mrs Simplon made to open the door and

get Ree away from the circling vulture-reporters.

"I'm afraid you can't wait in there with her. Them's the rules."

"Oh. But she's only a child," Mrs Simplon pleaded.

"Even so, today she is a witness and we must not tamper with the workings of the court." He flicked a finger at the reporters. "That goes for you lot as well. You must not interfere with the witness. I'll have you thrown out." With a disgruntled flutter, the journalists moved a few paces further off.

Recognizing a battle that she couldn't win, Mrs Simplon cupped Ree's face in her warm hands. "I'll be here when it's over. Have courage."

"Will you be in there watching?" asked Ree.

"I'm not allowed. Paul and my husband will be though. They're also called as witnesses. Go on now."

Ree walked through the door expecting to see her friend. Instead she found an empty chamber a little like a railway waiting room. A feeble fire burned in the grate, making no dent on the cold atmosphere. She could hear the rumble of voices through the wall on the far side. Walking to a second door, she saw that it opened onto the lowest level of the theatre. From the bellowed announcements, she could tell that the trial was just starting. Confused as to what was expected of her, she tried the handle. The door opened a crack before being pulled smartly closed.

The clerk came in with his ledger. "Get away from there. I told you to wait."

"But the trial's starting! My father!" She had caught a glimpse of her da as he walked up to the platform on the far side of the room, wearing a pale orange prison uniform.

"Sit down. You will be the last one called, and the trustees instructed me to make sure you are kept away from their deliberations so your words are not influenced by previous witnesses."

"But I want to stand with him."

"What you want is immaterial." The clerk thumped the book

down on a side table. "Now do as you are told. Haven't you caused enough trouble?"

Her panic and terror fought silently like the rats in one of Mr Billibellary's sacks. Ree took a seat on a bench, fists clenched. Empty-headed. Innocent. She was neither.

Annoyed by the interruption to his research, Henri took his seat among the other senior scholars near the front of the lecture room. The spring holiday started at the end of the day and he didn't have long to solve the case before the boys dispersed. Why he had to be dragged away from his investigation when everyone already knew the outcome of the trial was beyond him. The Theophilus protestors had been condemned to transportation last week; he had no doubt this case would go the same way. He had plenty of work to do, as the pet killings had not stopped with Rainbow. A new boy's parrot had been found in a similar grisly fashion in a bathroom, and this morning Ramon had reported his ancient white-bellied tabby cat missing, evidence of ill-doing in the bloodstains on the carpet in his set of rooms. The scholars were all very upset but when they had appealed to the teachers, they were told that they kept pets at their own risk and that the animals were probably just killing each other as creatures were programmed to do in the survival of the fittest.

But it wasn't that; Henri was sure something darker was at play.

"All rise for the chancellor of the museum!" shouted Simplicius Shelley, who always seemed to be insinuating himself into official business.

With a rumble of boots shifting on the floorboards, the audience rose for the entrance of Chancellor Grassmann. At least this made a change from the usual pantomime. Henri hadn't seen the museum chancellor for months. Four footmen carried Grassmann in his scarlet and gold palanquin, an ornate litter bought from India and used by the ancient Sanskrit scholar to get about the island now that he could no longer walk. Grassmann sat bundled up in it like a very old squirrel in a drey, nibbling on a few nuts of knowledge while he slept through most of his winter. The trustees followed and took seats either side of the palanquin. Lord John was already present, sitting at a table with a pile of documents in front of him. He had volunteered to act as the stonemason's defence, while Professor Gall was to put the case for the prosecution.

Just an elaborate play, thought Henri. They could go straight to the verdict but they had to pretend they were going to examine the facts with scientific rigour.

"Bring in the accused!" bellowed Shelley.

A door leading up from the vaults opened, and a short man with a strong build walked into the court. Blinking in the light, he took one brief look around the room as if searching for someone then continued to his place in the dock.

Professor Gall got to his feet and bowed to the museum chancellor. "With your permission?"

A claw-like hand emerged from the folds of the chancellor's robes and waved him on.

"Your name is James Altamira, foreman of the works?" asked the professor.

The man took off his cap and scrunched it in white-knuckled fingers. "Yes, sir."

"Do you swear to tell the truth, the whole truth, and nothing but the truth?"

"Yes, sir."

"You know that to lie before this court is perjury and in the worst instances is punishable by death?"

The man swallowed, again looking for someone in the crowd but not finding whoever it was that he sought. "Yes, sir."

Henri sighed and studied his nails. It was a farce. Watching the stonemason in the dock was like seeing a worm in the path of the plough.

"I am going to read you an account of the facts as we understand them from our interviews with your workmates." Professor Gall gestured to a row of men and boys sitting at the foot of the platform. They were set apart by their rough clothes and capable hands from the ranks of scholars. Henri's eye stopped on a boy of his own age who was sitting with head hung, face flushed. His hair was so short you could see that the skin of his scalp was also reddened. "You may ask your defence to cross-examine them at any time."

"If my workmates gave their account on oath, then I'm satisfied they told the truth," the prisoner declared loyally. He went up a notch in Henri's estimation. The workmen exchanged glances. Some now sat up straighter, no longer so ashamed to be there.

Professor Gall shook out his page to turn attention back to himself. "The accusations are twofold. The first is that you have for two years allowed a female – your daughter, Maria Altamira – to work in the guise of a boy. She has been receiving the pay for doing the same tasks as a male apprentice. The second is that you did encourage the said Maria Altamira to carve forbidden figures on the walls of the museum, implying that a deity had a hand in creation. Your intent was secretly to undermine the foundations of the museum as you are a supporter of the banned Theophilus movement. How do you plead?"

The man stood with head held high. "Guilty to the first, sir. Not guilty to the second."

Professor Gall turned to the trustees with an extravagant gesture. "See what we are dealing with? He has admitted his guilt. If that man breaks one solemn law, why should we believe him innocent of violating another? Going against our laws as to the appropriate conduct of the sexes is enough to earn a life sentence in a penal colony. But if we add to that the charge of vandalizing our institution in the worst possible way, surely we must consider the ultimate sanction as fitting the crime?"

Henri felt a throb of horror in his chest. An excited mutter ran around the audience. This was far more dramatic than they had expected. The man in the dock went parchment white, feeling blindly out for the front of the dock to steady himself. Lord John got to his feet, looking very harassed. Clearly, he hadn't expected this turn either.

"But respectfully, professor, I must remind you that the museum has not considered the death penalty for any offence, not since 1863."

Gall stroked his beard, preening. "Just because we haven't employed it does not mean that it should not be used in this case. I've never come across a more blatant challenge to our delicate social fabric. Our gains are fragile. It has taken us decades to overturn centuries of superstition: we mustn't slip now or we will fall back into darkness. And it is not only the museum Altamira has damaged: he has ruined the mind of a defenceless female, his own daughter. What has she gained but the roughened hands and muscles of a workman? What young man would marry such a monster?"

Tell that to the women who manage the museum laundry, thought Henri wryly. He wouldn't fancy a stonemason's chances in an arm-wrestling competition with those terrifying laundresses, bane of every Monday when he had to collect his washing. They never let the scholars go without at least making them blush.

"I wish to call my first witness," said the professor. "Jan Simplon, master stonemason."

The workman sitting next to the red-faced boy got to his feet and took his place in the witness box. He swore his oath to tell the truth then waited with bowed head for the questions to begin.

"Simplon, how long have you known the accused?"

"Fifteen years, your excellency."

"So you would say you know him well?"

"Yes, sir." The stonemason looked over at his friend. "He's a good man."

"I beg to differ, as he has already admitted to allowing his daughter to work among you. Did you know about that?"

Simplon pulled at his collar. "Yes, sir. You see, James is a fool when it comes to Maria, thinks she's a genius. You have to allow for the partiality of a father."

"I don't have to allow anything."

"Er, yes, well, it blinded him to what he was doing. I think it was the grief that did it, sent him off on the wrong path."

Seizing on the excuse, Lord John leaped to his feet. "Grief? You think he might not have been in his right mind?"

"Yes, your lordship, driven by his grief for his wife and babe that died two years back. Taken by typhoid. That's when he decided he wouldn't let Maria out of his sight."

"So he was protecting her? As any father would?" Lord John asked.

"I suppose that's how it started."

"But not how it finished," interrupted Professor Gall. "Did you challenge him?"

"Yes, sir, but he was the boss, wasn't he? Besides, Maria never made no trouble."

"A female not making trouble? That has to be a first," said the professor with a glance at the audience, some of whom obligingly sniggered. "And now we have reached this crisis. Trouble is definitely what that girl is today. Did you ever see any sign that Altamira was a sympathizer with the Theophilus movement?"

"No, sir. He always said we should leave such matters to you, sir, meaning you and the authorities. Our job was to do our work to the best of our ability."

"So, how do you explain the carving she did?"

Simplon looked down and pulled at his sleeves, uncomfortable before so many eyes in his best jacket and shirt. "My son said she meant it as a tribute to our craft of making something from the stone."

"Your son? Then we'd better talk to him rather than go by

hearsay." Professor Gall turned to the row of stonemasons. "Come forward, young man."

The apprentice took over his father's position in the box and swore his oath.

"Explain what the girl told you she was doing."

The boy recounted his conversation, then concluded: "But, sir, Maria's just a little daftie." That comment provoked a titter of laughter among the younger scholars. "She had no idea how others would see what she had done. She didn't think. She gets lost in her imagination. She's only a girl after all."

"Indeed, only a girl." Professor Gall addressed Lord John. "Have you any questions for the witness or shall we summon the daughter? It appears she holds the key to this particular mystery of motivation."

Lord John agreed they could proceed directly to the last witness. Henri thought that a wise move, as the boy had done a good job at downplaying the idea of there being any Theophilus plot at work.

"Summon Maria Altamira!" called Shelley.

An usher hurried off to a door at the back of the stage and returned with the final witness. Like the other boys in the audience, Henri craned his neck to get a good glimpse of this rare creature who had sent the museum authorities into an uproar. Was this the monster Professor Gall had described? All were taken aback by the elfin girl with waist-length black hair as she stepped into the witness box. She looked so frail, swamped in her white blouse and overlong skirt. She also couldn't see over the top of the box built for an adult male unless she stood on tip-toe.

"Fetch something for the accused – I mean, the witness – to stand on," demanded Gall. A chair was duly brought and now the girl was too high, the barrier reaching her at her waist, leaving her horribly exposed. If she swooned, as girls were said to do when distressed, then there would be nothing to break her fall.

Henri found himself feeling unaccountably worried for her.

Stop being so foolish. The girl has been a stonemason for two years. She's hardly likely to faint at standing on a chair for five minutes, Henri reminded himself.

"Maria Altamira, do you promise to tell the truth, the whole truth, and nothing but the truth?" asked Professor Gall.

"Yes, sir." The girl was looking at her father, not at her accusers. The stonemason gave her a smile of reassurance, their loving connection plain.

Did she know he was facing the death penalty? Henri wondered. Of course not. She hadn't been in the courtroom when that surprise had been sprung.

"Your father has admitted to employing you as an apprentice for two years, Miss Altamira," said Gall, "but looking at you, I have to admit it would be very hard to believe unless I hadn't witnessed it with my own eyes. Or did you mostly make the tea and tidy up after the men?"

"I... I did what I was told," she said, taking a quick look at her father who nodded at her answer.

No, no, thought Henri, don't go along that path or they will say your father told you to carve the deity in the stone!

Lord John got to his feet. "So, Maria, you were with him only so that he could look after you? With no mother at home, what else was he to do?" He addressed this to the audience.

"Ask a neighbour to mind her, or find her decent employment," cut in Professor Gall. "Instead he let her play with dangerous tools, dressed in boys' clothes. She could have been exposed to all manner of rude talk mixing with the men as their equal."

The girl twisted her hands before her, eyes lowered. "I'm sorry, sir, but what do you mean by rude talk? I don't understand."

The professor actually blushed. "Never you mind, miss."

Clever girl, or was she genuinely that innocent? Henri narrowed his eyes, trying to read the clues from her expression. Her eyes, he saw now, were big and blue-grey like her father's.

He didn't quite believe they were as devoid of knowledge as she was pretending.

"We are straying from the point," continued Professor Gall. "We've established that the witness has been working illegally as an apprentice because she has been drawing the wage for two years." He thumped a pile of account books embossed with the museum seal. "Whether or not she did much of the actual work or just swept up is immaterial. The law has been broken. Now to the carving that all admit she did do. Miss Altamira, whose design were you following?"

She touched her fingers lightly to her chest. "Why, mine, sir."

"Did your father ask you to include a hand in the design?"

"No, sir. All he said was that, on the orders of Lord John, we were to let our imaginations run wild."

"And yours ran wild in the direction of a forbidden subject: a god." Professor Gall gestured to her father. "We have to ask what that man has been teaching her."

"The idea didn't come from my father but from my own head," she said quickly, proving to Henri that she wasn't as witless as she was making out. She understood her father's peril. "I heard someone talking about looking for a finger in nature, and I went from there."

Simplicius Shelley raised his hand and received a gesture to proceed from the professor. "If I may add, sir, I was present when the last group of Theophilus protestors were shouting such slogans in the great entrance hall. I perceive that their poison has done its work, acting on the uninformed mind of a female to produce such an error. This is why they must be eradicated as a movement."

"Maybe so. But that apprentice over there, Paul Simplon, said you did it to honour your craft, Miss Altamira," said Professor Gall. "Was he lying?"

"Oh no – and yes, I did. I told Paul that. I suppose I got all muddled." She brushed her hair back in her agitation, dislodging a ribbon so that the silk mane fell about her face in charming disarray. The ribbon fluttered to the floor at Gall's feet. "Oh, I'm sorry, sir."

Forced into gallantry, the professor picked up the ribbon and handed it back. "You got muddled?"

She wound the black ribbon around her fingers nervously. "After those scary men yelled things in the entrance hall, I was thinking of hands and how I was using mine to work the stone, and it all became one in my mind somehow. I'm really very sorry. I've never been to school as you know so I didn't understand how others might see it. My da explained how wrong it was as soon as he saw what I'd done and I was trying to put it right, but then you came, and it was all too late, and everyone was shouting and Philoponus the dodo stole my hat..." She wiped her wrist across her eyes. "I'm so sorry. It's all my fault."

Despite usually being able to trust his detective instincts, Henri couldn't tell what was false and what was true about her performance. The sequence of events sounded correct, and the regret. However, her eyes were still bright with intelligence, her chin raised just a little too high, for him to trust the tumbled series of sentences said in a breathless voice. He decided she was faking it. She was playing the part of a poor confused girl begging for protection. He wished she were a better actress as there was a danger the trustees might not believe her.

Except Henri hadn't allowed for their ingrained prejudice against females. They saw what they expected to see.

"Look, my fellow trustees, how the female mind is unable to keep things straight!" declared Professor Gall. "They need a man to guide them or they veer into error. I'm sure if I conducted a phrenological examination of her head, I would find an overdeveloped ideality bump and a deficiency in her logic."

Henri sighed with relief. Professor Gall had shifted ground, deciding this case had more importance as proof of the correct division of work between the sexes as proved by his pet subject of phrenology. He'd lost interest in making a poor stonemason pay with his life for vandalism he had not instigated.

Seizing his chance, Lord John came forward. "With my honoured colleague's agreement, I think we can dismiss the witness. I have no further questions for her." He offered her a hand, which, after a moment's pause, she accepted and stepped down from her perch.

"Might I join my da?" she asked the peer.

He patted her hand. "Not now, my dear. I'll make sure you get to see him after we have agreed our verdict."

Reluctantly, the girl let a court clerk lead her back out into the room beyond. The door closed.

"James Altamira, we now come to you," said Professor Gall severely. "We've all seen the little female you've led astray. I'm sure all here were struck by how unsuited she so obviously is to the craft into which you forced her. You failed her as a father."

The man bowed his head. "Yes, sir. It's all my fault. Don't blame Maria."

Professor Gall gave a curt nod. "Indeed not. Her testimony suggests that she remains remarkably innocent considering the life to which you exposed her. However, I remind all that we are here today to test the evidence and make our observations drawing from the facts. We must not be swayed by emotion. My conclusion is that your plea is correct – you are indeed guilty of the first count, but not guilty of the second. However, surely you should have anticipated such a disaster might befall once you set off on the path of involving a female in your craft? You may be not guilty in the strict legal sense, but that is not the same as innocent. What do you think, Lord John?"

The peer was looking at the foreman sorrowfully. "I fear I have to agree, Professor. I was sadly mistaken in the man I trusted to run the works on my behalf."

"Then I suggest we proceed to the verdict. Do we need to retire for further deliberations?" Professor Gall's gaze swept the trustees. "I see not. Then, by a show of hands, who judges Foreman James Altamira guilty of the charge of employing a female in a man's profession?"

All hands went up.

"On the second count, of instigating her to make a forbidden image, who believes him guilty?"

This time no hands were raised.

"Then we are unanimous. Chancellor, we leave the punishment to you as it is written in the museum's constitution."

The old man appeared to have gone to sleep and had to be woken by a discreet shake of his arm. "What-what?"

"The punishment, sir? Guilty only on the count of employing a female," Lord John quickly repeated.

"Oh, transportation for life, of course." The museum chancellor's voice grated like a gate in need of oil. "First five years hard labour. No chance of return. Take the prisoner away. I want my dinner." Altamira was marched back to the lockups as the footmen carried the chancellor off to dine.

"He got off lightly. He should've been strung up," commented Kurt Spurzheim, one of Henri's classmates. He barged into Henri on his way down the corridor, hands shoved nonchalantly in his pockets. Spurzheim, Professor Gall's favourite in Henri's year, fancied himself as a leader and had developed a dislike of the senior scholar that made itself felt in frequent push-and-shove matches.

"You think?" Henri kept his thoughts to himself that the penalty was far too severe. Spurzheim was always looking for an excuse to undermine him, and Henri had no desire to find himself in the dock charged with Theophilus sympathies.

"Obviously. Need to cut out the rot if the rest of us are going to flourish." Spurzheim surged on to join the others packing for their holidays, leaving Henri walking beside Ramon.

"*Oye*, imagine putting that little creature to working stone.

Obviously a bad idea," remarked Ramon, ever the gallant when it came to girls.

"I'm sorry to hear about your cat," said Henri, for whom girls were something of a mystery and not one he thought would be solved by his usual investigative techniques. "No sign?"

Ramon shook his head. "You stop this *canalla*, Henri, this murderer of innocent creatures. We are counting on you."

Henri gave a nod, feeling the weight of expectation. Ever since he revealed his interest in detective work to his classmates, he had earned a place for himself at the academy as the person the boys went to whenever there was a petty crime to be solved. These, though, had either been minor thefts or misplaced belongings. Never had he been presented so serious a case before.

Henri separated from his classmate to go back to his room to think some more. He was staying on over the holidays, Algeria being too far to go for a short holiday. What was frustrating him was that he couldn't find the logical thread – mouse, parrot, and cat only had in common the fact that they were pets. The owners did not fall into the same friendship groups: Hans was a popular junior, the parrot belonged to a new boy few had yet met, and Ramon was in the fourth year with Henri. There was no link there that he could see.

"So if it's not logical then it must be illogical – and therefore almost impossible to solve unless the person is caught red-handed," he muttered to himself as he opened his door.

The first thing he noticed was the added mess in the already untidy room. His apparatus had been knocked over, a bottle of hydrogen peroxide left dripping onto the floor, a rack of test tubes shattered.

"What the – ?" Even Zena at her most bored had never managed anything like this. *The only thing they had in common was the fact that they were pets.* "Zena? Zena!" Henri began a frantic search of her favourite hiding spots – in his wardrobe, under his desk, in his bed. Tossing back the bedspread he found a bloody handprint on the sheet and on the open pages of a book he had definitely not left there. It looked like it had been thrown at something. "Oh, Zena!" Lost in his own cleverness, he hadn't stopped to consider that the killer might come for the detective next. He would never forgive himself.

A chattering from the windowsill broke the silence, the most wonderful sound he had ever heard. Henri rushed to the window and found his monkey crouched on the ledge outside. Henri hated heights but from her fierce cries and shivering stance he could tell she was too scared to come back in. He made himself lean out to coax her inside. He reached out a hand.

"Come on, Zena. I'm here now. I'm so sorry. I didn't think." He gulped, keeping his eyes fixed on the stone, not the ground far below.

Zena bared her teeth at him in fear and displeasure.

He reached in his pocket and placed a peanut on the sill. "What did you do? Fight him off?" Henri could see no sign of injury on the monkey, so maybe the blood on the sheet had to be from the attacker? His macaque had had a narrow escape. It also told him that the pet killer didn't know much about the ferocity of a monkey when cornered. "Clever, clever girl."

The macaque was now looking at the peanut. Clearly this was a two-peanut situation. He'd happily give her the whole bag for her escape if it wasn't bad for her to eat too many in one go.

Zena tipped her head sideways.

"All right, three. But that's absolutely my final offer." Henri placed the third one on the ledge and sighed with relief as the macaque took a flying leap back into the room. She retreated to the top of the wardrobe with her haul.

"Right, let's see what we can find out," said Henri, stripping the sheet off the bed.

From the smeared print, he worked out the size of attacker's hand span (large enough to fit an adult or older student). The killer had been left with a deep monkey bite to at least one of his fingers. He was able to capture a fingerprint too from the marks on the book. Unfortunately, Henri had found the evidence too late. His fellow students were already leaving for home, and by the time they returned any injuries would've had a chance to heal. He'd have to look out for scars, but most of them sported lab injuries in the shape of cuts and burns so that would be hard to detect.

"Unless you learn to speak so you can tell me who did it, I'll just have to log it with the other evidence," Henri said to Zena.

The monkey glared at him.

"Sorry. Of course, you do speak – your own language. I'm stupid, though, and I don't understand."

To Henri and Zena's great frustration, the case then went cold as no more pet murders took place after the holidays. Scared off by a victim who turned out able to defend herself, the killer stopped or moved on to other less obvious prey. Henri didn't forget though. He was biding his time, waiting for the criminal to make one more mistake.

Chapter 5

A Prisoner's Last Request

Back in the courtroom waiting room, Ree couldn't sit still. She paced up and down, pausing by the door in the hope of catching a word or two, but all she could hear was the rumble of voices and then the movement of people. It had to be over. They were leaving. Quickly sitting down on a bench, she folded her hands in her lap.

The entrance from the theatre opened and Paul and his father came in. Ree shot to her feet.

"Yes?"

Mr Simplon dug his hands in his pockets. "It's good news, Maria."

A wave of relief swept her. "They dismissed the case? He's free?"

Paul glanced at his father. "She doesn't understand. Sit down, Ree." He took a seat next to her on the bench and pulled her around to face him.

"What, Paul?" Smile trembling on her lips, Ree didn't want him to say what he was going to say next. "Your da said it was good news." Her voice was a plea.

"Yes, it is: your father won't face the death penalty. They found him not guilty of the charge that he was a Theophilus sympathizer."

"Death penalty?" That didn't make sense. Surely people weren't put to death for carving hands – or even having someone else carve hands – on stone columns?

"Professor Gall said a death sentence fitted the crime if your father were guilty."

"What?"

"You must know that the king has given the museum authorities permission to self-govern the island? They can decide all punishments for what happens here."

Ree nodded, shivering.

"But he's not going to be hanged, so you can rest easy."

"Then he's free?" No, of course he wasn't. Ree already read that from Paul's expression.

Mr Simplon rocked on his heels, steeling himself to deliver the bad news. "I'm afraid not. It's transportation for life – five years' hard labour, no chance of return."

"No!" She pushed Paul away, determined to rush back to the theatre and make the trustees change their mind. "They can't. It was me. I did it!"

Paul caught her by the back of her skirt. "Stop it, Ree! You can't help him like this. It was his mistake to let you work – that's what he's being punished for. In the end, the matter of the carving was dropped. Count your blessings."

"My blessings!" Ree rounded on him, fury boiling up and spilling out. "My ma and baby brother are dead and now Da is

80

being sent to the other side of the world – punished – just for letting me work. How is that just? How is that fair?"

"It's the law, Maria," said Mr Simplon quietly.

"Then I hate the law!"

Paul put a hand over her mouth. "Hush! You'll find yourself in the lockup next."

She pushed his palm down. "Then at least I'll be with him!"

"But is that what he wants? Don't you think he's sacrificed enough for you?" Paul countered.

Ree sank down on the bench, all the strength drained from her. "I want to go with him."

"They won't allow that, not at first," said Mr Simplon. "Maybe after the five years of hard labour he'll be able to send for you, but not until then. He'll be in chains, in a prison camp far from civilization."

Ree hugged herself. She had to keep the sobs locked inside.

"At least he'll be alive," added Paul, managing again to say the wrong thing.

"Do you know where you'll go, Ree?" asked Mr Simplon. "I know James has no family, but what about on your ma's side?"

What did it matter what happened to her? Ree shook her head.

"You can stay with us for a few days, while you get yourself sorted," Mr Simplon offered.

"Can't she stay in her cabin?" asked Paul in a low voice.

"I'm afraid not. A convicted prisoner's belongings are confiscated and sold. The proceeds are used to pay for his passage. Besides, she'd never be able to keep up with the rent."

Paul cleared his throat. "Right then. Well, I can share a bed with Felix and Julian. She can have mine."

His father nodded. "Yes, we'll do something like that. Until we can make a better arrangement."

The clerk came back in, interrupting this attempt to absorb her into the already stretched Simplon family. "Lord John wants to see the witness. Follow me."

Paul and Mr Simplon stepped back, deferring to the official.

"You'd better go," said Mr Simplon. "Shouldn't keep him waiting."

"We'll stay here until you've finished," Paul promised.

Ree forced herself to get up. Maybe Lord John had a solution they hadn't thought of? Maybe he would say she could go with her father? She trailed the clerk back into the now empty theatre to where Lord John was waiting. She dropped an awkward curtsey.

"Bad business this, bad business," said the nobleman. "Still, no good crying over spilt milk."

Was that supposed to comfort her or was he merely warning her not to try tears? She met his gaze, letting him see that her cheeks were dry.

Her gaze unsettled him. He patted his pockets, finally producing a gold watch on a chain. "Your father asked to see you, Maria. I've a few minutes before my next appointment so volunteered to take you." He led the way to the cellar door. "Mind your step."

The stairs were narrow and damp, worn on the treads, showing that they had been used for centuries, long before the theatre above had been built. Ree ran her fingers over the rough walls, trying to root her mind in the here and now. Shock was making her thoughts drift off like a wisp of cloud. She had to sharpen her wits.

"There are passageways like this all under the museum," Lord John explained to fill the silence. "You have to be very careful not to get lost." He tapped at a sign with an arrow pointing to the lockups one way and the academy the other. "Keep to these and don't wander off."

"Yes, sir," Ree said quietly, reminding herself that she might still need the man's support and he had tried to help her father in the trial.

They turned into a row of whitewashed cells like the

chambers in a giant honeycomb. All appeared to be occupied by solitary bee prisoners. The red-haired man Ree remembered from the Theophilus protest sat with head bowed in the first cell. He looked up on their approach.

"Ah, John, you're imprisoning them young now, aren't you?"

"Quiet, Luc." Lord John glanced over his shoulder to check no guards were within earshot. "The girl's father's just been sentenced. He'll be going on your ship the day after tomorrow. She's here to say goodbye."

The man's brown eyes rested on her face for a moment, his expression missing the earlier satirical glint. "Poor lass – then I'll pray for her."

Lord John huffed. "Don't say such things. That's what got you into this trouble to start with. But no, you always have to go on and on, pushing things further until there's a crisis."

The man rested empty hands on his knees, a sign of resignation. "Cousin, cousin, you know I'll never change."

Ree glanced up at Lord John. Cousin?

"I'm sorry for that. But this time the family couldn't hush it up," Lord John said, confirming the truth of the prisoner's words.

"That was rather the point."

Lord John shook his head in exasperation. "Then I wish you luck in the New World."

The man called Luc gave his cousin a quick grin. "I don't need luck. My God will look after me."

"Well, he doesn't seem to be doing a very good job so far, does he?"

Luc shrugged philosophically. "How he sees things is not the same as our limited vision – but then you never understood that."

Lord John opened his mouth as if to argue but then decided on another tack. "Luc, I sincerely wish you all the best."

"God bless you, John. You always were my favourite cousin."

Lord John hurried her further along the row of cells. "I'm sorry you had to hear that, Maria. He's the black sheep of the family but he means no harm. I'd be grateful if you didn't mention his relationship to me."

"Yes, sir." Ree wasn't sure what to make of that request. The peer was linked to one of the ringleaders of the banned movement. Could she use his secret to help her father? She couldn't see how. No one would listen to her, so he had nothing to fear from her telling tales.

They reached the cell in which her father waited. He was standing at the door, straining to see who was approaching.

"Maria! Thank goodness! I thought they might not let me see you."

"Da!" She ran the last few paces and grabbed his hand through the bars. "Oh please, sir, can't I go inside?"

Lord John beckoned to the warden who was standing at his post at the end of the corridor. "I can't see that it would do any harm. He's not a dangerous man."

The burly guard nodded and unlocked the door. Ree slipped in as soon as the gap was wide enough and threw herself at her father.

"Oh, Da!"

He bent down and hugged her. Putting his lips to her ears, he whispered.

"Ree, there's something I've got to do for you. Everything I say from now on, I want you to know I mean the opposite. Understood?"

Ree pulled back, meeting his sad blue eyes.

"Understood?"

She nodded reluctantly.

"Let's practice. I don't love you more than anyone else in the world," he whispered.

She smiled but it felt stiff, like tears drying on her cheeks. "And I don't love you more than anyone else in the world either."

"See, it's easy, isn't it?"

No, it felt like deliberately sticking pins in her fingers. Ree wasn't sure what the point of this game could possibly be until Lord John cleared his throat.

"Terribly sorry to see you in this fix, Altamira."

"Lord John, I have a favour to beg of you," her father began humbly. "My daughter has no family beside me and won't manage on her own. I'm sure you don't mean to leave her destitute?"

The peer fingered his gold watch. "I suppose not. No, of course, that wouldn't do."

"I've heard that there are orphans taken in by the museum." Ree's father sifted his fingers through the hair lying flat on her back, letting her know by his touch that she should trust him. The game was about to begin again.

Lord John frowned. "We do sometimes make provision, that's true. When explorers go missing in the Congo, or scientists blow themselves up doing experiments, occasionally we take in their children. The boys go into the academy and the girls are trained in the domestic arts and are found husbands. But these positions are for children of a higher class of person, you understand."

"But my little girl, she's a biddable child. Cannot something appropriate be found for her? She'll make a good servant. I see now that this was her true calling, not that of stonemason."

Ree bit her lip. Her da said he meant the opposite. Was he saying she was stubborn and would be a terrible servant? That was true enough. But did he even now believe that her vocation was to be a craftswoman?

The peer scratched at the gold casing to his watch with a short clean nail. "I see. Well, I could raise it with the housekeeper."

"A word from you would surely be enough?"

"Yes, yes, I suppose that is true." Lord John popped the watch back into a pocket. "Why not? I have to admit I have my doubts about the punishment fitting the crime. Professor Gall was very passionate today. He swayed the trustees when I was hoping to give your case more of an airing. Still, it could've been worse – far, far worse."

"I know, sir, and I'm grateful."

"The girl did show talent – that little starfish was exquisite. As an artist myself, I can't deny that. You should have directed her toward embroidery or watercolours."

"Yes, my lord. You are, as ever, very wise. I was very wrong to do what I did." James rubbed his daughter's arm, silently telling her that he had no regrets. "Watercolours would've been just the thing."

Lord John smoothed down the front of his satin waistcoat. "Perhaps in due course she'll be allowed to help colour the prints of my pictures. Goodness knows the current bunch of colourists are as ham-fisted as a troop of monkeys with paintbrushes. But for the moment I'll see she starts as a maid. She'll get a roof over her head, three meals a day, and a secure future."

Ree felt the tension go from her father's body. This was the promise he had been waiting for. All along he had been concerned for her and not his own fate.

"Thank you, my lord. I knew I could rely on you." James turned to his daughter and hugged her tightly, her cheek pressed against his rough jacket. "Maria, look after yourself."

"Of course, Da. I'll come and join you as soon as I'm allowed."

He shook his head. "Your life is here. Please, sir, take her away." He pushed her gently toward the peer. "And Ree, you know the rules of our game? When I'm gone, remember me."

"Da?"

"I don't love you, not one tiny little bit." He smiled through shining eyes.

"I... I don't love you one crumb either."

"That's my girl." He turned away and sat down on the bed in a dark corner of his cell. Ree wasn't sure but she thought she saw him put a sleeve to his face.

"Well now, what an odd pair you two are," murmured Lord John. "I would've said you were devoted to each other. Still, the lower classes and whatnot." He shrugged as if the life of those so much beneath him on the social ladder were a mystery and would remain so.

"We are, sir. He… he was just teasing."

Stumbling back down the corridor in the footsteps of Lord John, Ree struggled to make sense of her father's parting words. He had said she must understand that he meant the opposite. If that were true, then he was telling her to forget him.

A sob broke out before she could keep it stifled. *No, Da!*

"There, there, girl. It's all for the best," said Lord John. "He's made sure you've got your chance at a proper female profession. Now it's up to you not to waste it."

Ree couldn't speak. If she had her mallet she would've hit Lord John over the head with it – hang the consequences. A new cause burned fiercely in her chest. She had been given a chance, had she? Then she would use it to make sure her father was allowed to return home or she would go to him. And she wouldn't be waiting five years to make it happen.

Part II

Mesozoic

Mesozoic era: from the Greek *meso*,
meaning "between", and *zoe*, meaning "life".
Also known as the Age of Reptiles.

Extract from Henri's notebooks

Chapter 6

Why Tasmanian Wolves Do Not Make Good Pets

Phil was not speaking to her. Not that the bird did speak, but he was giving her the dodo equivalent of the cold shoulder, perched huffily on a case displaying an early microscope next to an illustration of a giant flea.

"It's not my fault Mr Billibellary asked me to train her." The keeper had not stopped recruiting his favourites among the museum staff to help out with any tricky animal-handling issues. In the two years since her father's ship sailed, Ree had been foster mother to a golden toad, chief dispenser of fish to a Caribbean monk seal, and an occasional rescuer of a Pyrenean ibex when he got stuck on the cliffs at the eastern end of the island. None of these relationships had mattered to Phil, as she always returned to him, but he appeared to regard her time spent with the Tasmanian wolf as the last straw.

Ree soaked the mop in the bucket, then squeezed it out on the drainer. The offending wolf nosed obliviously along the bottom of the cases, hoping for a forgotten sandwich crust or, even better, a rind of bacon. Ree had to admit Ziggy wasn't the most beautiful specimen. She started quite well with a dog-like snout, big eyes, and pricked ears, but then it all went wrong somewhere halfway down her back, when the tiger stripes started and her tail ended up whip-like, hindquarters just a bit too pointy. She looked dangerous, until you spotted the pouch on her belly where she carried her joey, Zag. Then Ziggy just looked rightly defensive about anyone approaching her. Ree liked Ziggy for just not obeying any of the usual rules expected of mammals and being a grumpy example of the largest meat-eating marsupial.

But Ziggy also had the bad habit of biting people she didn't much like, which was why Mr Billibellary had asked Ree if she could train her, his own attempts having failed. Ziggy wouldn't be allowed to roam if she didn't learn to keep her teeth to herself.

Thinking through her problem with Phil and Ziggy, Ree sloshed her mop around half-heartedly, kicking the bucket along to keep pace.

"I mean, Ziggy's nocturnal and you're not, Phil. Why don't you let her follow me around at night when I work and then you can be with me all day when I'm off-duty and she's asleep?" Ree suggested reasonably. The dodo wouldn't understand her words, but it was a way of thinking through her options. "And of course, you're still my best friend. Ziggy will never be a friend. She's too wild for that."

Ziggy growled, hair pricking on her spine ridge. Looking around for the cause, Ree saw Maggie the Javan tiger stalking through the hallways, heading into the depths of the museum.

No longer a cute cub but a full-grown female, she rarely came to be petted and certainly not when other creatures were present. One day, Ree would follow her and find out what she did down there. But not today: not when she still had the whole floor to clean before the housekeeper made her dawn inspection. Mopping the big Thirtieth Hall, devoted to the proceedings of the seventeenth-century instrument makers, had been set as punishment for annoying Mrs Mantell, the housekeeper – a mammoth task as the room was built like a temple with a white paved floor that showed every speck.

Did the trustees know the extent to which Mr Billibellary allowed the creatures free range when the museum was closed? Ree wondered as she swirled her mop. He gave the maids a generous payment to keep their silence and to clean up, money taken from the menagerie entrance fee. He also taught the girls not to fear the animals. He explained that the museum was like a watering hole in the desert outback; the animals were good fellas, knowing they had to observe a truce if they wished to get what they needed from their keepers. With only the very occasional lapse, the arrangement worked; the zoo animals were kept from being bored and remained relatively content with their unnatural surroundings. Ree had long since realized that Mr Billibellary saw the world in reverse to most people. The trustees thought the animals served as illustrations to the museum's story of evolution; Mr Billbellary regarded the museum as serving the animals' need for protection.

Three hours later, reaching the far corner of the room, Ree took a break to admire her work. In the soft glow of the dim gas lights, her floor gleamed like the Arctic wastes, brass instruments in their cases like so many steamships trapped in the ice.

"Not bad," she murmured.

Ziggy lifted her head from where she lay curled up on a dry patch, sniffing in the direction the tiger had gone.

"Don't start. You can't take on Maggie." Ree scratched Ziggy's head, then gently stroked Zag when the joey ventured out of the pouch, which opened to the rear.

Ziggy yawned, as if she had never contemplated such a thing.

Odd; normally the tiger sent the Tasmanian wolf into a fret. Ree tried to see what had caught her attention in the shadows at the far end of the hall. A grey hooded and cloaked figure was moving stealthily along the wall, but on two feet not four, so it had to be human rather than feline.

A shiver ran down Ree's spine. A ghost?

There was no such thing as ghosts, said the scientists. But they'd never cleaned the museum alone at night and seen the strange silent figures flitting about as she and the other maids had.

Ree looked back at the animals. Phil was roosting on his glass case out of harm's way, Ziggy asleep. Either they didn't sense the apparition or it didn't alarm them.

"Hey, you! Anyone there?" Her voice sounded tiny in the echoing hall.

"Are you talking to me, Maria?" asked Mrs Mantell, entering from the direction of the servants' wing. A woman large in all dimensions, she took up a lot of space when she strode anywhere and had a booming voice to match. "If so, you will address me with more respect or I'll think of another floor that needs cleaning."

Ree jumped to her feet. "Sorry, Mrs Mantell. I just thought I saw something over there, in the shadows."

"Very likely. Since Mr Billibellary took over the menagerie I've never know what to expect on my rounds." She ran a finger over a ledge that Ree had fortunately already dusted. "I saw that python of his just yesterday wrapped around one of the dinosaurs. I can understand that four-legged creatures might need exercise, but a legless one? As for Mr Billibellary being a keeper: he's a let-looser and he's gone too far. One day one of you will end up as a snake's supper and then where will we be? Short-handed, that's what!"

Ree thought that probably wasn't the main problem with a snake-eating-a-maid scenario but knew better than to stop Mrs Mantell on one of her rants. She and Mr Billibellary were usually at loggerheads and only the sizeable personal fee she received from him for her silence had so far kept her protests from reaching the museum authorities.

Mrs Mantell surveyed the gleaming expanse of floor, finding nothing to criticize. "You can go. Remember in future that lateness will not be tolerated."

Ree had only been late because Ziggy had stolen a string of sausages from Ingrid's kitchen, and she had been held up making profuse apologies. "Yes, Mrs Mantell."

"And take that mangy dog with you."

Ree bit back the words that Ziggy was not a dog – that was not an argument worth having and certainly not with her employer. "Yes, ma'am." She clicked her fingers. "Ziggy? Breakfast?"

Ziggy leaped to her feet and stretched her hind legs one after the other. Mrs Mantell stomped away to continue her round, while Ree headed in the opposite direction carrying the mop and bucket. Phil scuttled after the housekeeper rather than go with Ziggy. Disposing of her equipment in the scullery, Ree entered Ingrid's kitchen.

"You'd better stay out here," she told the wolf. "You aren't in the cook's good books."

Ziggy lay down, tongue lolling. Little Zag stared with trusting dark eyes from the belly pouch.

"Good morning." Ree hovered at the entrance to the kitchen like a swimmer testing the temperature of the water before plunging in. A second woman was sitting on a chair at the table as Ingrid stirred porridge on the coal-fired range. "Mrs Simplon!"

Her old neighbour got up and gave her a quick hug. "How are you, Maria? Not grown much yet?"

Ree wrinkled her nose. It was a sore point that she hadn't yet reached five feet unlike all the other maids. "Not yet."

"There's no rush. Cheaper on uniform material and at least you're not outgrowing your boots like Paul seems to be every month."

Ree smoothed down the grey cotton dress and white apron she wore. The cost came out of her wages. "That's true. How is Paul?" She avoided going anywhere near her old workmates. To see them doing what she had once done so well was too painful. In her opinion, the standard of carving had dipped since no Altamira worked among them. Appearing before them in her uniform would be an embarrassing reminder that she was reduced to a mere drudge rather than progressing to be a respected stonemason.

"He's well. Wonders when you're going to come to spend a free day with us. You've been quite the stranger."

Ree had spent the New Year's holiday over at the builders' settlement four months ago but it had been a bitter experience. Another family occupied her cabin and the stone seats had been thrown out onto the bank, to be used by fishermen to scrape their boots of river mud. "Tell him I said 'hello'."

"I suppose you've come for that creature's breakfast?" said Ingrid, bringing a dish out of the meat safe. "Not that she deserves it after stealing the scholars' sausages."

"She's very sorry about that," Ree said, not completely truthfully.

"Humph! Why Mr Billibellary landed you with that cursed pet, I don't know."

"He knows Ree has a soft heart for the difficult cases," said Mrs Simplon, smiling fondly at Ree.

"Well, go on now: take it its meal and then come back for your own."

Ree placed the dish on the scullery tiles. Ziggy would now eat and then curl up on her favourite old sack under the stone sink to sleep the day away. That meant Ree's shift as Tasmanian wolf watcher was over; she had to admit it was something of a relief.

She returned to the kitchen, finding it filled with the mouth-watering scent of fried sausages. Ingrid slapped one on a plate in front of her.

"For me?" marvelled Ree. The maids normally had porridge.

"There weren't enough for the scholars after that creature had been at them, so I kept what was left back for the servants to share. They don't complain if they get half a one each."

The white cat jumped up onto the mantlepiece and eyed Ree's plate. "But I've got a whole one."

A smiled twitched the corner of Ingrid's mouth. "Compensation for having to put up with that beast all night."

Deciding it would be foolish to question her good luck, Ree set about her breakfast with a hearty appetite. The egg that Ingrid added to the side had been cooked to perfection, golden yoke running out to meet the dam of toast and sausage. Happily, Ree ground some pepper into the mix and ate the lot with an appetite Ziggy would approve.

"Where's your other shadow?" asked Mrs Simplon.

"Who?" Ree's thoughts went back briefly to the grey figure she'd seen at dawn.

"The dodo."

"Oh, Phil? Went off with Mrs Mantell. He's determined to convert her into a friend. He's not talking to me. He's got in a flutter about Ziggy."

Mrs Simplon smiled over the rim of her teacup. "He'll get over it."

"It would help if Ziggy stopped nipping at his tail feathers. He doesn't understand that it's just for fun."

Mrs Simplon rolled her eyes. "This place is a madhouse. Still, you haven't asked me why I'm here, Ree. I've a letter." She patted her pocket and produced a yellowed envelope that looked like it had been doused with weak tea on one corner.

"From Da?" Ree reached out to take it. His letters came so rarely. This was only the third she had received in two years.

"Who else would be writing to you, lamb?" Mrs Simplon pressed it into her hand. "There now. You'll want to read that immediately, I expect. Don't feel you have to stay to talk with me."

"Thank you!" Hugging the letter to her chest, Ree ran out of the kitchen. She couldn't take it to the maids' tower: there would be too many girls there all wanting to know the news before she had a chance to absorb it. She hurried to her favourite room in the administration block, a rarely used little committee chamber decorated with shells like a sea cave, *trompe-l'oeil* openings painted with seascapes, and a little golden beach where wet footprints stretched into an illusory distance. It had a circular balcony running around the domed roof reached by a rope ladder. Once up there you could pretend you were in a bird's nest high on a sea cliff. She scrambled up and sat cross-legged by the porthole-shaped window. She ran her finger over her father's firm handwriting, her name written with such care across the centre, the downstrokes of the M with a little flick to the end, the wide stance of the A like a stepladder. She turned it over, finding it unsealed as the previous letters had been. Prisoners' correspondence was checked and censored before it was allowed out of the camp. It was dated six months ago.

Dearest Maria,

I hope this finds you safe and well. Thank you for your letters. I have received six, though from the numbers you put on the front of each I fear three may have gone astray. No doubt they will eventually turn up like migrating birds blown off course in a storm.

I am in good health and have continued to do well here.

Oh, Da, was that true?

I've recently made some new friends. My best mate in the camp, Luc, tells me he saw you briefly when he was in the lockups so asks me to send you his regards. He says he still ▓▓▓▓▓▓ for you. Unfortunately, he has not been well and may be transferred to lighter duties elsewhere. If he is sent away, then I will sorely miss him. He has been a cheerful presence and a determined optimist even on the darkest days.

Unintentionally, Ree felt sure, Da had given her more of a hint of just how bleak life was in the labour camp. She had to get him out – had to!

The governor of the camp tells me you are still writing to him and every member of the government on a weekly basis. You have become quite famous and I am known as the man with the persistent daughter. Bless you, but I fear it will not do. You must be spending all your wages on stamps.

Not all. Only two-thirds. She scavenged the paper from the academy so didn't have to buy that.

Do you not remember what I told you in our opposites game? I hoped you would understand that I meant you to forget about me and get on with your life. Ask Lord John about the colouring he mentioned. That surely will be better than cleaning and more suited to your talents?

Maybe, but she couldn't see the point of colouring in someone else's designs. She wanted to create her own. The frustration of not being able to do so was like carrying Zag inside her dress and feeling her squirming to get out.

If you go on making a nuisance of yourself then he won't want to help you any more. And your letters won't change anything. The facts of my case still stand no matter how many times you plead for mercy.

Ree grimaced. Da was as plain-speaking as he had always been, but she matched that with her stubbornness. She could no more forget him than she could stop writing the letters, useless though they were at present. Her hope was that just once, maybe, one would get through, like a strange quirk in a creature proving to be the very thing to give the species an evolutionary advantage as conditions changed. It only took one shift in the official environment for a letter to win out. She had long ago accepted that most of them were destined for mass extinction.

She finished the rest of the letter in a happy gulp of news like the pelican painted on the rock behind her, swallowing a fish whole. She would come back to it again and again to savour the words at more leisure, but for now she could bask in the feeling that he was all right – or had been six months ago when he wrote those words to her.

Putting the letter in her apron pocket, she was about to go in search of some paper to start another round of appeals when the door to the committee room opened. Scooting back into the shadows of the balcony, Ree lay on her stomach so she couldn't be seen. It was not the first time she had been caught where she had no right to be and she knew some good hiding places. This, fortunately, was one of the best. The officials of the museum thought it below their dignity to climb the rope ladder and there was no other way she could be seen.

"Why are we holding the meeting in here, Simplicius?" Professor Gall walked in followed by nine other men. "The Displays Committee normally meets in the founder's gallery."

"I thought you would appreciate a rather more private venue for our discussion," said Simplicius Shelley, the guide who had told off the schoolboy on the day of the Theophilus protest. He

99

had gained his wish of promotion to full curator shortly after her father's trial and had then progressed much more quickly than normal to be made a trustee and head of one of the museum's committees. There had been much muttering about his meteoric rise, achieved largely, it was rumoured, by the sponsorship of Lord John and by making himself indispensable to the chancellor. Ree had heard that he had learned Sanskrit to impress his patron, even though his own field of geology was nothing to do with ancient languages.

Gall tutted. "I can't see why. We usually allow the public to listen to our debates. We have nothing to hide."

"Please, gentlemen, sit down." Simplicius wasn't to be budged. Ree resigned herself to the fact that she would have to doze here while they talked.

"Oh, very well," growled the professor.

Chairs scraped and the men took their seats.

Shelley tapped his papers on the table. "We have three main items on our agenda. First is the report from the menagerie. I regret to say that takings are still way below the estimated income. It is only just breaking even."

That was because Mr Billibellary spent any extra on bribes and treats for his charges.

"However, it is paying for itself and is undoubtedly a draw so I suggest we review the situation in the autumn.

"The second item I wish to bring to your attention is that the stonework in the entrance hall is now complete, unfortunately late and well over budget – a matter I have raised with the foreman. As most of you will recall, I took over control of the workmen after that unfortunate incident. I've threatened the foreman with dismissal if this situation carries on."

Poor Mr Simplon.

"I have instructed the workers to start on the external work facing the railway station and told them they have to be more economical from now on."

By which he meant lower wages and tighter belts in the builders' encampment, thought Ree grimly.

"I trust there has been no repeat of Lord John's foolish idea that the men should decide their own designs?" asked one of the trustees, whom Ree didn't know but she remembered him as he wore a monocle. He had been on the platform when Phil stole her hat.

"Of course not, Professor André. But it was not the *men*, may I remind you, that caused that problem?"

There was a rumble of laughter. Ree clenched her fists. How dare they reduce her case to a joke?

"The point being that we are free now to remove all dust sheets from the remaining display cases and think about refreshing their contents. Some of those exhibits haven't been looked at for years. What are we saying to young minds as they come into our great palace of knowledge? That science is all about dead reptiles and stuffed animals?"

"You have to admit the dinosaurs are very popular with the boys," ventured one man, whom Ree knew to be an expert fossil hunter. He had happily given the stonemasons pointers on their carvings of ancient creatures when they worked on the entrance hall.

"Indeed, but it gives a false impression of the age of the earth, and of the universe. If they leave believing that it all started with your terrible lizards, Joseph, then we are doing them a disservice," Shelley continued.

"It is only an appetizer," argued the fossil man. "Still, why don't you tell us what you've been thinking?"

"Rocks. A huge cliff face representing the different geological ages of the earth."

Ree shook her head in disbelief. The man really thought children would like to look at a heap of stones? Not unless they were allowed to climb them, which she doubted he had in mind.

"Hmm, I'm not sure," said Joseph.

"I've drawn up a proposal, which I will leave with you all for you to consider for a decision at our next meeting." From his pile of papers Shelley handed out a large folded sheet.

Joseph spread out the plan on the table before him. "But what about the diplodocus? Where will you put it if you mount your cross-section as you propose?"

"Don't worry, Joseph. I thought we could find a home for it in the new octagonal room."

Professor Gall slammed the paper describing the proposal on the table. "Hang on a moment – that's my room!"

"*Your* room?" Shelley asked icily.

"You know dashed well that it was destined to be the new phrenological room. I've worked for months on the display."

Shelley gave him a thin smile. "Ah, that brings us to the third and final item on our agenda: the current scientific standing of phrenology."

A sticky silence fell in the room. Ree held her breath.

"What?" Professor Gall's voice was like the venomous spit of a cobra.

"Come now, Franz, surely you can't have failed to notice that there has been doubt cast on the recent claims made for your discipline?" Shelley spoke as a patronizing father to his ignorant child.

"Doubts that I have only last month challenged in my article in *The Phrenologists' Journal*!" Gall countered.

"But that hardly has the standing of the peer-reviewed process of the *Proceedings of the Royal Society*. Unless you bring your evidence forward to be judged by those with a more sceptical outlook on your – I hesitate to use the word – 'science', how can you expect the museum to devote a whole room to it?"

"You dare to question – ?"

"Of course, *I dare*. That is what we all do, what we all teach – science is only that which can be proved in a laboratory with repeated experimental data. It is not a pet theory that disintegrates like a paper umbrella under the first shower of challenging questions."

Oh, this was excellent. Thank goodness she had got trapped here to hear this. Ree well remembered Professor Gall's campaign against her father. Paul had told her he was the one asking for the death penalty. It was a pleasure to see the professor having something he cared for taken away as he had taken everything from her.

The professor acted like a kettle, lid rattling as it came to the boil. "You've had it in for my subject since the beginning! You know nothing about it – you with your rocks and hammers."

"It was men like me with rocks and hammers who started to unravel the ridiculous lies told about the age of the Earth." Shelley thumped the table, causing a landslide of his pile of papers he only just caught.

Gall pointed a finger at him. "You look at the lumps and bumps in a cliff and use that to declare your truth; I look at the surface of a person's head to do the same. If my method is suspect, then so is yours."

Shelley straightened his papers with two sharp taps. "An analogy doesn't make it the same at all."

They'd lost Ree. But what she did understand was that they were arguing over what was a proper science and that Professor Gall was losing.

"Look, Franz, I understand this is a difficult time of adjustment for you," continued Shelley.

"A… adjustment!" spluttered Gall.

"And I don't dispute that there may be depths to your discipline that are yet to be sounded, evidence that will validate its speculations. I haven't said we should scrap the phrenological display, but I was merely going to suggest it is moved."

"Moved where?" Gall's voice was a growl like Ziggy gave before she bit. Shelley should look out.

"In with Animal Mesmerism in the antechamber to the Fortieth Hall."

"Animal Mesmerism! But that is pretty much accepted to be a pseudoscience after its theories were discredited."

"Steady on!" said Professor André. "I'm rather partial to mesmerism. Cured me of my gout."

Gall was oblivious to this protest. "Gentlemen, you can't let him do this to my subject. If he can do this to phrenology, where will he stop? Yours will be next!"

"Oh, come now!" muttered André.

"Let's not lose our tempers," said Joseph. "Nothing is decided yet."

"Nor will be until the next meeting," added Shelley.

The professor rapped on the table. "I want it recorded in the minutes that I make the most strenuous protests against any attempt to relegate phrenology to a fringe interest. It should and must be given its due place in the museum."

"I can certainly agree with you on that," said Shelley with a snide smile.

"You'll destroy the reputation of my subject at your peril, Shelley! You're nothing but a jumped-up guide getting unearned promotion through taking advantage of an old man's weakness. What do you know about true science?"

The angrier Gall became the more gloating his rival. "Professor, calm yourself. Nothing is going to be done without a rigorous peer-reviewed process weighing the merits of the subjects about which we are disagreeing."

"And I suppose you'll be heading the review!"

"Gentlemen," intervened Joseph firmly, "I suggest we defer this discussion until we've all had a chance to think about it without the issue being clouded by hot tempers."

Gall yanked on his beard, probably to give himself a sharp reminder that he would win nothing this way, and potentially lose the respect of his peers. "Yes, Joseph, you're right. We all need to step back and give this the rational consideration it deserves. Personally, I have always thought your diplodocus a fine way to introduce our guests to the museum and see no need to change anything."

"Then we will adjourn until next Wednesday," said Shelley. "Gentlemen, I bid you good morning. I have a meeting with the chancellor now." Gathering up his papers, Shelley swept out with the air of a busy man with many vital tasks to perform.

Ree waited for the room to empty, then waited another five minutes to check no one was returning to collect something they had forgotten. Once she was convinced it was safe, she clambered down the rope ladder and slipped out of the room. If Professor Gall, main accuser in her father's trial, was losing ground in scientific circles, then maybe opposition to her father's return would be less strong? It was certainly worth hinting as much in her next letters.

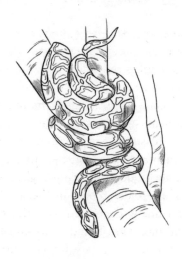

Chapter 7
Head to Head

Pacing the scholars' library, Zena on his shoulder, Henri checked he had all his equipment with him: notebooks recording his experiments, the prototype of the apparatus he required, estimate of the funds needed to cover his costs. He couldn't think of anything else and he was certain he knew his subject inside out. His main worry was that it was a little speculative and unproven. But surely the trustees should want science to be advanced? The museum was supposed to be the world leader in research.

The other scholars applying for the funding allocated to the new intake of junior curators watched Henri with envious gazes. He could feel them follow his every pace. He knew from the mutterings in the academy common room that, despite his young age, he was expected to walk away with the lion's share of the money. He was the only one to have once been to tea with the trustees, not that he had ever admitted that his triumph then had been more to do with his ability to catch a cake stand than to impress the elders with his learning.

The double doors to the library opened and three men came in: Professor Gall, Dr Erasmus – the old botanist, now almost completely deaf – and Master Ricardo. Henri could tell at once that the professor was in a bad mood. He practically flattened the footman who had hurried to pull out a chair for him at the table under the stained glass window. The library was one of the older rooms in the academy wing of the museum, the window decorated with the shields of the noble families who had contributed to its construction. The light coming into the room was flush with warm tones from the Ansbach family coat of arms, but unfortunately the stripe that fell across Gall's head made his face look as though he was wearing a bloodstained mask. He looked quite fierce, a red-tailed hawk waiting to fall on its prey. Some of Henri's confidence leeched away.

"I don't like the look of this," he murmured to Zena.

She grimaced, clambered down his back, and jumped on the nearest bookcase.

"Coward," Henri muttered.

"Let's get on with it then," snapped Gall.

Henri hoped that Master Ricardo would choose one of the others so that the professor had time to work off his ire, but he was not so fortunate.

"Volp, come to the front," said the teacher. "Dr Erasmus, Professor Gall, you will remember our senior scholar from Algeria? Volp will graduate early with honours at the ceremony at the end of the month. He's been named chief wrangler and swept the board with the academy prizes."

Gall glared at Henri. Dr Erasmus stuck his hearing trumpet in his ear.

"Speak up, man. Stop mumbling!" he shouted at Ricardo.

"Of course, sir." The master beckoned Henri forward. "Volp, make your case."

Henri spread out his exhibits, notebooks, and equipment. "My proposal," he began in the loudest voice he could manage, short of bellowing, "concerns the invention of a process by which we can lift fingerprints from objects left at a crime scene." He hadn't forgotten the pet murders two years ago and the difficulty of getting the school authorities to accept that a human had been responsible. "So far we can only record prints made in something we can see – ink, blood, powder – which we then photograph and catalogue. It is my theory that the natural oils on our fingers also leave hidden prints behind. If I can find the right chemical compound to reveal those to a camera lens then these too can be compared with the prints of suspects, making a conviction much more likely."

"More likely!" spluttered Gall, examining the accounts. "Time-wasting, more like. As I've been saying for years, all you need to do is examine the scalps of your suspects and the guilty party will reveal him or herself. I was expecting a serious scientific project from you – not this nonsense!"

Humiliation crawled like fire ants below Henri's collar. "But, sir, forensic science has proved very useful in recent years. Ballistics, handwriting analysis, poison detection – all have been used in the courts to secure convictions. I'm certain fingerprinting is the next big advance. All I need is lab space to conduct my experiment safely and on a larger scale than I can at present, and funds for the chemicals involved."

"You are going to commandeer an entire room to yourself?" fumed Gall. "You, a wet-behind-the-ears scholar?"

"Indeed, sir, that is part of the proposal. I was thinking that one of the unused rooms that won't be missed could be dedicated to it. Maybe over in the Fortieth Hall near Animal Magnetism? No one goes there."

"Preposterous!" Gall got to his feet. 'I'm not wasting my time listening to this claptrap. Who is this boy again? The senior scholar? Well, if this is the best the senior scholar is able to come up with then I fear I'm wasting my time here."

Zena let out a stream of monkey abuse in Gall's direction.

Ricardo saw that the annual division of grants was about to be cancelled. "Please, Professor, do take your seat again. This is only the first proposal and I put the most ambitious at the head before we get to more normal fare. Volp has a tendency to overestimate his own intelligence. Thank you for bringing the weakness of his idea to my attention. As you know, this is not my field. Volp, go away. Johansen, come forward. Johansen here has a very nice little project to do with the propagation of peas that might interest you."

"Peas?" queried Dr Erasmus, brightening up at the mention of a botanical specimen. "Did you say 'peas'? Jolly good."

Henri gaped. That was it? His ideas had been dismissed without any more consideration than that? "But sir!"

Professor Gall scowled at him. "Remove yourself, boy. Observing your scalp, I see you have a pronounced organ of self-love and a distinct lacking in the region of sagacity and mechanical skill. That tells me that no experiment you propose will ever succeed."

"But that's just foolishness!" said Henri, against his better judgment feeling his head for the bumps and dips the professor claimed to have detected.

"I'd say it goes with your heritage. What scientific truths have ever come out of the African continent? You have been encouraged beyond your capacity. I won't spend any more time on you. Get out of my sight!"

Henri's gaze went to Ricardo in appeal, but he saw that he was going to get no help from his teacher, who was outranked here and unwilling to spend what little influence he did have on a pupil he had never much liked.

Furious, Henri clicked his fingers to summon Zena, who

leaped to his shoulder. Keeping his spine straight, he gathered his notebooks and walked out. He would collect the apparatus later when no one else was about.

"How did it go, Henri?" asked Hans, leader of the little group of juniors Henri helped tutor.

"How much did they give you?" asked one of the newest pupils, a fair-haired scholar called Maxwell. It was rare for him to pipe up; he always kept quiet in class as if afraid of drawing attention to himself by asking too many questions.

"Was it the full six hundred or did they cut it down like you thought they might?" Hans offered Zena a peanut.

Henri wished he could just walk past them, but they were his supporters and deserved better.

"They turned me down flat. I got nothing."

"What!" exclaimed Maxwell.

"Those old fossils!" said Hans.

"Not fossils – I like fossils – they're dung beetles!" muttered Maxwell.

"Henri, what are you going to do?" Hans asked.

"Try on my own, I suppose. I don't need them." He gave his young friends a brave smile. "Come on, I'm hungry. Let's go and see what's for dinner."

For all the show he put on for the juniors, Henri was still fuming as he ate his meal of meat pie and mashed potatoes. Zena amused herself, flicking peas at the boys in Henri's year, much to their annoyance, but he was too downhearted to stop her. The meal sat like a boulder in his stomach. He had never been treated so dismissively before. He had known his nationality in this part of the world had counted against him in small ways, but usually people had ignored that once they realized how able he was. This time was different: Professor Gall hadn't asked more than a cursory question, having decided against his project before Henri had done anything, and then he had come out with his outrageous assertion about scalps! Henri had always considered phrenology suspect; now he saw that it was dangerous.

In the afternoon study period, Henri noticed that he had already lost status with the other scholars in his year. All graduating in a few weeks, some were going back to their home countries to go on to university, others staying on to take further studies in the elite fellowship of junior curators. Henri already had a confirmed place among this number, having come top in all his subjects. But now he had no official research project so no purpose for being here while others had their funding sorted.

"So, Igor, you got the money for your peas?" asked Ramon. Careless in the lab, the Spaniard was guaranteed to knock over the sulphuric acid or crush a seedling so knew his future didn't lie in research. Henri would miss him when he left. As the year's clown, Ramon made up for his lack of brains with jokes, often at his own expense.

"More than I could have wished for. I'll be able to construct my own greenhouse in the botanical garden." Igor Johansen was glowing with pride.

Ramon gave an appreciative whistle. "I hope you said *peas* and thank you. That will cost a packet."

Igor groaned at the terrible pun. "They gave me three hundred guineas. They didn't even blink at the amount. I think I got it only because, well, you know, what happened to Henri?"

"Yes, I heard. Apparently to decide guilt we only need to check for bumps, not bother with the little matter of evidence." Ramon cast Henri a sympathetic glance.

Pretending he wasn't upset, Henri leafed through Dr Joseph Bell's book on anatomy, a volume he already knew from cover to cover. It was horrible to feel so jealous of the pea proposal. He didn't dislike Igor, but right then he felt like planting him in a greenhouse and turning on the sprinklers.

"I heard that Professor Gall announced that no proposal from Henri Volp had a chance of succeeding, that his head is all wrong." This came – unsurprisingly – from Kurt Spurzheim,

Gall's top student. He, of course, had his proposal to measure the scalps of criminals in the city jails fully funded and commended by the professor.

Ramon rocked back on his chair. "*Es la verdad*? Then there is no hope for the rest of us." He grinned at Henri, who smiled slightly in reply.

"I have to say that I didn't understand Henri's idea either," said Igor, not appreciating having his moment of success tarnished by any sense that the play had not been fair. "It sounded a bit like magic – making invisible prints visible."

Ramon slapped his friend on the arm, a big smile heralding one of his jokes. "But I looked at your greenhouse experiment and I didn't understand that one either. So you know what they say?"

"No?" Igor was too slow to see the elephant trap waiting for him.

"People who live in glass houses shouldn't throw stones!" Ramon cackled at his own joke, making everyone join in because his laugh was so infectious.

Henri silently thanked Ramon for teasing him about his disappointment. The Spaniard was right: it was a situation that you could only turn into a joke. Henri didn't respect the judgment of those who had refused him so he would simply have to find another way.

"So where are you going to live, Henri, when you lose your senior scholar set?" asked Spurzheim, his blue eyes glinting maliciously. "Those rooms come with your scholarship, which ends next month. I hear Billibellary has an opening in the menagerie – in one of the cages."

"Hilarious, Spurzheim. Tell me, are your insults the result of the moment or do you spend all night coming up with them to use later?" Henri said it with disdain, but his classmate's attitude was becoming increasingly disturbing since he'd caught the phrenology bug from Professor Gall. Henri sincerely hoped

Spurzheim never got into a position of power as he would do nothing but abuse it.

Spurzheim stuck a finger right under Henri's nose. "Watch it, Volp: your days as a favoured son of this place are numbered. Once you're down, I'll make sure you're out for good."

"Steady on, Kurt," said Ramon.

Zena threw a peanut shell at Spurzheim and screeched.

Henri didn't need the Spaniard or even his monkey to defend him. He pushed the finger away with a yawn. "Really? Threats now? I would ask 'what ever did I do to you but beat you in every single subject?' but I suppose I've just answered my own question."

"I'm not jealous of a rat like you!"

Henri lifted Zena to her usual perch on his shoulder. "Good to know. And let me assure you that I'm not the slightest bit envious of a *pulex irritans* like you."

"A what?"

"Look it up. You'll find it in the Latin dictionary in the library, if you know where that is." Thinking the next move after this swapping of insults would be an exchange of blows, Henri gathered up his books.

"Just you wait, Volp, I'll get you!" spluttered Spurzheim when one of his more intelligent friends whispered the translation: a human flea.

"I doubt that very much." Henri swept out, clutching his books to his chest. Zena screeched ear-splitting threats. He might have appeared confident to his fellow students but inside he was shaking. Spurzheim had always been slyly hostile, but now he was bringing that battle out into the open. The academy had suddenly got much more dangerous for a student from Algeria.

Henri waited until the boys had settled down for the night before beginning his exploration. If the trustees wouldn't grant him a room, then he would have to find one for himself. This

wasn't as unlikely as it might sound, as there were vast areas of
the museum that were no longer on anyone's daily patrol, lying
beyond the reach of visitors who only had a few hours to spend
on their tour. Rather than maintain these dusty rooms of arcane
knowledge, the doors were locked. Some chambers, Henri was
convinced, had been forgotten entirely as no one appeared to
have kept an architectural plan of the whole building in the early
days of construction, and the museum now had become so big,
no one could know the full extent.

Leaving Zena curled up on his bed, he took a lantern and went
out into the corridor. Passing the refectory, he glanced inside
and saw the maids busy cleaning the tables and floors. One was
singing, the others joining in for the chorus, something about
milkmaids and seafaring lovers. It was odd to see so many girls
in one place. His life in the academy meant that the only women
he spoke to during the day were the cooks and laundresses, and
then but rarely; maids he glimpsed when he had been studying
late, but they always ignored him. He couldn't remember the last
time he had actually had a proper conversation with a female.
Was that a logical state of affairs, to shut the students off from
half of the population like they were monks in a cloister?

His lips curved at the image. He guessed that Master Ricardo
would not appreciate Henri complaining that the boys in the
academy had less freedom than women in Henri's country.

Careful not to be seen, Henri left the part of the museum
he knew well and forged on in the direction of the Fortieth
Hall. This was the outer limit of guided tours, reached only by
those with the greatest stamina. His room, if he could find it,
would lie beyond. He needed to find steps leading down to a
basement, an underground room being ideal as less likely to be
found. There was a real risk of getting lost, however, so he had
brought a ball of thread with him. Being encouraged to study
the classics by his father had served a useful purpose: Ariadne
had provided Theseus with thread so he could find his way out

of the minotaur's labyrinth. Henri was about to borrow her idea.

The clatter of a metal bucket in the Fortieth Hall alerted him to the presence of yet another maid. Henri covered his lantern and stepped into the shadows, hoping to creep around the edge of the room. His plan was thwarted when a thick log tripped him, then began to move over him.

Panic set it in: it was no log, but a very large snake! He yelled and leaped up, all thoughts of being quiet vanishing.

"Who's there?" The gas lights flared brighter as the maid turned up the supply on the wall control. Dazzled briefly, he saw now that the room had a chequered floor of black and white tiles, and a display of chains linked to old-fashioned wet batteries, as well as a giant model of a frog. He was in the animal magnetism chamber, face to face with a scowling girl, mop held like a soldier's pike, ready to gut him. Her floppy mob cap framed an oval face with snapping blue eyes. She looked familiar but Henri couldn't place her. He was too busy getting out of the way of the snake, which slithered out of the shadows and moved between them like a slow-flowing brook, she on one side, he on the other. Henri climbed on a plinth holding the statue of a celebrated scientist, grabbing the elbow as an anchor.

"Oh, you tripped over Naidu." Balancing the mop in the bucket, she kneeled down and stroked the monster. "Did the clumsy boy upset you, you poor little python?"

The scene got even more ridiculous as the dodo glided down from a nearby display case and landed next to the maid, croaking with what sounded suspiciously like laughter, and an ugly-looking dog-creature prowled toward him, teeth bared. Henri swung his lantern out in front of him, ready to thrust it at the beast if it got any closer.

"Ziggy, no!" ordered the girl.

The creature whined.

"Really, no. You must not bite the scholars."

Henri was regaining his composure. "I would rather expect you to say it mustn't bite *anyone*."

"Well, I have a few exceptions to the rule," admitted the girl, patting the dog. "Some people here definitely deserve to have her nip their ankles. But that's beside the point. What are you doing here scaring the life out of me?"

"Me, scaring you?" Henri had rather thought it had been the other way around. This small maid came with three formidable guardians. "What is that thing anyway?"

"Ziggy? Oh, she's a Tasmanian wolf. Lovely, isn't she?" The girl had expertly found the scratch spot on the beast's neck, making its hind leg rise in a reflex shiver. A little face became visible on its stomach.

"There's another of them?"

"Yes, they're marsupials. That means they carry their young in their pouch."

"I know what a marsupial is." He didn't need this girl to educate him. He felt ridiculous stuck on this statue.

"All right then. You'd better get back to your wing, scholar. You're not supposed to be wandering the corridors late at night."

He bristled at her tone of command and risked jumping to the floor. "And you are?"

"The cleaning is always done on the nightshift. You're in *my* territory during my time." She dunked the mop in her bucket and splashed it on the floor, purposely close to his feet so he had to step back smartly.

"I hadn't really thought about it before," admitted Henri. He had assumed it was only the academy that was tidied when the students were asleep and he had given scant attention to what happened in the rest of the building.

"This place doesn't clean itself, scholar." The girl's movements with the mop were jerky, as if she was battling with her temper.

"Of course, it doesn't. I apologize for disturbing you. I'll let you get on."

"That's so kind of you, sir." Her sarcasm was cutting. "I get rather bored to tell the truth, so seeing you trip over the python and then clinging onto Mr Mesmer at least broke the monotony."

Henri struggled with his dignity as the senior scholar and his own sense that he must have made quite a ridiculous sight, floundering in panic on the floor. Humour won out. "You will forgive me for not approving of your choice of doorstop."

Giving him a surprised glance, she rewarded him with a chuckle. She unbent enough to give him some advice. "Look, Master Scholar, the museum is a wild place at night. If you're going to make a habit of wandering, you'll have to watch where you put your feet. It's not just the animals but what they leave behind that might be an unpleasant surprise."

Henri had to allow she had a point. She was beginning to interest him. This wasn't how he thought girls would behave at all. "You seem very at ease talking to me. I thought maids weren't supposed to speak to us?"

She shrugged. "We're not, but you wandered into my domain, remember? What am I to do? Pretend you don't exist? That's just stupid. I've talked to boys before, worked alongside them. I know they're not a different species."

It suddenly fell into place where he'd seen her before. "You're that girl!"

She kicked the mop bucket away from him. "Good night, sir."

"No, no, don't run off. I wanted to say at the time that I thought it wrong."

"Then why didn't you? No one stood up for us; no one said I should've been allowed to carve stone."

Her belief that he could have made a difference was flattering but very ill-informed. "What? Me, a mere scholar? And an outsider from Algeria? Believe me, my support would not have worked in your favour."

She put the mop back in the bucket. Henri wondered if he had just escaped being dowsed in dirty water. "Algeria? That's

North Africa, isn't it?" Her eyes reconsidered him, noting his darker skin. He was pleased that she hadn't taken any notice of that before. It was tiresome having it as the first thing people saw about him. "So you're African?"

"Half. My father is French, my mother's from Algiers. You know a lot for a maid."

He meant it as a compliment but she did not take it that way. "I do have a brain, you know, and eyes. There are globes in the Thirtieth Hall. I bet I could name more capital cities than you can."

"I don't doubt it. That's not information I've ever considered worth memorizing."

"It's much more useful than some of the things I hear you scholars chanting in your classrooms."

She wouldn't understand what she was listening to and was obviously deluded about her own future prospects. She was a maid, for heaven's sake! "Why do you study globes? Are you going to travel the world then? Go up the Amazon or along the Silk Road into China?"

"Maybe. One day. Why shouldn't I?" she challenged.

Such adventures weren't possible for her in the world they lived in. She didn't need him to point that out though. In her heart, she must realize that. "Well, good luck, Miss Altamira. I'll leave you to your cleaning."

Taking his lantern, Henri retraced his steps. His exploration of the forbidden parts of the museum would have to take place on another night when she wasn't watching. Those blue eyes saw too much.

Chapter 8

White Chalk and Rebel Talk

Ree kicked the bucket a second time once the boy had retreated. After a brief hope that he might be different, with his sympathy for her cause, he had revealed himself to be an arrogant so-and-so like the rest of them.

"Why do you study globes?" she mimicked his voice, though admittedly his had a nice quality to it but she wasn't in the mood to allow him any positives. She studied globes, Mr Scholar, because they were interesting and one of her links to her father. She could trace the shoreline of the country to which Da had been sent and feel as though she were blessing him from afar. The boy doubtless would disapprove of such a sentimental notion, but she was as much a part of this world as he; she had every right to know what was in it. The scholars seemed

to expect the maids to move through the museum like a placid flock of sheep, providing for the needs of the men without one single intelligent thought between them. She knew for a fact that one senior maid, Mary, had taught herself about fossils from cleaning the glass cases in the First Hall, and Beata had begun to work out some basic mathematics from the Tenth Hall, which was devoted to some old Greek called Euclid. Mrs Mantell had put Beata on to the housekeeping accounts as a result, saving a great deal of time and errors for their employers.

Giving the bucket a satisfying rattle and kick, she let her anger go. She had learned a hard lesson over the last two years that there was no use fretting over such slights; she just had to take what action she could and be content with that.

"What do you think Mr Scholar was doing down here?" Ree asked Phil.

The dodo looked up at her quizzically.

"Exploring? I'm surprised we don't see more boys going on walkabout. I couldn't live in a building for years like them and not get to know it. I bet I've explored more rooms than they have." Ree retrieved from her apron pocket a plan of the various chambers she had charted so far, a different sheet for each floor, pinned together so you could flip between them, keeping track of your position if you took stairs up or down. She'd learned that trick from the architectural drawings she'd seen as a stonemason. When she had time, she added a new area to her guide, partly for her own safety in case she ever got lost, but partly out of pure curiosity. She had never forgotten Lord John's throwaway remark that the museum had a labyrinth running beneath it that you wandered at your own risk. She had long since left the arrows behind and forged her own paths. "So, what shall we visit tonight?" Ree, Phil, and, more recently Ziggy, had explored all the many antechambers off the main halls that formed the heart of the museum, well over two hundred rooms on her last count if you included the unnumbered storage rooms and attics; it was time to see if there was a Fiftieth Hall beyond this one.

Propping her mop against the plaster model with instructions that the giant frog look after it for her, Ree went to the heavy doors leading out of the hall at the west end. She knew from experience that these would be locked but it was always worth checking.

The handle rattled but didn't move.

The tunnels underneath it would have to be. She had discovered that usually there was a way around locked doors if you were prepared to go up or down. But which of the many side doors was the one she required?

As she was pondering her choices, Maggie padded regally through the chamber, nosed a door at the far right of the chamber, and disappeared.

"Thank you, Maggie," murmured Ree. She tapped Phil on the beak. "You'd better stay here, as Maggie is a little unpredictable. You too, Ziggy. No fighting!" With that warning reinforced by the shake of a finger, Ree hurried after the Javan tiger. As she expected, the door opened on to one of the spiral staircases that led down to the cellars. She glanced behind once to check that Ziggy and Phil were behaving themselves, then ventured down. Maggie was waiting for her at the bottom and accepted the scratch between her ears that she wouldn't allow with others looking on.

"So what do you want to show me?" asked Ree.

The tiger turned and walked soundlessly further west. Ree noticed that the floor was clear of dust, suggesting someone was using it. Many of the other passageways were so clogged with leaves blown there from who knew where that mushrooms were growing in the mulch.

Maggie led her through a complex series of passages, over what appeared to be an underground river spanned by an arched bridge, and past a statue of a seahorse man in a fountain. She paused briefly at the bottom of the next flight of stairs to check

Ree understood her intention, then bounded swiftly up the stone treads. Ree followed the tip of her tail, excitement growing. What was attracting Maggie to go so far from the menagerie each night? Ree felt sure she was about to find out.

Tiger and girl came out into a huge hexagonal chamber: the Fiftieth Hall, surely? Ree held up her lamp but it wasn't powerful enough to illuminate such a large space. There appeared to be a glazed roof-lantern high above, as she could glimpse stars and a thin crescent moon dodging between fast moving clouds.

Not paying full attention to her footing, Ree missed the clue that prompted Maggie to leap forward. Instead, she tripped over an obstacle on the floor. Next thing she knew she was lifted high in the air, caught in a rope net.

What on earth…? "Help!"

No one answered. Ree twirled in the silence. Maggie padded below and looked up at her disapprovingly. Apparently it was a cub's mistake to get caught in such an obvious trap.

"Well, I wouldn't've done if you'd warned me!" grumbled Ree. The lantern, fortunately still alight, had been caught at an awkward angle and was burning her calf. She wiggled it through a hole, then hooked it from the net so that her hands were free. She attempted to rearrange her limbs so she could climb up to the top and see if there was a release. Looked at from this height, the floor was revealed as a mosaic pavement, a little distorted into ripples like a pebbled beach after the passage of the tide. Four dividers like compass points stretched from a central star. Each quarter of the room appeared to have a theme: water in the area where sea creatures swam, fire opposite that, earth in the third, facing air in the last. Some fragments were missing. An odd creature, part human, part fish – a mermaid, Ree guessed, though talk of these was now forbidden – was without her eyes and nose, giving her a most sinister look.

Maggie rumbled and bounded off into the shadows.

"Maggie!" called Ree. "Wait!"

"So, what critter have we caught, Maggie?" A tall figure in a wide-brimmed hat strode toward her, the tiger pacing alongside. Whoever it was looked ready for jungle exploration in their beige shirt and trousers, a wide-bladed knife hanging from a belt, a revolver in its holster.

Ree gulped. She'd been caught. After so many nights of rambling, she had finally crossed the line and would be facing dismissal. "Could you help me down, sir?"

Hands on hips, the person laughed, an oddly high-pitched sound from so tall a man. "Sir? Please, I prefer to be called doctor."

"Doctor."

"All right – drop that lantern down to me."

Ree unhooked it and the doctor caught it deftly in gloved hands.

"Now brace yourself!" Whipping the knife from the belt, the doctor slashed the rope that was keeping the net suspended. Before she had time to fear what would come next, Ree took the quick way down, ending up on her back, staring up at the newcomer.

"Hurt?" the doctor asked, putting the light down beside her. There was something distinctly different about this doctor from any Ree had met. An American accent lightly laced the alto voice.

"Um, no?" Ree rubbed her bruises. Her behind had taken the worst of it.

"So, Mags, that didn't fool you, huh?" The doctor scratched the tiger between the ears. "I'll have to hope the critters of the Orinoco River are more gullible. It seems it works perfectly on humans."

As threats of dismissal were not forthcoming after all, Ree plucked up the courage to ask her most urgent questions. "Excuse me, doctor, but who are you and where are we?"

The doctor straightened up and offered Ree a hand as she got to her feet. "You are standing in the Hall of the Four Humours, or Fiftieth, in the museum numbering system." The doctor did a slow turn, taking in all points of the compass. "Four humours: I always thought it an interesting idea. It has a kind of poetry to it that much of our science is losing."

A second, deeper voice echoed through the chamber. "Hypatia, you're not misleading the poor girl, are you? You should first explain that it was a load of nonsense."

The doctor spun around and grinned cheekily. "Hamid, darling, your idea of nonsense and mine will never agree."

A short statured man emerged from the shadows, dressed in a white robe belted with black rope. Handsome, with a neat beard, he wore a headdress also of white, held on his temples with scarlet braid. Arriving at a surprisingly athletic pace, he bowed to Ree. "I'm Dr Hamid Al-Ghazali, named in honour of the great mathematician. My colleague here rejoices in being named after the most famous female scientist of antiquity. Peace be with you, child."

Not sure what to do, Ree bowed back. "Um, peace be with you too." She was still reeling. A female animal collector and a mysterious doctor in exotic dress! Hidden in the museum and she'd never suspected a thing!

"I'd be surprised if you really were at peace – not after that trip to the rafters. Hypatia, you need to reconsider the wisdom of boobytrapping the halls. I know you'll say it's all research into trapping techniques, and that we want to keep people out, but logic should tell you that we do have to let them go eventually – and then they see us. What are we going to do now she's found us?" Compared with his friend, Hamid talked twice as fast.

His companion tipped back the hat with a forefinger, revealing conclusively that it was a woman who stood there. "Nothing, Hamid."

"Nothing? But if she tells, they'll send people to clear us out."

"You won't tell, will you, Ree?" Hypatia turned an astute gaze on her. The woman, probably no more than in her early forties, had cropped dark brown hair and strong eyebrows, olive skinned like her companion.

"How do you know who I am?" Ree was still recovering from the shock of finding a woman who claimed the title of doctor.

"Our friend, Mr Billibellary, mentioned you to us. I collect rare animals for him. You are Maria Altamira, nicknamed Ree, best friend of that dodo I rescued. How is he these days?"

"Um… fine." Hypatia was responsible for bringing Philoponus to the museum? When? How?

"Come; sit while we sort this out." Hypatia sat cross-legged on the floor as if they were exchanging tales around some forest campfire. Maggie sprawled beside her. "I wondered how long it would take you to make your way toward us. I wagered you'd be here by the end of April, Mr Billibellary said it would be this month – so dang it all, he was right." She gave a rueful smile. "That means I have to give Maggie her bath and that's no easy task."

On the word "bath" the tiger's ears pricked and an unhappy growl rumbled in her throat.

"Mr Billibellary said you were making a map. May I see?" Hypatia held out a hand.

Ree kneeled down to join doctor and tiger on the floor. How had the keeper known that? A little reluctantly, Ree passed Hypatia the map, ashamed now of her work. She often had to add to it, drawing against a wall or her own thigh. The lady unfolded it and held it up to Ree's lamp. She hummed in pleasure as she discovered the method of flipping between the various floors.

"Excellent. Do you mind if I add what you've discovered to our own chart? I've been up the Amazon and down the Nile, but it looks to me as if you've made a much more thorough exploration of the first forty halls than I've ever managed."

Ree found she did mind a little but couldn't think of a reason to refuse. "All right."

The lady smiled at her with understanding. "It's hard to let go of your research, isn't it? I'm a grizzly bear about the notes from my own explorations, guarding them until the day when I can publish them under my own name again. But Hamid likes to remind me that knowledge, or as the Greeks would have it, *scientia*, is for sharing."

"But there's no use having knowledge without wisdom," chimed in Hamid.

The lady rolled her eyes. "Yes, Hamid, I know. You've told me a thousand times."

"But now I have a new audience for my sayings." He smiled warmly at Ree. "That is certainly something to celebrate. We all get tired of seeing the same old faces over here."

Ree was beginning to realize she had stumbled into something far greater than she had suspected. "How many are there of you 'over here'?"

Hamid shrugged, wafting his sleeve in a vague manner. "Oh, no idea. Quite a few beyond the bridge. There's plenty of room for us to hide out. We're like Robin Hood and his merry men, outlaws in the museum's wild lands."

"Can you not estimate how many?" asked Ree.

Hamid's face lit with enthusiasm. He rubbed his hands. "Ah, she talks my language, Hypatia. Estimate. That's statistics, you know, young lady. So now, there are the alchemists – an odd bunch, I'd keep well away from them, far too many explosions – and the Sisters of Science, friends of Hypatia here; there's a surprising number these days as more ladies take refuge among us."

Hypatia picked a burr from Maggie's coat and flicked it away. "Some of us trained in the old days. Even then we had to struggle against the odds."

"You did?" asked Ree.

"Oh yes. I was born in poverty in Egypt – a street child, no parents – but I had the great good fortune of being adopted by an intrepid lady traveller. Thanks to her, I won a scholarship to

America, before this gender nonsense took over. Zoology is my specialist subject, saving endangered creatures."

"Quite remarkable, isn't she?" Hamid beamed proudly at his partner. "Now, who else is there?"

"Don't forget the Brotherhood of Scholastics – not the most reasonable of men," added Hypatia. "They like to argue only by logic, not experimentation."

"I think there are still a few Phlogistonites here too."

"Phlogistonites?" wondered Ree.

"People who still believe that air contains a flammable substance called phlogiston and is the reason why things burn. They are a sad bunch. They won't change their mind even though we identified oxygen many decades ago. They like the idea too much to let it go." Hamid pointed to the region of the room decorated with a bird coming out of an egg surrounded by fire. "Like the phoenix, the concept keeps coming back."

"And don't forget the Flat Earthers. There's a surprising number of them in the most distant chambers," added Hypatia.

"So are you all followers of old theories?" Ree was trying to calculate just how many crackpots the museum housed. She was going to add "useless theories" but thought that sounded rude.

"I suppose we are." Hamid rocked on the balls of his feet. "Not that I'd ever thought of myself as in the same boat as the Phlogistonites and Flat Earthers. Most of my kind were chased down here when they told us we could not be Theophilus followers and scientists – that God was the last thing about which we were allowed to be curious. I was not going to imperil my mortal soul and denounce the foundations of my science so I left."

"I came because I was told my gender made me irrational and I was no longer allowed to hold an academy post." Hypatia gave Ree a cold smile that seemed to promise unpleasantness for anyone who repeated the charge. "Believe me, the closest I have ever come to being irrational was when that idiot Grassmann told me I couldn't continue to practise science as I was a member of the weaker sex – that from a man who couldn't fight his way out of a paper bag."

"You taught in the academy?"

Hypatia nodded. "You bet I did. I was the youngest ever head of the Biological Sciences department. Briefly. And then progress for our gender went into reverse rather brutally and they chucked me out."

"But you aren't listed on the wall of past masters." Ree had polished the brass enough times to know.

Hypatia took out the revolver, opened the chamber and spun it, before closing it again – a habit, Ree guessed, as it hadn't held any bullets. "I'm not surprised, though it's very small-minded of them. I was the first woman to hold the post. I hope I am not the last."

This was all fascinating, but Ree was aware that the skies above the lantern roof were getting lighter. "I'm really sorry but I have to get back before the housekeeper notices I'm missing. May I visit you again?"

"Of course; you'll have to come back. I'm holding your splendid map as hostage." Hypatia patted the pocket into which she had slid the plan.

"Is there anything I can bring you? Anything you need?" Ree wondered how so many people survived beneath the noses of the trustees.

Hypatia shook her head. "Don't worry about that. We have an arrangement with sympathetic servants."

"If you could bring me a recent newspaper, that would be most gratifying. I miss the daily crossword," added Hamid.

Ree turned to go. "Oh, I think I should warn you: I found a scholar nosing around tonight. He might try again and possibly get to this hall."

The two doctors exchanged a look.

"They usually get lost first. And it would be a shame to

block the lower passageways," mused Hypatia.

"But no more traps, Hypatia, no matter how entertaining they are! We'll just have to keep an eye on the comings and goings, make sure he doesn't see anyone he shouldn't. Thank you for the warning." Hamid bowed again. Ree, prepared for it this time, made a creditable one in reply.

"God bless you, my child," he said. "Wisdom guide your path."

Ree grinned. "I'll settle for Maggie. I've never been all that wise."

Hypatia chuckled throatily. "I like this kid, Hamid. Shows some grit."

Sensing it was close to breakfast time in the menagerie, Maggie butted Hypatia in farewell and headed back the way she had brought Ree. The girl had to hurry to keep up.

"Thank you for showing me your friends," Ree said. "That was a brilliant adventure." No longer having her map to help her, Ree made sure she took careful note of the route Maggie took through the underground labyrinth and was a little disorientated to find they emerged through a different door than the one they went down. "Just trying to confuse me, huh?"

The tiger yawned and loped off, her stomach's call now louder than her enjoyment of prowling the underground jungle. Ziggy and Phil ran into the hall to greet Ree. As all tail feathers were present and correct, Ree assumed they had got on much better in her absence than they usually did with her present.

Ree found her bucket just where she had left it; the splayed frog looked like he was doing a star jump while mopping. She was just about to pat him in thanks when she noticed her clean floor had words scrawled on it.

"Oh no!" Ree quickly dampened the mop. That wretched student must've come back and made a mess on purpose to annoy her. She quickly started rubbing at them before realizing what they spelled: "GOD IS." God is what? Had the person been interrupted by her return before having a chance to finish it? They could've been intending to say the standard "GOD IS DEAD", or the dangerous "GOD IS ALIVE" or even something absurd like "GOD IS A TEAPOT". Mockery or heresy: either would get her into trouble. Fortunately the words were in chalk so they were fairly easy to erase, but it was full daylight by the time she had cleaned up to her satisfaction.

Odd. Mrs Mantell still hadn't come. Ree was not allowed to go back to the maids' quarters until she had had her work approved. Exhausted by her exertions, she curled up at the base of the frog, allowing Ziggy to rest her snout on a thigh and Phil to roost his warm body on the other side. Before she knew it, she was drifting off to sleep.

"Maria!"

She had only managed a very short doze before she was roughly woken by Mrs Mantell shaking her shoulder.

"I'm sorry, Mrs Mantell. I must've just dropped off for a moment waiting for you." Ree gathered her wits enough to see that the housekeeper wasn't alone. She had two of the museum police with her, creaking in their highly polished boots.

"This is the girl?" asked one.

Ziggy started growling.

"Quiet," warned Ree. "No biting!"

Mrs Mantell looked extremely upset. "Yes, inspector. But she's never been any trouble since joining my staff."

That was rather generous of Mrs Mantell, thought Ree.

"Everyone is being searched, no exceptions." The policeman indicated that she should stand. "Turn out your pockets."

Ree had only a second to thank her lucky stars that she had left the map with Hypatia or it would've been discovered. She turned her empty apron pocket inside out to show it was quite bare apart from a pencil stub and the menagerie key. Fortunately, the officer wasn't interested in the latter.

"Show me your hands."

Beginning to wonder now if hers was the only floor to be defaced that night, Ree held out her palms. Though a little grubby, there was no chalk on them as she had used the mop to clear up the graffiti.

"Where were you between the hours of four and six this morning?" asked the policeman.

"Cleaning in here," Ree replied, skirting around the truth.

"Can anyone vouch for that?"

Ree wondered if she could risk mentioning the boy, but if he had been the one chalking the floors then she would be ending his school career and possibly getting him transported. "Sorry, sir, but no one else will work with me."

"Why not? What's wrong with you?"

Mrs Mantell stepped forward to defend her charge. "It's not Maria, Inspector Gideon. It's that blasted dog."

"Tasmanian wolf," muttered Ree.

"It bites the other girls and Maria has been asked to train it out of its bad habits."

"Another of Billibellary's schemes, eh?" The policeman scowled at the wolf, who scowled back much more effectively as she had teeth and a mean look that he could not match. "Then I'll have to ask you directly. Did you leave this hall and chalk forbidden words on the floors of the First, Twentieth, and Thirtieth halls?"

"No, sir." Ree held his eye. She had left the hall but not to do that.

"Did you see anyone do so?"

Again he had phrased his question in such a way as to make her reply the truth. "No, sir." She couldn't confess she had just cleared up similar chalk words as that would lead to questions as to where she was while they were being written.

"Are you sure?"

"I did see Maggie and Naidu," offered Ree.

"The tiger and the snake," translated Mrs Mantell.

"They spent most of the night in here. If anyone had wanted to come to this hall, they probably scared them off."

Inspector Gideon nodded, accepting that explanation. "Still, you remain a person of interest in our enquiries, Miss Altamira. It's a puzzle. You did have the opportunity but not the means, unless you disposed of your chalk between here and the Thirtieth Hall?"

"No, sir. Please, why do you think it was me?"

When the inspector wasn't going to explain, Mrs Mantell stepped in, speaking in hushed tones. "Someone has written 'GOD IS' many times throughout the museum."

"Just that? 'GOD IS'? How strange. What does that even mean?"

"We hoped you could tell us." The policeman's look was severe but Ree, bolstered by innocence in this matter, didn't flinch.

"I'm sorry, but I can't. It doesn't make sense to me." But there was a whole group of Theophilus refugees in the Fiftieth Hall and beyond who might know. The secret lay hot in her heart and she bit the inside of her mouth so no word escaped.

"In that case, I'll leave it for now. But be warned, Miss Altamira – you are my prime suspect."

"Why me?"

The policeman tucked his thumbs into his broad black belt. "Because you carved a hand of God on the walls of the museum, of course! You remain on our lists as a potential rebel."

"Oh." Was someone trying to make her look guilty? wondered Ree.

"And we have been kept informed of your letter-writing campaign. You might look like butter wouldn't melt in your mouth but in my book you are down as a Troublemaker with a capital T."

Normally, Ree would take that as a compliment but there was too much at stake here. "Please, sir, I really did have nothing to do with it. I don't even understand why the person did it."

"We'll see. I'll catch them, I promise you, and it better not be you or there will be another Altamira for transportation." The policeman marched off, followed by his junior.

Silence flowed back into the hall with their departure. Ree felt the wonderful discoveries of the night being crushed by the more imminent problem of coming under suspicion.

"It really wasn't me, Mrs Mantell."

The lady sighed. "I don't suppose it was. It's not your style of trouble. Now run along and get rid of that dirty water before the visitors start arriving."

"Thank you, ma'am." Ree bobbed a curtsey and took her dismissal as a signal to flee. *Stupid scholar*, she thought as she tipped the grey water down the scullery sink. Had it been him, though? He had seemed intent on exploring, not chalking messages. Was it fair to leap to a conclusion that he was to blame just because he was taking a midnight stroll? Should she mention him to anyone, Mrs Mantell for example?

But you don't even know his name, Ree reminded herself. It wouldn't be hard to find out, as it sounded by his account that scholars from Africa were rare, but she had no obligation to tell tales. However, if the police persisted in persecuting her because she appeared to fit the profile of the person they were looking for, she would do well to discover who the mystery student was and gather any evidence against him she could. The last thing she needed in her campaign to get her father free was to find herself the recipient of a sentence of transportation for a crime she hadn't committed.

Chapter 9

Sailing Boats and Sisters

A few days after the chalk writer first struck, the academy had an afternoon holiday to mark Founder's Day. Henri decided to spend it as far from the museum as he could. Besides, Zena would enjoy the expedition.

Taking the easternmost bridge to the north bank of the city, Zena on his shoulder, Henri amused them both by walking the broad pavements of the government district, a place of white stone buildings and dark-clad civil servants hurrying in and out of offices. Needing to put yet more distance between himself and the museum, he climbed the steep street that led to one of the parks with a good view across the city. He'd been here before on days off and particularly enjoyed the raspberry ices sold by the kiosk near the boating pond. He let Zena go off to explore the leaf-canopy as he walked the paths beneath. Even wandering the tree-shaded alleys, though, he could feel the power of the museum like the heat of a furnace behind him. He knew he only had to turn to look down on the turrets, square towers, and shining roofs of his home and all his joy in the day would vanish.

"Hello, Henri."

He glanced down to see the young student Maxwell standing beside him, hands dug in his pockets. Even here he couldn't escape the museum.

"I hope you didn't follow me?" he asked stiffly.

"Oh no, Henri." The boy blushed a fierce red against his blond hair. "I mean, not on purpose. My family live over there." He pointed to one of the tall mansions that hemmed the park to the north. "I'm meeting my mother and sisters but saw you and thought I'd better say hello. Sorry, I'll go."

Henri now regretted his tone. "No, don't leave, Maxwell. I apologize for snapping like that. I was feeling a bit out of sorts."

Zena dropped on his head from the canopy overhead and chattered in triumph to have caught him out.

"Wretch!" groaned Henri.

Maxwell smiled warily and offered her a nut from his pocket. Zena was a fan of Maxwell, as he always remembered to travel with treats. "Horrid, isn't it? To feel under suspicion like that? Have our rooms searched and the chalk locked up in all the classrooms."

Henri nodded. He'd had a narrow escape on the night that the graffiti had started appearing. No one had noticed him slip back into his room late. He hadn't roamed since due to the new night patrols by the police, but the messages had not stopped and were always the same: "GOD IS." He just wished the person would finish the sentence for once. It was driving him mad, like listening to a piece of music that paused before the last chord.

"They gave me a real grilling when they questioned me," admitted the younger boy.

"They questioned you?" Henri was surprised. As far as he knew, none of the other boys had been singled out.

"Yes. Curator Shelley marked my card before admission as a potential rebel. I only got into the academy because my family had influence with the king."

"What on earth made Shelley do that?"

Maxwell flushed a deeper red. "I asked a forbidden question on my first visit to the museum."

"Ah. That would do it. You were unlucky to get Shelley as your guide. Most of them would overlook a single mistake."

"I know that now, and I had no idea I wasn't supposed to ask a 'why' question, just stick to the 'how' of things."

"So you know better now?"

The boy shrugged and scuffed at the gravel, shooting a few stones into the pond. "Yes, I suppose."

Henri understood Maxwell's problem. Looking around to check they weren't overheard, he decided to confess. "It is a stupid rule. I ask 'why' all the time in private. That's what detectives do – we have to detect motive."

"But when you ask for motive in pure science, doesn't it mean that you leave the possibility of there being something like a… like a god behind it all?" Maxwell said the word with a visible shudder. This conversation could get them both into serious trouble.

"Who knows? It's not something I can prove either way. I see science as the best tool to solve the 'how' but maybe we need different tools for 'why', like they tried in Philosophy and Theology before they were banned. We certainly shouldn't be made to feel bad or unscientific for talking about what matters to us like we are now." Zena pulled on his ear, reminding him he was supposed to be entertaining her. "Do you want to have a go at one of the boats? I've got some pocket money with me."

"Oh, yes please! I'm completely penniless." Maxwell took the offered coins and hurried over to the old lady in charge of the model boats. He surprised Henri by hiring two, a pirate ship for himself and a three-masted naval frigate of the old-fashioned sort for Henri. "Come on, Henri. Let's play, sailors versus pirates!"

That hadn't been what Henri meant at all. Surely at sixteen he was too old for such things?

"Please, Henri?" begged Maxwell. If anyone else from the academy had been around in the park Henri would have remembered his dignity as senior scholar, but Maxwell looked so eager to have fun, Henri couldn't resist.

"All right. But you'd better not tell anyone." He pushed his boat away from the bank with a long cane for the purpose, calculating the direction of the wind so that it would follow in the pirate ship's wake. "What are you and your dastardly crew smuggling?"

"Stolen treasure and slaves!"

"Then I charge you in the name of the law to surrender!" ordered Henri.

Zena shrieked her agreement – or was she on Maxwell's side?

"Never! Pox on you and all revenue men!" cried Maxwell in mock pirate accent.

"Then prepare for a broadside!"

The combat continued, both boys losing themselves in the story, until, that was, Maxwell's ship washed up on the bank.

"Aha, you've run aground on the shoals. Now I have you!" declared Henri, sprinting around the pond to reach the vessel first. "That's jail for you and freedom for your slaves!" He lifted the dripping boat out of the water, not caring that dirty pond water was running down his sleeves.

"So this is where you got to, Maxwell." A lady arrived at the lake, accompanied by three elegantly dressed girls who had to be his sisters.

"Mother!" Maxwell barrelled into her, hugging her fiercely around the waist while she kissed the top of his head.

"He forgot he was supposed to be meeting us," said one of

the girls in an amused tone. "Typical!" They all looked older than their brother, impossibly fashionable and refined compared with the scallywag they each took a turn in hugging.

"Who's your friend?" Maxwell's mother eyed the embarrassed Henri curiously.

He bowed, aware of his disadvantage of bearing a monkey on his shoulder while carrying a weed-draped pirate boat. His own frigate spun in circles behind him.

"This is the Henri I told you about, Mother. He is quite the most intelligent boy in our school, youngest person ever to win a senior scholarship, and he's graduating this year, can you imagine it? And that is Zena, his macaque. Isn't she just the most splendid creature?"

Zena had leaped to the shoulder of one of his sisters and begun grooming her hair for bugs.

"Don't take it personally," Henri muttered to the wide-eyed girl.

"You didn't mention that he was…" The lady changed her mind as to what she was going to say. "Well then, ask your friend to tea, Maxwell." She gave her son a little push between the shoulder blades.

Maxwell frowned. "I didn't mention what?"

His oldest sister, or so Henri judged, nudged him. "Ssh, Maxie."

"But…?" It was obvious to everyone but Maxwell. Henri was African.

"Henri, and Zena of course, would you like to take tea with us?" asked Maxwell's mother. "We have plenty of cakes."

"Thank you, ma'am. I'd like that very much."

It felt like a true holiday to be in the drawing room of Maxwell's comfortable home. His sisters were all charming, able to ask intelligent questions about life at the academy while having their intricate hairstyles picked apart by Zena. They were clearly not that interested in museum politics. They were more engaged by his tales of Algiers and had many questions about how the people lived in such a warm climate. From feeling the power of the museum looming over him, it was as though Henri had turned the telescope and now its concerns seemed very petty.

Maxwell's mother, however, was more alert to the potential dangers that accompanied the high-prestige career of a museum scholar.

"So this mysterious chalk person has not been caught?" She offered Henri a plate of iced cake slices. "Have a *mille-feuille*."

"You've heard about that?" He took a piece and broke into the crust like a geologist excavating the layers of a most luscious-looking rock-face. Vanilla custard and almonds leaked out of the fissure.

"The papers have been giving it a lot of room – that and the news from the colonies, of course." Maxwell's mother poured her guest a cup of tea. "Did you read about the terrible outbreak of cholera there this past winter? As many as a quarter of the prisoners and guards have died of it."

Maxwell put down his plate. "Is Uncle Luc all right?"

Who was Uncle Luc? wondered Henri.

She shook her head slightly. "The prisoners may have earned transportation," she continued, "but they did not deserve being dumped in a disease-ridden camp. The governor has launched an enquiry. Our cousin, Lord John, is making his own protests and seeing what he can do for... for some of the prisoners."

It fitted that Maxwell would be related to the lord: all the most important families in the city appeared to be linked by marriage, which would be an advantage to his younger friend. But the rest of her news was bad. Henri thought of the people he'd seen sentenced from the museum, the stonemason most particularly. Was he one of the casualties? How might his daughter take that news?

"If only the people in charge would accept germ theory, then the right treatments could be used to stop diseases," muttered the middle of Maxwell's sisters, a serious-looking girl of Henri's age whose light brown hair was now being searched by an equally earnest macaque. "And Uncle Luc would be safe."

Well now. That is a surprise. Henri kept his eyes fixed on his teacup.

"Hush now, Florence," murmured her mother, with a warning look at Henri.

The girl went back to her embroidery hoop with a false smile at her mother. Henri didn't need to be told that further questions as to their connection to this mysterious Luc were not welcome. It sounded as though he was involved in the camps in some way? Judging by the status of the family, that was likely to be as a warden or some other senior post. Under the cover of eating his cake, Henri took a closer look at Florence's sewing box. Was that a copy of John Snow's article on cholera peeking out of the tangle of threads? Recent developments in biology suggested microscopic organisms carried disease, rather than it being spread by bad smells as had been believed under the old theory. Still, it was none of his business. If Maxwell did come from a family that flouted the law on female education, then it was better if Henri didn't know too much.

"I wish I knew who was making the chalk marks," said Maxwell, diverting them back on to the safer ground of the original topic. "It's very annoying for us all to be blamed for it." He reached for another cake.

"The paper said the police had a suspect in custody." His mother offered Henri sugar, which he politely declined. Zena took an impolite handful and disappeared under Florence's skirt with her contraband.

"They arrested a girl briefly after the second night, but she was able to prove she'd been with the other maids all the time," he explained. Henri had been interested in that story, as the maid had been none other than the stonemason's girl. Fortunately for

Maria Altamira, the housekeeper had started sending the maids out in teams for the overnight cleaning so they all had alibis.

"But according to the story, she defaced the museum a few years ago," said the oldest sister, Elizabeth. "She sounds a likely candidate, don't you think?"

"That's why they arrested her, Lizzie, but they can't just blame her because they want to, not when there's not so much as a scrap of evidence against her," declared Maxwell, clearly still smarting from his own experience at the hands of the investigating police.

"They should be looking for fingerprints, not making wild accusations. Besides, as far as I could tell from talking to her, she's not the kind to do something so… so pointless." Henri wondered why he was defending the maid, whom he hadn't very much liked, but it did seem a particularly foolish form of protest, like kicking a wasps' nest, and she hadn't struck him as stupid.

"So you've met her?" asked the youngest sister, a cheerful freckle-faced girl with curly hair.

"Once, Miss Eleanor. I bumped into her in one of the halls when I tripped over a python." This encounter fortunately sounded so intriguing that Henri's listeners went off on the track of asking questions about the large snake, and on to Zena and the other animal inhabitants of the museum, rather than the issue of his brush with Maria Altamira.

Maxwell, however, had guessed more than Henri wished he had. On their way back to the museum, the younger boy returned to the subject of the maid.

"When did you meet Maria Altamira, Henri? I've never talked to one of the female servants or even seen the python."

Henri wondered how far he could trust his younger friend. Maxwell had shown great faith in him in letting him meet his family, and the secret of Henri's night-time ramblings was no great matter compared to the scandal of having educated sisters. "I met her a few nights ago. I decided to find my own room for my fingerprint experiment, as the trustees won't give me one."

141

"Of course you are! I knew they couldn't stop you."

"I was just beginning to look for an unused corner I could borrow when I came across her cleaning the Fortieth Hall. Truth be told, we had a bit of an argument."

"Really?" Maxwell seemed pleased by that piece of information. "I didn't know maids were as full of opinions as sisters."

"I detect that we are woefully ignorant about girls," said Henri.

"True. What happened after the argument?"

"What with the maid and the python, I decided to put off the exploration to another night."

"Don't blame you. Scary stuff." Maxwell's voice was a mixture of awe and apprehension.

"Just as well, or I might've been discovered out of bed on the first night the message writer struck. It's very annoying that they've doubled the guard."

"Oh, I wouldn't worry too much about them: they're useless. The message writer always strikes when they are somewhere else. The museum is just too big to patrol. It's just like that pet killer a few years ago – the one you told me about; in a place that size you can hide all sorts of wrongdoing."

Maxwell was right. Maybe, thought Henri, he had been too cautious? If the chalk writer had got away with it, then Henri certainly should be able to slip past the police and carry on with his much more important mission of making progress on his work. He had come too far to be stopped now, and, if he got some interesting results that detectives could use, even Professor Gall would have to take notice. Criminals like the chalk writer and the pet killer would be stopped before they could strike again. But it would be risky. He would be helped if he had someone prepared to cover for him back in the academy. He glanced down at the blond head of the boy kicking a stone along the road beside him, Zena disloyally riding on Maxwell's shoulder as provider of more nuts than the empty-pocketed Henri.

"Maxwell, I was wondering, would you do me a favour?"

It was just not fair. Ree had made the discovery of a lifetime that there were other people living in the museum, and then the messages had started appearing and her night-time cleaning now always took place under the eyes of others. What was much worse, she was the prime suspect despite there not being a scrap of evidence. Mrs Mantell, with the best intentions, included Ree on the biggest crews – the ones cleaning the kitchens, bathrooms, and dining rooms in the academy and administration buildings that got the dirtiest during the day. That hadn't stopped the guard arresting her on the second night of the graffiti attacks and Ree thanked Mrs Mantell's foresight in giving her a cast-iron alibi. After a few hours of questioning in the lockups, she had been released, hot with humiliation and not a little scared. Being monitored every second was difficult. Ree turned up for staff roll call without much hope tonight would be any different. Standing on the raised platform under the portrait of the museum founder, Mrs Mantell looked down her list.

"Girls, we have a busy night ahead. The students have been on a half-day holiday so I anticipate that their quarters will be more untidy than usual." She read off the work teams, Ree finding her name among those expected to clean the bathhouse. "Before you set to, I've a special request from the head gardener in charge of the botanical exhibits. He asks that I send one of you to help clean the windows of the grand glasshouse. It's a big task, as you might imagine. He anticipates it will take at least a week."

The vast new greenhouse for tropical plants was shaped like a sultan's palace with domes and minarets. Cleaning such a big expanse would be no picnic. Everyone shuffled and looked down.

Mrs Mantell smiled sourly. "Don't all rush at once. There is a special aspect that might appeal to some of you. Because of the nature of the job, it is to be carried out during the day. Ah, I thought that might make it more attractive." Ree and most of the other maids had raised their hands as soon as they heard that condition. All of them missed daylight. Mrs Mantell's gaze swept the ranks of maids. "There are a few more special conditions. Mr Olmsted requires the person to wear the uniform of the gardeners, as she will have to climb scaffolding, with an overskirt, of course." A few of the hands went down. Ree stuck hers up even more firmly. *Oh, to be in trousers for a few days!* "You need to have a good head for heights." Some hesitated and dropped out of contention. "And Mr Olmsted was most particular that he didn't want any of what he called 'girlish humours', whatever they are." Her mouth bent in a wry expression while her gaze sought out and found Ree. "Ah, good, Maria; I was hoping you would like the sound of the task. You have proven yourself equal to ladders in your time. I trust you will behave yourself if I send you over there?"

"Yes, Mrs Mantell."

"Why her, Miss?" grumbled another maid.

"Because I said so, Doris. It's hardly a treat. Now run along all of you. Maria, report to Mr Olmsted at dawn. I suggest you sleep now, as you've a long day ahead of you. I don't want to see you wandering the museum on your own."

"No, ma'am." She certainly wouldn't be seen.

Mrs Mantell was no fool. She pressed her thumbnail to her bottom lip in thought. "In fact, just to be sure, I'll lock you in."

"But what about Ziggy?"

"I'll tell Mr Billibellary that he'll have to find another minder for the week. I'm not having that creature up in the maids' dormitories."

Ree accepted this with as good a grace as she could manage. Ziggy would find her despite Mrs Mantell's views on the subject. She climbed the stairs back to the dormitory she had left only a few minutes ago, Mrs Mantell puffing on her heels. Ree shared a room at the top of the tower with Beata and Mary – "all the lively minds in one place", as the housekeeper put it. Ree's two roommates were also to be trusted not to tell tales on a fellow maid if she happened somehow to find a way out, say, by jumping to the next building, crossing the tiles, and going over the gothic battlement and down the backstairs to the kitchen courtyard.

Ree turned and smiled meekly at the housekeeper when she reached the door. "Thank you, Mrs Mantell. Good night."

The housekeeper huffed. "After them arresting you for no reason at all, I thought you deserved this chance. Also it's better you're not in the museum at night for a while. Don't let me down."

That gave Ree a moment's pause. Understanding now that Mrs Mantell was a tough but fair taskmistress, she was beginning to warm to her employer. It would be terrible to be caught abusing this privilege. "I'll try very hard not to."

"Get some sleep, Maria. Mr Olmsted works his people hard."

Ree waited to hear the key turn in the lock. She didn't feel sleepy and she wanted to ask her new friends if they could help her clear her name. They might know who was really responsible, moving as they did in the shadows of the museum without detection. Taking off her apron and mob cap, she dug around in her trunk. There at the bottom she found her last pair of boy's breeches. They were a squeeze now but she still just about fitted them. The stair was quiet. There shouldn't be anyone returning until dawn, which gave her a good nine hours before she had to be back. Making a mound under the bedclothes with a rolled blanket, she went to the window in the maids' tower. It was indeed a good thing that she had a head for heights because the first part of her escape relied on her keeping her footing on a narrow ledge to make a leap to the first tiled roof. She'd done it before but never lost the heart-in-the-mouth sensation as she crossed the gap between the high buildings. It was a kind of awful fun.

Making the leap with no mishap, Ree scuttled across the roof of what was the scholars' wing to reach the battlements of the kitchen tower. She guessed she wasn't the first person to use this route as a plank lay ready to bridge the space between the two. No doubt some adventurous student after kitchen treats in the middle of the night had brought it up here many moons ago. Checking no boy was out and about now, she slid the plank with the aim of resting it in the crenellation opposite. It was heavy, so she had to be careful not to lose her grip. Not only would that endanger anyone who happened to be walking below, but it would also betray her position to any watcher. On the whole, people didn't look up so she should be safe as long as she made no noise. With a snick, the plank reached home, as firm a bridge as she could ask for considering the circumstances. Not giving herself time for second thoughts, Ree walked across, not once looking down.

After that, her route got easier. The main difficulty was dodging patrols and her fellow maids. She thought that maybe Beata had seen her as she borrowed a lamp and a recent newspaper from the pile of discards in the scullery, but her friend merely rattled her coal scuttle with more vigour as she refilled one of the buckets by the kitchen fireplace, covering any sound that Ree made on the stairs. Ree breathed more easily by the time she reached the doorway to the underground passages. She wasn't going to risk passing through the First to Fortieth halls but was going to go under. Without her map, this was quite dangerous, but she had a fairly good sense of direction and had been down here a number of times so hoped it would be familiar.

Just as she was about to take the plunge, Maggie appeared at her side.

"Excellent timing," murmured Ree. "I just hope you are going to the same place I am."

It seemed that Maggie was. Sniffing the air a few times, the tiger set off with confident tread. They must have walked for half an hour, following the doublings where passageways had been curved around a room or obstruction, taking deviations where the roof had collapsed through lack of maintenance, using stepping stones across the river, until Maggie took a set of stairs leading upwards. Ree had to trust that the tiger wasn't going to land her right in the middle of a patrol. Instead, they emerged into the Hall of the Four Humours, exactly where she wanted to be.

"You brilliant cat!" crooned Ree, rubbing Maggie under the chin. "I definitely would've got lost if it hadn't been for you. You saved me from making a fatal error."

A scuffling behind her caused Ree a moment's alarm, until she saw the yellow reflection from Ziggy's night eyes and then heard the croak of an indignant dodo. Her two friends emerged from the cellar stairs, looking a little dusty from their travels.

"I couldn't keep you out of the adventure this time, it seems. And now the crew's all here," said Ree, deeply amused that her secret excursion was no secret from her animal companions. She brushed the dust off her breeches. Just as well the patrols didn't have as good a sense of smell as a Tasmanian wolf. "Best behaviour, everyone. No feather nipping, no pecking, and definitely no chasing. I need these people to want to help me, not run me off." Not sure that her words would make any difference, Ree headed for the far side of the hall, the direction from which her new acquaintances had emerged that first night. "Maggie, find Hypatia."

Maggie took an arched doorway that had the statues of two muscular men holding up the lintel. It led to a long corridor with many portraits, but Ree was in too much of a hurry to pay much attention to them, just registering pointed faces and white ruffs. The tiger then scratched at an oak door on the right-hand side. After a few moments, it opened, and Dr Hypatia stood in the entrance.

"Now there's a sight for sore eyes. The kid's back." There

was a broad smile on the lady's face. Ree felt reassured that she hadn't been wrong to come.

"I am. I've come for my map." Ree pulled the newspaper out from behind her back. "And to bring you the crossword."

Hypatia stood aside to let her in. "Only that? I was hoping you'd like some tea. Hamid was just going to put the kettle on."

The man in question looked up from a desk covered in papers, a little pair of wire-bound spectacles perched on the end of his nose, which didn't detract from his good looks but made him more owlishly adorable. "I was? Ah-ha!" He pounced on the newspaper with glee.

"It's your turn." Hypatia scratched Maggie on the neck and fed her a treat from a pocket hidden in her jacket. Ziggy sat on her haunches in hope and was rewarded with a titbit thrown her way. "Well now, what an unlikely critter, or should I say critters – not one of my collections." Hypatia turned to her companion. "Hamid, you know me: having been bitten and scratched by most of creation, I rarely admit that anything is sweet. Yet I have to say that this Tasmanian wolf mother with a baby tucked in a pouch like a kangaroo is the darnedest thing. You must take a look."

"But she'd take your hand off if you try to stroke Baby Zag," warned Ree.

Hypatia wisely put her hands on her hips and gave the wolf an assessing look. "I see you are right. What an excellent example of motherhood."

"My dear, you are offending the dodo by ignoring him." Hamid reached into a jar over the little fireplace and threw a handful of yellow pellets towards Phil. "Dried pineapple. I see he likes it as much as I do."

The animals settled down now they had been given their due, Ziggy curled on one side of the hearth rug, Maggie on the other. Phil hopped up on to Hamid's desk and roosted among the papers, something the scientist did not seem to mind at all. Hypatia cleared a space on a side table for Hamid, who set out a quaint little silver tea service with a swan's neck spout.

"Mint tea with honey," he explained as he poured the steaming water into the pot. "A little indulgence of ours."

Ree relaxed into the cushions of the low chair she had been invited to take, close to the fire and with a good view of the rest of the room. It was a library, she realized, lined with shelves of ancient tomes chained in their places.

"Why are the books on chains?" she asked.

"In the early days of books, before printing, books were extremely expensive," explained Hypatia. "They had to be copied by hand. To stop scholars stealing them, the librarians went for a very direct method." She ran her finger over the top of a few of them and then frowned at the dust she disturbed. 'Hamid, you didn't do your job.'

"I know, dearest. I just really hate dusting."

"Don't we all? So I'll not do sweeping then and we'll just live in squalor. Like warthogs."

"Tomorrow: I'll get to them tomorrow." Hamid patted Hypatia's arm in passing.

"Why are they here and not with the rest of the library's collection?" asked Ree. She'd dusted her fair share of books, enough to know how vast the holdings of the main library were.

Hypatia gestured to the shelf in front of her. "They said these were no longer relevant in the new scientific era. Still, they are beautiful works. Take a look."

Ree got up, drawn to one with a gold and green spine. Opening it up, she found an eagle on a cactus surrounded by figures dressed in white.

Hypatia came to stand at her shoulder. "Ah yes, the book of the conquest of Mexico from the sixteenth century, made by priests for the Spanish emperor."

Ree flipped through the pages, finding more with pictures and writing in Spanish explaining what was going on.

"Such a shame the Christian invaders destroyed the books

written by the natives, claiming the Mexicans were devil worshippers because they followed a different faith." Hypatia crossed her arms. "Never trust a society that starts burning books."

Hamid poured tea into the tiny cups. "As you may have gathered, my beloved is no supporter of religion."

"Not when it imposes its ideas." Their tone was of two people who had had this argument many times before and could anticipate what the other was going to say next. There was little heat in the exchange.

"Quite so. No sane person would agree with that. But I find it ironic that our era of No Faith uses the worse lessons of the past rather than following the many examples where science and faith worked well together. You would've thought they would want to reject such things as burning books as a sign of religious extremism, but instead they praised scientific publications that reflected their views, and made a great bonfire of religious books. We're living in a culture of scientific extremists. Have a biscuit, Ree." Hamid held out a box of delicate almond rounds so light they melted on the tongue.

Hypatia brushed her fingers affectionately over Hamid's cheek as he moved on to offer her a biscuit. "You know, you old Theophilus lover, that I'll defend your right to believe even if I don't agree with you."

He took her hand and gallantly kissed her knuckles. "I know, my dear. And I your right as a woman to study. That's why we work so well together."

Ree could feel the love between them, though to outsiders it might seem as unlikely as Ziggy falling for Phil. "I came back partly to check you are safe. Have you heard about the chalk messages?"

Hamid nodded. "Oh yes. Our friend in the kitchens warned us to be careful. None of us are wandering in the upper halls at night anymore."

"Did they also tell you that I'm blamed?"

Hypatia put her cup back on her saucer with a rattle. "Dang paper-pushers! I suppose it is because of your past?"

"Are you safe now, my dear?" asked Hamid, looking to the door as if he expected a posse of museum police to break in.

"I think so," said Ree, beginning to feel a little worried herself. What if her absence was noted? Was she being stupidly reckless?

"And did you do it?" asked Hypatia, sipping her tea.

"Me?" Ree began a shocked laugh, then realized the lady wasn't joking. "No! No, I don't even understand the point of the message. It's never finished."

Hamid raised a brow. "Indeed?"

"God is *what*?" said Ree, with obvious exasperation.

He looked to Hypatia. "O the young generation who have never read the great books of faith! That's how God in some religions introduces himself: 'I am.' God is. You see?"

Ree frowned. "Not really."

"Adding anything would close down the sentence – yes? – which makes God smaller. He just is. It's the closest language can come to eternity."

"So you are saying that the message is written by someone who understands all this? They must know your great books?"

"Exactly."

Ree looked down at her fingers. "Did you write it, Dr Al-Ghazali?"

"Oh, touché!" He beamed at her. "I invited that, I suppose. I'm a much better suspect than you, I agree. But no, I didn't. I have other things on my mind than baiting the museum authorities and making them look as though they can't control their building."

"We much prefer them to think they have everything in hand, leaving us to work away here without disturbance," added Hypatia.

"Is… is there anyone else here who might not be so cautious?" asked Ree.

"I can't speak for everyone, but I think it unlikely, unless one of the Brothers has entirely lost his reason," speculated Hamid.

Hypatia snorted derisively, indicating this was not unthinkable. "We'll hold a meeting of those in exile here and find out if anyone has noticed someone behaving oddly. If they live among us, we'll put a stop to it. We know what we risk if we're discovered."

Ree felt a little knot in the ball of tension inside unwind. "Thank you. It's not nice being under suspicion. And I need to be thought a good citizen, so I can make the case to get my father back."

Hypatia and Hamid exchanged pained looks. They evidently had heard about this and thought her hope a frail one.

"I'm going to do it. I know what I've got to do." Indeed, the idea had been taking shape since she'd heard of the female scientists like Hypatia proving women were up to the task. "Asking for mercy hasn't worked, so I've got to persuade the authorities that it wasn't such a bad thing to let a female work as a stonemason, that they need to be a bit more bendy in their interpretation of the rules."

Hypatia sighed. "You would take on the world to free one man?"

Ree nodded curtly. It wasn't just any man; it was her da.

The lady brushed the little dent in Ree's chin. "I like you, Ree Altamira, but I fear for you. Take it from one who has been fighting the system for decades: this is not a battle you are likely to win. You will get crushed in the process."

"Don't be the first to crush her hopes, Hypatia," said Hamid, unexpectedly coming in on Ree's side. "As long as she is subtle, she might be able to make them shift. With a long enough lever and a fulcrum to place it on – "

"One can move the world. Yes, yes, I know what Archimedes

said. The problem is, Hamid, where is the girl to turn when the men have taken all the levers and fulcrums for themselves?"

Chapter 10

Walking the Plank

Henri's palms were sweating and his head swam. Earlier, he had thanked his good fortune when he and Zena found a plank laid across the gap between the scholars' wing and the kitchen tower, saving him the job – that was until he had to make the crossing. It felt worse on this return trip as he now knew what it felt like to inch across the ravine.

"Come on, just do it," he told himself.

Sensing his fear, Zena sat silently on his shoulder, willing him across. The grip of her tiny hands in his hair was added encouragement: they were in this together, even though she could run across it without a second thought.

It would be more dangerous to sit and shuffle along. *Treat it like a narrow strip of pavement. Look ahead and not down.* Taking a deep breath, he forced himself across, vowing that on another night he wouldn't take this route. Though it was a famous secret among the students, a way to raid the kitchens for midnight feasts, it just wasn't worth it, in his opinion.

Reaching the other side, he wondered what he should do with the plank.

"It's almost dawn, Zena. Do you think the boy who pushed it out is back yet?" Had he just forgotten to pull it back or, worse, had he been caught by one of the patrols Henri had successfully avoided? Standing up to catch a glimpse of the sky to the east, Henri saw the first flush of light behind the distant hills. "Better to be safe than sorry, hey?" The scholars would blame him if the traditional sneaking out route was betrayed. Besides, if the other boy was late, all he need do at this time of the morning was go back through the kitchen pretending he had got up early for some reason. The servants rarely questioned the scholars. Zena jumped to the tiles as Henri bent down to begin shifting the plank to their side. When he got it safely stowed, he wiped his hands off on his trousers and began to think about bed.

"Wait! Stop!"

Henri looked up to find a small breeches-clad person standing on the roof opposite. Not a boy though. "Miss Altamira. What a surprise," he said dryly, finding he wasn't so very surprised to see her there after all.

The girl dug her hands in her pockets, shoulders hunched, obviously expecting the worst from him. "You're not supposed to move the plank unless you were the one to put it out."

"That's a rule, is it?"

"No, common sense."

Feeling that for once he had the advantage, he mimicked her posture, hands in pockets. "Really? But I understood it was our plank, the *scholars'* plank. What have you got to do with it?"

Zena leaped to the very edge of the roof and cocked her head with interest at this newcomer. She generally liked girls as they had long hair to groom.

The maid scuffed her toe on the debris of leaves and pigeon feathers that gathered in the gully.

"In fact, it would be much safer if you took yourself off down the stairs. I don't think I can let you risk yourself on the plank bridge." Now that he had said this, he realized it was true. What would happen if she fell? He would be partly responsible.

"I can't – not dressed like this. They'll dismiss me."

"And that is *my* problem?"

Teeth bit into lower lip. She shook her head.

Zena turned disappointed eyes on him. She didn't understand their conversation, but she got that he was denying the girl something she wanted very badly. That made him feel ashamed. If the maid had argued he would've stuck to his position that she should take the stairs, but seeing her and Zena so upset changed his mind.

"All right then. I guess you don't need more marks against you at the moment." He hefted the plank back across the gap.

Perhaps not trusting him to keep it there long, she ran as surefooted as a mountain goat across the bridge. Henri was pleased she hadn't been there to see his own super-cautious passage. Zena bounded immediately onto her back and set about undoing the nearest plait.

"Oh yes, sorry about that. Personal grooming – my macaque's life mission."

The girl gave a startled laugh. "I can hardly object. I'm always a mess."

"She's called Zena."

The maid reached up and cautiously stroked the monkey. "Hello, Zena."

"What've you been doing going about in those clothes?" he asked, reaching down to move the plank again.

"And what have you been doing out and about in yours?" She was studying his hands.

He gave a hollow laugh. "I'm not the chalk writer, if that's what you're thinking. Are you?"

"No." She showed him her palms in evidence. "I wish everyone would stop blaming me."

Henri didn't suppose it mattered if she knew what he was really up to. She had to be suspicious of him, having met him twice now after curfew. "And before you start thinking I've anything to do with it, I was just looking for a room to run an experiment. I need one out of the way where the trustees won't find me."

"Oh." From her expression he could tell she was taken aback that he'd actually explained himself.

"I was looking for one the first time we met but tonight I had more luck. So if you see me out after hours, that's what I'm doing. What about you?"

"I was seeing friends. I had the night off as I'm working in the greenhouses at dawn, a rare day shift." She glanced over his head. "Rats! I'd better hurry. Sorry, Zena, you'll have to complete the mission another night." Gently she scooped the monkey off her shoulder and ran lightly across the roof tiles; then she gave him a brief wave of farewell as she made a heart-stopping leap between Henri's building and the maids' quarters, using the ivy to steady herself as she landed.

Henri cursed under his breath. He would've tried to have stopped her if he had guessed what she was about to do. That was one gap he would never try to jump. Zena, however, gave a congratulatory shriek that might bring others to their windows.

"Hush now!" He watched until he saw the maid had safely wriggled through a window in the turret opposite. *Utterly insane*, Henri decided, making his way carefully to the skylight that enabled him to swing down in the attic of the scholars' wing. Slipping off his shoes, he tiptoed in his socks down the stairs to his rooms and got inside without anyone spotting him. He had left Maxwell with the cover story that he was suffering from a vile form of food poisoning, but it looked like no one had come in here. The hair he had stuck across in the inner door to his bedroom was still intact, meaning no one had opened it to check up on him. Zena climbed to the nest she had made herself on top of the wardrobe. Yawning, he stripped off his outer clothes and stretched out on the bed, determined to catch some sleep.

"Henri, Henri, you've got to hurry!"

Henri rolled over reluctantly, right into a beam of sunlight striping his pillow. That worked better than the arm-shake Maxwell was giving him.

"What time is it?"

"Last servings for breakfast, but that's not the hurry. There's another whole school assembly in the Grand Theatre."

Even though he knew he hadn't been spotted, Henri still felt a guilty tumble in his stomach. "I'd better get up then."

After splashing his face at his hand basin, he turned to face a worried Maxwell.

"They didn't see you, did they?"

"No, Max."

"Did you go out?"

"Yes. Zena and I found a perfect little room under the Fortieth Hall. It already has a stone sink in it, just right for washing equipment. I think it must've once been used for cleaning specimens." Henri ran a comb quickly through his hair. "I guess I don't have time for breakfast then?"

"No, but I grabbed a roll for you and fresh fruit for Her Majesty."

Maxwell really was turning out to be an excellent friend – so much sense for someone years younger than Henri.

"Thanks. We'd better get a move on."

Leaving Zena breakfasting on grapes and apple slices, they reached the theatre just before the doors closed and squeezed into the back row.

"Uh-oh, all the trustees are here too and most of the staff," murmured Maxwell, taking a seat next to Hans.

Henri turned to Ramon, who was lounging on the bench next to them. "Any idea what's going on?"

The Spaniard shrugged, a magnificent gesture that nodded to his heritage of arrogant conquistadors. "*No sé*. But it's not the chalk messages. There weren't any last night."

"How do you know that?" asked Henri.

"My friend in the police." Ramon was often seen sharing a smoke with the younger men on the museum staff in an out-of-the-way corner, as smoking was banned in the academy. Thanks to these connections, Ramon was well known for being able to obtain things the other students couldn't get, like sweets for the younger boys and forbidden tobacco and alcohol for the seniors. Even if Ramon never made a name for himself as a scientist, Henri was convinced that he had a bright future as a businessman ahead of him. Either that or he'd end up in prison.

Looking unusually sombre, dressed in a black swallow-tailed suit, Lord John came to the front of the stage and held up a hand. The ripple of conversation died away.

"Gentlemen and scholars, it is with great regret that I have to announce the passing of our esteemed chancellor, Professor Grassmann. He died quietly in his sleep last evening at the impressive age of ninety-six. A funeral will be held for him tomorrow." Lord John waited for the murmuring to die away. "The chancellor would be the first to say that life must continue even when death strikes down one of our number. The work we do here was too important to him for us to neglect it even for a moment. This museum is his true memorial. So, in the spirit of keeping our vital work running smoothly, I have a further announcement. Until elections for a new chancellor can take place, the museum sponsors have asked Curator Shelley to step up to the role of acting chancellor."

This appeared to be news to most of the trustees. Professor

Gall, as one of the senior members who might have been expecting to be asked to fill Grassmann's position, looked particularly thunderous. Professor André rubbed his monocle with furious concentration before sticking it back in to glare at the nobleman.

Lord John moved aside, turning to the new acting chancellor. "Curator, if you'd like to say a few words?"

Struggling not to smile at the achievement of his life's ambition, the curator swept to the front of the stage. How a man who had very little in the way of academic honours behind him had come to occupy such an influential position, Henri could not understand.

"Look at him: he's loving this," murmured Ramon.

"How did he of all people...?"

"It's a mystery, no?"

Maxwell was shifting uneasily next to Henri. Henri began to suspect his friend knew something about it, but now was not the moment to ask. Gazing at the men on the stage, Henri noticed the awkward hunch of Lord John's shoulders, almost as if he was expecting one of them to stab him in the back. He was acting oddly deferential toward the curator, who could not match him in social position or even in talent. Lord John was a famous artist as well as chairman of the committee of the museum's wealthy sponsors. He held a position of great influence, as he controlled the money. That's why they indulged him in his decorative schemes for the museum. Even the trustees had to listen to him when he spoke on behalf of the sponsors.

"Gentlemen, scholars." Shelley's voice was attempting statesmanlike but came out as platform announcer. "This is a sad day but one that we all knew was coming. Chancellor Grassmann lived a full and productive life, an example to us all. He would not wish us to grieve but move on swiftly to celebrate his achievements as a man of learning. After lying in state in the antechamber in the Twentieth Hall, devoted to his beloved subject of ancient languages, he will be buried in the museum's cemetery tomorrow evening. Please stand for two minutes' silence in honour of our colleague."

The audience rose and stood with heads bowed. Henri felt very awkward. To be honest, he did not care two hoots about the old man whom he had not even met. He imagined that most of the younger people in the room felt the same way.

"Please be seated." Shelley was obviously enjoying his power to get them to sit and stand on his command. He tucked his hands behind his back and puffed out his black robe like a peacock fluffing his tail. "I have a few announcements to make and, as we are all gathered, I think it only appropriate to let you know what changes I am introducing. To begin, it has come to my attention since we began night patrols of the museum that some of the menagerie animals are allowed to roam unchecked."

Hans made a furtive attempt to hide the speckled gecko peeking out of his pocket, the pet that replaced the much-mourned Rainbow.

"This is a glaring breach of the rules we have in place for the health and safety of scholars," continued Shelley.

Henri noticed he made no mention of the maids who surely were the ones at greatest risk as they worked at night.

"My first *act* as *acting* chancellor," Shelley preened at the wordplay, "is to order that all animals be kept strictly in their pens as was intended when our ancestors established the zoological section."

All eyes in the room went to Mr Billibellary among the staff, his dark face surrounded by a froth of white hair easy to spot. He was staring at the new acting chancellor as if contemplating feeding him to the python Naidu.

"Secondly, I'm pleased to announce I've been given approval to mount a new display in the entrance hall. This will entail a few weeks of upheaval as exhibits are moved, but I'm sure everyone will be satisfied that the displays are shown with the correct emphasis on their importance to science."

"He's moving Professor Gall's stuff to the Fortieth Hall," Ramon said in a low voice. "There've been furious arguments about it now for days."

"How do you know all this?" Henri marvelled.

Ramon grinned and tapped the side of his nose. "You might have your head in the clouds detecting invisible fingerprints, Henri, but I keep my ear to the ground."

"They're not really invisible," Henri replied without much heat. He knew Ramon was only teasing.

"And finally, I am going to begin the process of replacing all the remaining female members of staff with male appointees. It is not compatible with our reputation as the leading centre for serious manly scientific studies," Shelley tucked his thumbs in his waistcoat pockets, "to have our scholars at risk of meeting the weaker sex in the kitchen, laundry, and going about their cleaning duties. Advertisements will be placed in all the leading newspapers this week and subsequent weeks until all positions are filled."

"He's *loco*," muttered Ramon. "Taking on the laundry women?"

Henri stared incredulously at the flushed face of the curator. "Can he do that? Just throw all those women and girls out of their jobs? Some of them have nowhere else to go. I can say one thing for our new chancellor: he's not afraid of making enemies, is he?"

Having dropped his three bombshells, Shelley turned to leave. Professor Gall stood up and blocked his path.

"Curator, a word, if you please." His voice rang out in the room.

"I think the correct term of address, Professor, is Acting Chancellor." Shelley fluffed his tail.

"Acting Chancellor." Gall snarled the words as if he were saying "blue-bottomed baboon".

"Go ahead. I want my time at the head of this illustrious institution to be marked by an openness to debate, in the best traditions of scientific enquiry."

"Yeah, right," muttered Maxwell mutinously, making Henri smile.

Gall twitched his sleeves straight. "These are all very important matters, but I'm sure what we all want to know is what you are going to do about the most grave threat we face? You called it an illustrious institution but recently our reputation has been severely tarnished. How can we trust your hand on the helm, when under your time as head of displays you have not even been able to stop them being defaced by the unknown message writer? You seem remarkably at ease with the fact that someone has been scrawling Theophilus-inspired words all over our rational exhibits. I'm afraid I for one cannot have much confidence in your leadership while this situation is allowed to continue."

There was a murmur of agreement from some of the men on the stage. Spurzheim, sitting a few rows in front of Henri, gave a loud "hear, hear!".

Glancing quickly around him to gauge the strength of support for Gall, Shelley gave his colleague a tight smile. "Professor, I promise you that measures are in hand to have the guilty party caught and punished."

Gall rocked like a boxer limbering for a bout, clearly feeling he had landed a punch. "Then may you be judged on your success or otherwise in that area. You might consider yourself on probation."

The more confident Gall became, the stiffer Shelley reacted. "Quite. Now, if you will excuse me, I have a notice to write for the newspapers." Shelley swept out, not as convincingly as he had hoped. As the door shut behind him, the room burst into a buzz of conversation that made it sound like a vast overset hive. Henri sat quietly amid the speculation. This wasn't good.

Shelley had begun his reign by declaring war on key sections of the museum.

It was boiling so high up in the glasshouse. Ree had long since taken off the overskirt she had been told to wear. The loose linen tunic and baggy trousers were almost as good as a dress on her, and who, anyway, was to see?

"You're enjoying this, aren't you, Phil?" she said to the dodo, who was happily sunbathing beside her on the scaffold.

He croaked, as if to say finally she was being sensible, doing a job in the daylight and far away from Ziggy, who had slunk off to sleep in the cool stone scullery.

Ree dipped her sponge into the vinegar and water solution in the bucket and drew it across the next set of glass panes. It felt so like working with the stonemasons, being high up above the visitors, Phil for company; part of her half-expected to hear her father's voice asking her how she was getting along with her project.

Put it away. Don't think about him now, not with the gardeners about. It would be the ultimate humiliation if they caught her in a "girlish humour", as Mr Olmsted called it. He had been called away to a meeting in the museum but would be back at any moment.

Having cleaned off the dirt, she then went over the pane with the wiper, making sure it was sparkling.

A chattering in the tallest of the palm trees caught her attention. A troop of colobus monkeys was watching her and, from the sounds of it, making unflattering comments about her progress. This particular group was the black and white sort, who looked at her with their solemn dark faces framed in a white fur wimple and tufted cape – a convent of banned monkey nuns. Even though their hands only had a short little thumb, they had no difficulty taking great leaps across the canopy, screeching with glee or alarm as the mood took them. Phil obviously despised them but Ree found them very entertaining, as did the visitors.

They were not the only menagerie animals that had decided to move into the palm house. A flock of rainbow-coloured parakeets were sitting on a railing like spectators at a tennis match, heads bobbing between her and the monkeys. Butterflies bloomed and settled on the foliage in garlands. If it wasn't for the heat, this might just be her new favourite place in the museum.

"What? All of these animals back in their pens? But sir, that's impossible!" The under-gardener's voice reached her from below, where he stood talking to Mr Olmsted.

"That's what the new chancellor decided, Fred, so don't make a fuss."

The under-gardener scraped the ground irritably with a rake, like a tiger clawing her territory. "But the butterflies?"

"I suppose they can stay. We'll claim they're needed for the pollination."

"The parakeets?"

"'Fraid they have to go. I suggest a big net and lots of peanuts. Blinking bureaucrats: never think of the work they cause other people when they make their fancy declarations. I'd weed the whole lot of those pen-pushers if they were in my garden."

Ree frowned as she worked on the next pane. Surely Mr Olmsted didn't mean what she thought he meant? That there was a new chancellor was no surprise, as the last one was almost as old as some of the fossils in the museum – but he wanted the animals shut away? Mr Billibellary wouldn't stand for that.

The shaking of the ladder on her scaffold warned her that an inspection was about to be made. Ree dumped the sponge into the bucket and quickly donned the skirt.

"How are you getting on, Maria?" asked Mr Olmsted. With a balding crown and white hair, moustache, and beard, he looked like most of his curls had melted in the heat and slid down to rest under his chin. He mopped the sweat from his pate with a red and white spotted handkerchief.

"Good, sir," said Ree. "I've finished the top row and am

working my way down."

"Mrs Mantell told me you're a hard worker and I see she wasn't wrong. Take your break now. While you're at it, take this beastie back to the menagerie." He nodded to the sleeping dodo. "I've orders to see that all animals go back to their cages."

"What, even Philoponus?" Parakeets were one thing, but it hadn't crossed Ree's mind that the rule might involve the dodo. And did that mean Ziggy too?

"Aye, we've a new chancellor. Curator Shelley has taken over as Grassmann passed away yesterday."

"Mr Shelley?" Ree had warmed a little to the man when she heard him take down Gall in the committee meeting, but she still didn't think it boded well that he had been put in charge. He had no flexibility. Any appeal she could make on behalf of her father would be doomed.

"I'm afraid so, lass. That man must have friends in high places to rise so quickly." Olmsted glanced over the edge of the platform. "But not as high as this. I have to admit I've never been able to stomach heights. I'm going down. Take your dinner break early and don't forget to return the dodo!" With a creak and a sigh, he set off down the long chain of ladders leading to the floor.

"Blast it all." Ree sat next to Phil and nudged him awake. "Sorry, my friend, but you've got to go back to your pen. I don't know for how long but I can't see that rule lasting, so don't get too upset." Phil couldn't understand her, of course, but he did understand the bribe of one of Dr Hamid's pineapple chunks that Ree had in her pocket. He happily followed her, fluttering from platform to platform, from forest canopy down to the damp tiled floor. "Come along, Phil; it's time to take you back to the duchesses."

Ree found Mr Billibellary busily engaged in locking his charges back in their enclosures. A surprising number of creatures had slipped the curfew rule and taken up residence permanently in corners of the museum, not just the monkeys and the parakeets in the palm house. A tough-looking laundress was sniffing miserably as she handed over a basket of terrapins. Two of the younger boys from the academy looked devastated to be separated from the ring-tailed lemur pup they had been nurturing.

"Mr Billibellary, I was told to bring you Philoponus."

The zookeeper scowled, dark eyes practically vanishing in his wrinkles. "It's a bad day, Ree."

"I know, sir."

"Them fellas in there," he jerked his head to the museum buildings, "don't understand the first thing about these creatures. They need to go walkabout."

"I'm sorry."

He huffed and then offered her a faint smile. "Not your fault. Philoponus, you're under house arrest – for the time being." He ushered the confused-looking dodo into his pen. Phil immediately waddled over to his escape route, but the keeper had already removed the stack of crates. The dodo turned to stare at Ree and Mr Billibellary in shock. Ree felt awful. He was her oldest and truest friend in the museum.

"Phil, I'll come and visit you later."

Phil croaked then honked in distress as she made to go.

"I really will be back. With more treats."

He honked again.

"I'm really, really sorry."

When the dodo realized she was not going to let him out, Phil turned and shuffled over to the furthest corner and sat down, giving her his back. He let out an unhappy rumble.

Mr Billibellary patted Ree's shoulder awkwardly. "He'll be all right."

"But he hates it in his pen. It's like prison to him."

"He's not the only one. I'm as mad as a cut snake at what Acting Chancellor Shelley has done."

It was rare for the taciturn zookeeper to admit to any emotion to another human, though Ree knew he confided in the animals often enough. She'd heard him talking away to them, telling them stories of the Dreamtime of his people, when great spirit animals walked the land.

"I don't blame you, sir."

"You must be fit to be tied too, youngster, what with him putting all you girls out of a job?"

"What?" Ree felt like she'd just missed a step in the dark and tumbled all the way to the floor.

Mr Billibellary picked up his barrow, heading for the gate to receive more returnees. "Though who he's going to get to do the hard *yakka* like scrubbing floors is a mystery. Most blokes won't do it. Go and fetch Ziggy, will you? She'll only bite me if I try to get her back here."

Ree stared after him. If the zookeeper was right, not only had Shelley's appointment deprived her of any hope that a fresh campaign on behalf of her father would work, and the company of her best friends shut up in their cage-prisons, but he was also going to wreck her livelihood. She would be out of a job and a place to stay in short order if he got his way.

She squeezed handfuls of her skirts in her fists, powerlessness the worst of the stew of emotions inside her. "Oh, Phil. I could kill that man. I really could."

Chapter 11

Death Comes to the Dodo Pen

Ree grabbed Beata's sleeve as they passed each other in the corridor, Ree just returning from escorting Ziggy to her enclosure and her friend heading out. "Is it true, Bea?"

"That they're getting rid of us?" Beata's thin face looked strained. Like Ree she had no family. After several horrible placements with other families, experiences she still refused to talk about, Beata had flourished at the museum. Now all that was at risk. "Seems so."

"But what are we to do?" Ree squeezed her friend's hand in sympathy.

"I don't know. Mrs Mantell says it'll take time to find replacements, that maybe something will happen to change his mind." Beata didn't sound too hopeful. "I suppose we'll have to start looking for another job in the city somewhere." With an apologetic smile for Ree, she added, "I'd better go," then hurried off to the evening roll call.

Ree was too tired to sneak out immediately. She had been up for twenty-four hours and had spent the last part of the afternoon yawning. Only the antics of the gardeners trying to catch the monkey troop had kept her awake. They had failed miserably and concluded they would have to try a different strategy later.

There was time to eat before sleeping. Ree went by the kitchen to grab some supper and found Ingrid scraping burned stew into a big bowl.

"Is there anything I can have?"

"Not this swill," the cook said shortly. "Over on the warming plate; help yourself."

Ree found a pot of herb-flavoured lamb casserole, a rare event for a servant's supper. Not wanting to pass up the treat, she filled a bowl and sat down at the end of the kitchen table. Ingrid added a warm crusty roll and pat of creamy butter to the feast. Ree watched as Ingrid sent the charred stew off into the scholars' dining room with a nod of satisfaction.

"If they don't think us females are good enough to cook for them, then that's what they'll get," the cook declared.

Ree didn't think it was a good moment to argue that the scholars, like the boy she kept meeting, were blameless in this affair. "So you think it's serious – the new chancellor is getting rid of us?"

"Yes, Maria, I do. And that fool Jean-Paul in the first kitchen had the gall to laugh at me and Mildred over in the second kitchen. If Chef thinks he can feed all of these mouths with his fancy food, then he's got a shock coming; I don't care how many sous-chefs he employs to do the grunt work."

"Can we do anything? I mean, do we just have to accept it without a fight?"

"We're considering a strike, me and Mildred."

"Maybe we should all go on strike, the laundresses and maids too. That would really show them."

Ingrid gave her a sharp look. "Clever girl. You're right." She cut Ree a generous slice of poppyseed cake, added a dollop of cream, and placed it on the table for dessert. "I hadn't got that far in my thoughts, but it's clearly better if we stick together on this. I should go and talk to the other heads of department. We can't let the grass grow on this issue or we'll be out on our ear before you know it. Help yourself to tea while I'm gone."

Once the cook had left, Ree had second thoughts about her idea – not the idea itself, but the fact that she had been the one to suggest it. She should have steered the conversation that way, prompted Ingrid to come up with it herself. If word got out she had suggested the strike, her letters would never get a fair hearing.

Face it, Ree, the letters were never going to work, whispered a gloomy voice in her head. They are never going to forgive your father even if you are a model servant for the rest of your life.

Shut up. They will. They must. Ree sipped a cup of weak tea, breathing in the bergamot-scented steam. She imagined the vapour uncurling in her mind and chasing out the pessimist who lived somewhere inside her brain. Her chin dipped, eyes closing despite herself. *I'll be asleep if I sit here any longer.*

Shaking off this strange defeated mood, Ree jumped up and cleared her plates. She had to keep on fighting, no matter the obstacles. Take her friends over in the Fiftieth Hall. They hadn't given up. Hypatia was still secretly going on her exploratory voyages; Hamid was still investigating his mathematical universe. Had anyone warned the renegade scientists that a new man had taken control of the museum, she wondered? Ree could not imagine Shelley allowing vast areas of the building to remain out of his grasp for long. Next he would be sending search parties and demolition crews into the labyrinth to tidy everything up in the spirit of the new order he wanted to impose. She had to tell Hamid and Hypatia so they could take steps to protect themselves.

"First sleep, then another midnight walkabout," Ree muttered, running up the stairs to her room.

Mrs Mantell was waiting for her at the door to her dormitory. "Ah, there you are. I was just coming to look for you. All well at the glasshouse today, Maria?"

"Yes, ma'am."

"I suppose you heard the news?"

Ree nodded.

Mrs Mantell jingled her bunch of keys much as a porcupine would rattle its spikes to warn of a bad temper. "Well, never mind that now. Just one man saying things are going to change doesn't mean they will. Things can happen. Sleep well." She locked the door behind Ree and set off down the stairs.

Ree woke up as the clocks around the museum began to strike midnight. Splashing water on her face to drive away the last of her sleep, she prepared for another expedition across the rooftops. A light rain was falling, making the ledge slippery, but she was determined to go on with her plan.

Pushing off, she landed awkwardly on the scholars' roof, losing her footing on the tiles and slipping toward the gutter.

"Blast!" she hissed and threw herself flat to prevent her body shooting over the edge.

A hand grabbed the back of her shirt and hauled her away from the edge. The boy again, of course, accompanied by the pretty little monkey. "Newton's apple, girl, have you no sense?"

Ree decided not to snap back at him. She had to admit that she may have needed his help this time, just a little. "Good timing. I'm fine, by the way." She brushed off her shirt, now stained from close acquaintance with the moss that grew on the tiles. "Tell me, what *is* your name? I feel foolish as you know mine."

"Henri Volp." The scholar sketched a shallow bow. The things in his backpack chinked. "At your service." His macaque copied his gesture, making it rather absurd.

"Maria Altamira," replied Ree, playfully giving a matching gesture to boy and monkey. "Paid to be at yours."

He gave a huff of laughter at that. "I doubt very much you're ever really at anyone's service, Miss Altamira. I've watched you pull the wool over the eyes of the trustees at the trial but you don't fool me. You have a very independent spirit."

She liked the sound of that. "And you don't?"

"I suppose I might at that." He grinned, his usually serious face becoming much more approachable. "Are you going to visit friends again?" He began the process of moving the plank across the void. Ree kneeled to help him.

"That's right."

"Are they on or off the island?"

She sat back on her heels. "Why do you want to know?"

He shrugged. "I'm curious why you're risking it. I know why I am, Miss Altamira."

That name sounded ridiculous considering they were now conspirators in each other's law-breaking. "Ree. Please, call me Ree."

"You can call me Master Volp." He chuckled at her expression. "Just joking. I'm Henri." The plank was now in place and he gave a visible gulp. "Do you want to go first?"

"All right." She walked swiftly across the plank. "The trick is not to think too much about it."

"Says the girl who moves like a mountain goat."

"You'd be surprised. Some of them aren't so clever when it comes to climbing. There's a Pyrenean ibex in the menagerie who is forever getting stuck on the cliffs." By keeping up the banter about the height-challenged ibex, she hoped she was distracting Henri from the potential dangers of the plank. He managed it slowly without a wobble, Zena following him as if poised to catch him should he fall. Neither mentioned his cold sweat as they headed into the attics of the kitchen tower.

"She's not been sent back to the menagerie?" asked Ree, gesturing to his pet.

"Ah well, theoretically. I took her back – for five minutes. Decided that was enough to satisfy the letter of the law. I owe her far more than I do the new chancellor."

"Oh, that's exactly how I feel! I must go and fetch Phil and Ziggy. I'm sure Mr Billibellary will agree to let them go. They just can't be kept shut up like that. Seriously, I think it would kill Phil."

Henri had brought a lamp with him, but he waited while Ree dipped into the scullery to borrow one for herself.

"How did you get to your room last night?" asked Ree, pausing in the shadows of the kitchen court.

"Through the halls." Dressed in black, Henri merged well with the darkness – better than she did, in fact.

"I think you might have been lucky not to get caught. I've a better way if you want to try it."

"You have?" He sounded interested rather than sceptical.

"We go down."

"But I've been told that it's easy to get lost in the passageways. They don't follow the same plan as the rooms above."

"No, they don't. But I have this." She showed him her map, opening it out in a patch of moonlight so he could see the meticulous notes. A new handwriting in dark blue ink on the sheets showed where Hypatia had added her own information to the plan.

Henri reached for it. "This is wonderful, so detailed! Whose is this?"

Ree pulled it back from his eager fingers. "Mine. I made it."

"You've drawn it beautifully – so, so elegant!"

Ree actually considered it a fairly poor example of her design skills. "I was a stonemason before I became a maid. I know how to make an architectural drawing."

Henri was oblivious to her slight tone of offence. "Exactly! Your talents are wasted as a maid."

Well, if that was what he meant, she would forgive him his initial surprise. "So, Henri Volp, are you willing to risk yourself by accepting the guidance of a female mapmaker?"

"I can't see why not."

Exchanging a friendly grin, they headed for the nearest door that led down to the passages beneath.

"We have to go carefully in this section. Some of these lead to the lockups and are used by the police. You can tell which ways are known to the authorities because they have these little signs at the junctions." She held her lamp up to the painted hand pointing one way to the cells, the other to the exit. "But as it's dark, you can see their lights before they arrive and I've always had time to dodge around a corner."

Once they went beyond the passages most used by the police, Ree allowed herself to relax.

"There's little chance we'll meet anyone now. Could you hold up your lantern so I can check the map?" Light flooded the page. "We take the third right down here – where the roof looks like it wouldn't take much to bring it down."

"There speaks the stonemason."

She really liked him for giving her credit of her profession, far better than any other compliment he might have made. "Maybe, but anyone can see the ugly big crack running along the ceiling. I've put up some wooden props but I wouldn't trust too much to them. We'd best go silently. Try to keep Zena quiet."

"Ah, yes. Keep down sound vibrations. Good idea." Henri was excellent at taking her orders even if his footfall wasn't as soft as she would like.

"There, we're safe for the moment." Ree picked up her pace, knowing the next part of the journey involved no detours and the passageways were in a reasonable state. "So why are you setting up an experiment down here?"

"They refused my proposal."

"Why not just put in another one?"

"All the money for this year has been shared out… but it was worse than that." He paused, evidently not sure if she wanted to hear more.

He hadn't taken into account her insatiable curiosity. "Go on."

"Oh, it was just that Professor Gall was in a stinking mood. He went on to say that nothing I ever put forward would be of any use, because no African had ever come up with a scientific breakthrough and that my head shape was all wrong for a man of science."

Ree couldn't resist a chuckle. "You're in good company then. Mine is wrong too, according to him – something about an ideality bump. I suspect that the only skull he approves of is his own. I think his subject – what is it – phrenny-something?"

"Phrenology."

"Yes, that. It's a load of cobblers."

"I think you might just have hit the nail on the head." Henri sounded amused by her plain speaking.

"And as for no science coming out of Africa, I've a feeling he is wrong about that too." Could she risk it? It was a wonderful if reckless idea that might make a huge difference to her new friend. He *was* a friend, wasn't he? Yes, someone who put their monkey first and came with you on illegal night excursions was certainly that. "Henri, if you have time, do you want to meet some people?"

"The ones you've been visiting?"

"Yes. But you have to promise not to breathe a word of their existence."

"Ree, I give my promise. And if that's not enough, I stand to lose my place here if I admit to these night-time ramblings, so it really isn't in my interests to tell tales."

"Your word's good enough for me."

After a difficult journey where Ree had frequently to consult the map and backtrack, they finally made it to the Fiftieth Hall. She now understood why the renegade scientists preferred to risk travelling like grey ghosts through the corridors and chambers above ground when they had to emerge from their sanctuary for supplies. Going down was always risky; it was very easy to lose your way, even with a map, as so many passages looked exactly the same as another. A compass would be a good addition next time. Taking Henri swiftly through the portrait gallery, she reached the door behind which she hoped to find her two friends.

"Come!" called a voice.

"Dr Al-Ghazali, it's me. I've brought someone to visit you."

"A moment – I'm just chasing an idea. Yes, yes, got it!" Hamid noted something with his pen then looked up from his desk, light reflecting from his spectacles. "How interesting. You've brought me a scholar." He made it sound like the nicest possible present. "Henri Volp, isn't it?"

Henri bowed. "Yes, sir. And this is Zena, a crab-eating macaque."

"Not many crabs around here, but will she be happy with pineapple, I wonder?" Hamid held out a handful and Zena transferred her affections to his palm.

"But how do you know my name, sir?" asked Henri.

Hamid scratched his beard. "I do still have a few friends in the academy. They keep me abreast of what goes on there." He stood up, dislodging a precarious pile of papers. They scattered on the floor like a drift of autumn leaves. Ree and Henri rushed to rake them up. "Thank you. Hypatia despairs of me. She's always after me to have a proper filing system but I can't seem to get around to it."

"Is she here?" asked Ree.

"No, she's off with the Sisters of Science having one of their symposiums. I think they're over in the Hundredth Hall."

"There's a Hundredth Hall?" Ree realized that her idea of

the extent of the museum fell far short of the actuality. She had thought that maybe this hall and one or two others was the limit.

"Oh yes. That one was dedicated to Aristotle's model of the universe. It took them a long while to let go of his idea of celestial spheres with the Earth at the centre. Got poor Galileo in trouble, that did, but it was such a persuasive idea, no wonder they didn't want to abandon it. Look up into the sky and that's what it feels like – us at the centre, everything moving around us. Tea?"

"Thank you, sir." Henri arranged his pile neatly on the desk. "You're working on infinite series numbers?"

"Well done. You're as good as my colleague said. Yes, I am, but not getting anywhere." Hamid filled the kettle and put it on the hotplate. "I might have to turn to another area to see if I can make more progress. I feel that infinite series are beyond me at present."

"Is that... logical, to give up over a feeling?" Henri wondered.

"No, dear boy, it isn't, but haven't you yet discovered that the whole brain is used for scientific enquiry?"

"Yes, I suppose it is. I often reach my conclusions as a detective by a kind of intuition."

"Exactly. Mathematicians like me will tell you that very often our instincts take us to an answer first, while our logic runs to catch up. There are the most wonderful patterns underlying the universe. Physics can't exist without them. They govern such small things as making a cup of tea, as well as the grand things like the revolutions of the planets – and us humans are able to understand them. It's quite awe-inspiring when you think about it." With a wink at Ree, Hamid spooned tea leaves into a little pot.

"But isn't that just what's out there – Newton's laws and things like that? There isn't an alternative. It's reality," said Henri.

"How do we know that? Why should there be any pattern to

our everyday world? Because we assume there should be. Do you see what I mean? That's not logic; that's instinct."

Henri grinned. "Good point."

Hamid set out four cups on a tray, neatly lined up on saucers. "I see patterns and order in the universe, whereas my Hypatia sees evolutionary change happening by chance, or as being random." He offered them a little tin of leaf-shaped biscuits. "But, ah-ha, I ask her: where does chance come from? Chance conforms to mathematical laws too, if you look at the underlying probabilities. She gets annoyed with me when I do that. She tells me mathematicians can't always have the last word."

"I can imagine she might find that annoying," murmured Ree, thinking back to how irritating Henri had been when he had acted so superior with her on first meeting.

Hamid chuckled. "Yes, I can be most trying to live with, for at this point I usually go on to ask Hypatia: why is there anything at all? She hates that."

"You like looking for a motive." Henri sounded pleased. "Have you found it?"

"No, but the more I look at the universe, the more it seems to me like one great thought from a beautiful mind."

Ree found that rather poetic. She imagined a design for a carving of a godlike person thinking up the universe, much like Hamid sitting at his desk.

Leaving the mathematicians to make the tea and dabble in infinity, Ree occupied herself by examining some of the objects displayed on the shelves: a tiny model of the sun and planets that revolved as she turned it, a ship's compass pointing north, an abacus made of rows of coloured beads. The last item she picked up was a head divided up into sectors, but its dignity was somewhat undermined by the fact it sported a feathered bonnet placed at a jaunty angle.

"Don't tell me you study phrenology as well?" said Ree,

fearing that Hamid was about to plunge in her estimation.

"Good gracious, no. What made you think that?" Hamid saw what she was holding. "Oh, I see you've found Caligula. Hypatia swears by it as a hat stand. Best use for it in my view."

"Caligula?" asked Ree.

"The Roman emperor of that name was off his head, so it felt appropriate." Hamid handed her a cup of mint tea and put Caligula back on his shelf.

That recalled Ree to one of the reasons why they were here. "Henri's worried because Professor Gall said no scientific discoveries had been made by people from Africa. He says their skulls are wrong."

"That man gets more absurd by the day." Hamid sat in an armchair and poked at the fire, sending sparks up the chimney. "He is also woefully ignorant. Arabic scholars led the way in science for centuries in the first millennium AD, and the best university and library in the world was in Alexandria in Egypt for hundreds of years. And unless my geography is entirely up the spout, I'd say that was in Africa – wouldn't you, Henri?"

The door opened and Hypatia strode in, bristling with her usual energy.

"Hello, Ree. Who's this?" asked Hypatia, accepting a cup from Hamid and taking the chair opposite him.

Understandably looking somewhat dumbfounded by the trouser-clad lady doctor, Henri introduced himself again, explaining a little more this time about his desire to find a room of his own to run his experiment. Ree was amused to see that he was flustered in a way that had been missing when he talked to Hamid.

If she noticed the boy's admiration, Hypatia did not embarrass him further by making any mention of it. "So that's why you were setting up shop in that old specimens laboratory last night." Hypatia sipped her tea. "I did wonder."

Henri looked alarmed. "You saw me?"

"We keep watch on the halls. For our own safety. Don't worry: none of us will interfere, though Hamid here might want to as your enterprise sounds like something he would enjoy. Invisible fingerprints made visible: almost magic, wouldn't you say?"

Hamid laced his fingers across his middle. "You know me so well, dear. I was just working myself up to asking if I could take a peek at his plans."

"I'm afraid that will have to wait, Hamid. We can't go beyond the Fiftieth Hall at the moment. There's been a development – a new chancellor who's making the feathers fly within seconds of his appointment."

"So you know already!" Ree was pleased that word had reached the renegades, relieving her of some of the burden of explanation.

"Indeed. When Maggie failed to show for her evening visit, I sent a message to Mr Billibellary and got something of an incendiary letter back. Simplicius Shelley? Who is he, I ask you? What contributions has he made to science to be worthy of the honour of being appointed head of the museum? He's a nobody." Hypatia cracked open her revolver and checked the chamber for bullets.

"He made himself somebody very quickly," said Henri, watching her every move with the gun. To see someone with a revolver in the museum was odd enough; to see a woman handling it so expertly was unheard of. "Got on all the right committees. Positioned himself the chancellor's right-hand man."

"It's an old story, Hypatia," said Hamid mildly. "Shelley is a politician; his sort inherit the earth because our kind are too busy thinking about our research to notice."

"I think we'll all be made to notice now. The Sisters suggested that you and I move further in. We're too exposed here, in one of the first places they'll look if they decide to go beyond what they already know."

Hamid swept a sad gaze around their comfortable study with its chained books. "I suppose we must, but the accommodation in the older halls is so spartan, plumbing positively medieval."

"That's because it *is* medieval. We'll manage."

"Indeed. I suppose we'd better pack?"

"Will we be able to visit you?" asked Ree, not liking the implication that they would be moving beyond her reach too.

The lady nodded. "I do hope so. When the dust settles and the animals are free again, come with Maggie. She'll sniff us out."

"And if it doesn't settle?" Ree tried to conceal the worry in her voice.

Hypatia tapped Ree's forehead. "You'll work it out, Maria Altamira. You found us the first time. This Shelley can't have eyes everywhere in a place this size. There is no way that someone with your mapping skills will be defeated by a few more passages."

As Hamid and Hypatia refused help in packing, Ree and Henri took the hint that they should leave them to it.

"I like your friends," Henri said when they regained the Hall of the Four Humours. He paused over the eyeless mermaid. From her perch on his shoulder, Zena bared her teeth in challenge to the creature. "That's… rather unfortunate. I see there's so much more going on in the museum than I realized."

"Than anyone realizes," added Ree. "If you're ready for more outrage, do you want to break into the menagerie with me to liberate Phil and Ziggy?"

"An illegal night-time call on a dodo and a wolf: what could be better?"

After leaving the equipment Henri was carrying in the room he had selected for his experiment, the three explorers set off in this new direction. Hypatia's ink marks proved very helpful in suggesting a shortcut to the southern side of the island, taking them down previously unknown bypaths.

"Do you know what this feels like?" Henri asked after they consulted the map for the tenth time. "It feels like we're walking around inside one giant brain – all these layers and connections."

Ree grimaced. She had also seen the cross-sectional diagrams of the human brain in the anatomy theatre in the academy. She avoided volunteering for cleaning duty in there, as the jars of specimens and body parts gave her nightmares. "Thanks for that thought, Henri. Just what I needed in my head to feel good about wandering around in the labyrinth."

He chuckled, then dodged the retaliatory elbow she sent his way.

They emerged near the side gate, to which Ree already had a key. She didn't need to use it, however, as the entrance was ajar.

"It looks like someone else might've been this way earlier. We'd better keep an eye out."

From the worried hum from her companion, she guessed Henri was having doubts about the idea. "You remember that detective intuition thing I mentioned to Hamid? Well, it's asking me if I'm sure we should carry on with this."

"I can't let Phil and Ziggy down. If you prefer, you could wait here."

Henri cast an anxious look around him at the unfamiliar stacks in the builders' yard. There were plenty of places for someone to hide. "We should stick together."

There was no need of a lamp as there was a full moon. Knowing the path well, Ree led the way to the dodo's pen. She was just about to call Phil when Henri grabbed her sleeve.

"Wait!"

"What?"

"There's something lying on the path over there. Something bundled up in cloth."

Zena gave a whimper and covered Henri's eyes with her hands.

Phil had noticed their arrival. He scuttled across the pen, giving soft hoots that sounded most unlike him. Ree offered him a handful of pineapple through the bars but he ignored the treat and settled instead for nestling against her palm.

"Something's wrong," said Ree.

Henri stroked Zena in reassurance. "It's that thing on the path there. We'd better look."

"I don't think I want to." She made herself anyway.

They rounded the corner of the pen, Phil following them on the inside of the railings until they reached the section where the bars joined a brick wall. At its foot was a cloth bundle. They could see now it was a cloak covering a man who was lying at full stretch on the ground. Something dark and wet leaked out to one side.

"Sir? Sir? Are you all right?" called Ree, hesitantly touching his ankle. She didn't want to go anywhere near the stain at the head. He was cool but not cold.

"Ree, I don't think he's the least bit all right." Henri used a stick to flip back the edge of the cloak covering the man's face.

Acting Chancellor Simplicius Shelley sprawled before them, the side of his head stoved in by a stone axe. The weapon was still embedded in the wound.

Henri took a quick step back. "I'd go so far as to say he was dead, wouldn't you?"

Ree bit back a scream. "Henri, what do we do now?"

Part III

Cenozoic

Cenozoic era: from the Greek *kainos*, meaning "new", and *zoe*, meaning "life". Also known as the Age of Mammals.

Extract from Henri's notebooks

Chapter 12

Stone Axes to Grind

What they did was agree that Ree should guard the murder scene while Henri went off to find help. It was tempting just to vanish into the night, but Henri discovered they both were burdened with an inconvenient sense of right and wrong. Any idea of hiding their presence to avoid trouble was rejected on the grounds that reporting a murder was far more important. Besides, as Ree argued when Henri suggested she disappear and leave him to deal with it, she could not live with herself if any delay meant the murderer had more time to cover his tracks.

"Stay in the pen with Phil and Zena," Henri told Ree. "If the one who did this is still around, he'll think twice of approaching you in there." He gave her a boost over the wall as Zena scrambled over unaided. "Phil, Zena: look after her."

Phil clacked his beak in an impressive manner.

Ree landed on the sandy ground inside. "I don't think the one who did it is still here. We didn't exactly keep our voices down, did we?" Zena climbed on Ree's shoulder and started grooming.

Worried that he might be leaving them in danger, Henri ran as fast as he could to the police station, which was housed in a building close to the entrance hall. He found a whole patrol inside, on their break from walking the corridors.

"Please: you've got… to come!" Henri called, his breath coming in pants.

"What are you doing out of bed, scholar?" asked the officer in charge. He grabbed Henri's hands and held them up to the light, looking for chalk marks.

Henri tugged them out of the man's grip. "There's been a murder!"

That galvanized the police into action. Mugs were put down, belts refastened.

"Are you sure? Where? In the scholars' wing?" asked the officer, heading in that direction and not waiting for Henri to answer.

Henri pulled him in the opposite direction. "No, sir. In the menagerie. Please, come: it's the acting chancellor."

The officer drew back. "Is this your idea of a joke, young man?"

Henri wanted to explode with frustration. They just had to come and look and they would see this was the furthest thing from a jest. "No! He's been murdered. Come on: I left my friend alone there by the body." He began running.

"Did your friend do it?" puffed the officer.

Why was this man intent on getting absolutely everything wrong? "No, of course not. We found the body when we went to see the dodo."

Like an avalanche gathering momentum, the police swung into action. Lights were summoned, backup called in. By the time Henri returned to the menagerie with his entourage, they numbered more than twenty.

The officer held Henri back as they approached the pen. "Where's your friend? I don't see him."

"She's in with the dodo. I thought it the safest place for her to keep watch."

"Her? Oh-ho!" The policeman now thought he had the reason why Henri had been sneaking around at night. "Tell her to stay where she is. I don't want anyone disturbing the area around the body," ordered the officer.

"Ree?" Henri could see her peeking over the top of the wall, Phil and Zena beside her. She appeared to have built a staircase of boxes to reach the top.

"Yes?"

"Isn't that…?" queried the officer.

Of course, the policeman recognized his prime suspect in the chalk case. "Yes, but she didn't do anything but find the body with me," Henri said quickly. "Stay there for the moment, Ree. I've brought the police."

"All right." Her head ducked down below the parapet.

The officer held up a hand to get his squad's attention. "Men, I'll go forward and make a visual inspection of the site and confirm that there is indeed a victim and that he has been murdered."

Henri thought the axe in the head was a bit of a clue.

The officer walked carefully forward, scanning the ground with his lantern. "Too many footmarks here to distinguish any particular prints," he called out. Henri noticed that a junior officer was taking notes. Maybe they weren't as hopeless at investigating as he had assumed. "The body is lying on its front, head to one side. Sign of significant trauma to the left-hand side of the head. Weapon still present on the scene. I can confirm that the victim is indeed our acting chancellor." The officer took a moment to gather himself. He was used to dealing with protestors, not violent crimes, and could be forgiven for wondering what the correct procedure would be. "Fenelon, summon one of the medical professors and wake all the senior staff. I want a roll call taken of everybody on the island and note made of where they have been this night. Jones, pick five men and search the menagerie in case our killer is still here. Once that is finished it will be light. Return then and start a fingertip examination of the ground around this pen and any access routes the victim and murderer may have used. Schmidt, take these two witnesses to our office and begin taking statements. Their clothes should be taken into evidence and they must be searched. I'll want to talk to them as soon as I've finished here." He turned away and began setting up a perimeter around the body with a yellow cotton tape supplied by an underling. "Fetch the photographer. I don't care if you have to pull him out of bed in his nightclothes: I want him here at the double."

The officer that Henri thought had to be Schmidt took his arm just above the elbow. He was a well-built man with big hands worthy of a prizefighter. "Come along, boy. Let's fetch your accomplice."

That sounded ominous. "But we didn't do anything!"

"We'll see. Miss, time to come out of there."

Ree appeared at the top of the wall and dropped down. Phil fluttered to the ground beside her.

"Put that thing back in the pen," ordered Schmidt.

"I'm afraid I can't, sir," Ree said, scratching Phil's head. "He doesn't do what I say. Besides, he's a witness."

"Witness, my eye!" spluttered the policeman.

"He saw who did it."

"And I suppose he told you, did he?" Schmidt folded his arms.

"Of course he didn't. He's a bird. He can't talk." She gave the man a look that said he was an idiot. "But he's upset and won't easily be parted from me."

Over in the marsupial pen, Ziggy howled, adding her protest to the confusion.

"And I suppose that creature is a witness too?" sneered Schmidt.

Henri didn't think it was a good idea for Ree and Schmidt to launch into an argument right on the scene of a murder. "Please, she's right. You have to know what Philoponus is like. It'll be more trouble than it's worth trying to get him back in the pen." Zena scrambled up his leg and curled her tail possessively around Henri's neck.

Schmidt wiggled his pursed lips, left to right, before relenting. "Oh, all right. Let's get on with the rather more important business of investigating a murder, shall we?" Herding them in front, he took them back to the museum and into the police station. He snapped an order to the man who had remained there on duty. "Fetch a female – the housekeeper will do. We need to make a search and give them a fresh set of clothes."

Henri and Zena were parted from Ree and Philoponus as they were taken into separate rooms. Schmidt examined each of Henri's garments with care and rooted through his empty backpack. He sniffed it suspiciously.

"What did you have in there?"

Henri had been carrying bottles of the most promising chemicals for fingerprint detection but fortunately had offloaded them in his experimental chamber. "Sandwiches," he improvised. "For a late supper." That would explain why there was nothing left.

"Not a stone axe then?"

It was obvious where Schmidt's thoughts were going.

"No, not an axe," said Henri quietly, pulling on the set of clothes normally handed out to prisoners: pale orange trousers and shirt.

Schmidt bagged up his black trousers and jumper. "These will be tested for bloodstains."

"You won't find any. As I said, we only discovered the body. We didn't do it."

"Maybe he surprised you when you were kissing the maid, eh? Maybe you killed him to stop yourselves getting into trouble?"

"So why would my first act be to run and fetch the police?" asked Henri logically.

"You panicked. Or you wanted to give the impression you were innocent by acting like someone who wasn't guilty."

"Or maybe we're just not guilty?"

Schmidt sniffed again and put pen and paper in front of Henri. "Write down everything that happened tonight. Leave nothing out. I'm going to see what the girl can tell me."

Henri sat down at the table and rested his head briefly in his hands. Newton's apple, what a muddle. He and Ree had to tell the same story, but they hadn't had a chance to agree what they would include and what to leave out. He had to guess what she would say. Obviously, she wouldn't mention her renegade scientist friends, so neither would he. The story held together well enough if he omitted that and just went straight to the visit to see the dodo. They met on the roof, then went through the passages for an innocent little adventure. Yes, that would be best. He just had to hope that Ree was clever enough to know not to embroider or take departures that he couldn't guess.

"I'm very disappointed in you, Maria." Mrs Mantell had been going on like this ever since she had been hurried into the room. She folded Ree's gardener's uniform and put it in the bag the policeman had given her. "To go out when you knew how dangerous it was for you!"

Ree pulled on the drawstring that held the pale orange skirt around her waist. There seemed to be acres of material. "I'm sorry, ma'am. We were just visiting Philoponus. I was hoping to get him and Ziggy freed."

"I should've guessed your devotion to those animals would make you do something foolish, but still it doesn't explain what you were doing with that boy."

"We met by chance. I hardly know him." That was true enough. "Isn't it better that we found the body so quickly?"

"It would've been better if you'd stayed tucked up in bed where I left you!"

She had a point. Ree was very aware that she was already under suspicion.

Officer Schmidt knocked and walked in. "Maria Altamira, it just had to be you, didn't it?" He nodded to Mrs Mantell. "Thank you for assisting us. We'll take it from here."

"She really is a good girl," said the housekeeper, handing over the parcel of clothes.

"So you keep telling us." He waited until Mrs Mantell had left the room before starting his questions. "Inspector Gideon will be with us shortly, but before he comes he has asked you to make a statement. I assume you are no hand with the pen so I will write your replies for you."

Maria opened her mouth to deny this, then thought better of it. Never offer more information than they asked seemed a good tactic. She just hoped Henri was astute enough to keep what he said to a minimum and not take paths she couldn't guess. She had to trust him.

He uncapped his fountain pen and took a sheet of clean paper. "So, explain what brought you to the dodo pen?"

"We were visiting Phil."

The dodo gave a croak from his corner, recognizing his name.

"And how long have you been seeing Volp?"

"We're not seeing each other. We met by chance on the roof."

"On the roof?"

"It's a way out after dark."

"I see. Did you invite him to accompany you?"

Ree wrinkled her brow, trying to remember. One thing had just flowed naturally from another. "I suppose I did. I was worried about Phil."

"You didn't arrange to meet anyone else at the menagerie?"

"Of course not."

"You hadn't been there earlier?"

Ree could see where he was going with his questions. He was wondering if she had been responsible for the attack on the acting chancellor and then only pretended to discover the body with a witness in tow. "I was last there at noon when I took Phil back to Mr Billibellary."

"Did you see the keeper at all this evening?"

"No, sir."

"Did you hear him issue threats against the acting chancellor?"

"No, sir." The keeper had been angry, it was true, but enough to do murder? Surely not.

"Now talk me through every step of your journey from the roof to finding the body."

Ree pieced together her excursion, leaving the part in the cellars as a vague "we went through the corridors" without mentioning which ones. Before Henri had returned with the police, she had hidden her map in Phil's nest among the shredded newspaper that formed the dodo's bedding material. She hoped the police, if they did look in there, would assume it was just a dry liner. Again she had to trust that Henri had the sense not to mention it.

"The gate was ajar?"

"Yes sir." Her spare key was also tucked in Phil's shelter, shoved deep in a pile of fruit skins and droppings that formed his toilet area. Good luck to the policeman who looked through that mound.

"And you didn't see anyone else?"

"No, sir. No humans."

He sat back in his chair. Ree stood awkwardly twisting her fingers together. She would prefer to sit but he hadn't invited her to take a seat. Phil waddled forward and sat on her toes, an awkward if comforting gesture.

"Tell me, Maria: what did you feel toward the acting chancellor?"

"Me? I don't know. I barely knew him."

"But he was at your father's trial."

"I don't remember him speaking against Da." He hadn't, had he? All Ree could remember was Professor Gall's attempts to make her confess Theophilus sympathies.

"And he had just ordered your animal friends to be incarcerated."

"I didn't like that much but I was hoping it wouldn't last long." It would be a lie to say she didn't mind that decision, and she sensed Schmidt was waiting to pounce on the first fib he detected.

"And he had just announced that all the females on the staff were to be replaced."

"I heard that too, but Mrs Mantell said we were to wait and see."

"What do you think she meant by that?" Schmidt held his pen poised over the paper.

"That boys were unlikely to apply to be maids when they could do so many other jobs in the museum and elsewhere in the city."

"Not that she was going to take matters into her own hands?"

What could Ree say to that? The idea that the housekeeper would take an axe to Shelley was so outlandish she didn't even want to acknowledge it. She shook her head.

"Did you hear anything about a planned strike by female staff members?"

Yes, because she had suggested it, hadn't she? "I had heard a few whispers about that but I've been on the day shift in the greenhouses so wasn't around for much of the time. That was why I was wearing trousers, by the way. It's my uniform." She felt she had to put in a good word for her own behaviour when he wasn't looking for anything to excuse her.

"I see." Schmidt asked her for a few more details and wrote them down. He then stood up and handed her the paper. "Read this. Tell me if you have any difficulty understanding any of the long words, then sign if you think it an accurate account of what you have just told me."

Ree carefully read through his neat handwriting. He had been fair to her in this at least. "Yes, that seems right." She took the pen and signed, then on second thought struck through any spare room on the paper so nothing could be added.

He raised a brow at her caution. "Sharp one, aren't you? Stay here." He left, taking the statement with him. Ree guessed he was going to compare it with Henri's account. Biting a nail, she sat down next to Phil and prepared herself for an anxious wait.

Officer Schmidt took up Henri's account and ostentatiously placed it next to the one he had brought in from Ree's room.

"Has anyone mentioned to you, scholar, that you have appalling handwriting?" he asked.

"Yes, sir. Frequently." And Henri had made sure he gave a particularly poor sample so that he had a second chance to explain away any discrepancies.

"What does this say? You met where?" He pointed to a blurred word. Henri meanwhile had been quickly reading Ree's statement upside down.

"That says scholars' wing. We met up on the roof. Do you want me to add that?"

Schmidt shook his head. "How did you find your way to the menagerie?"

"Through the passageways under the museum."

"And you didn't get lost?"

"We followed our noses."

Schmidt tapped the statement. "What does that mean?"

Good question, thought Henri. "The animal stench is quite strong, you know. I've a particularly good sense of smell."

"So you led the way?"

Had Ree mentioned her map? Henri thought that unlikely. He had to hope they hadn't found it when they searched her.

"We went together but, yes, I did take the lead when we weren't sure." That would fit what they expected from a boy and a girl. It would be doing Ree no favours to say she was in charge of the expedition.

"Humph! Tell me, Volp, what did you think of our new acting chancellor?"

So they were going straight to motive, were they? Henri knew he had far less against the man than many in the museum. "I didn't know him, officer. I've not taken Geology so not been taught by him."

"That's it? You must have some thoughts about his promotion?"

"Only that it had been quick. He must have extraordinary talents. Have had, I mean."

Schmidt stared at him for a long time, hoping perhaps that a confession would gush out. It would make the policeman's life much easier if the case could be solved the same night as it was discovered. "What I don't understand is why you – a boy without a blot on your record – should see fit to cavort around the museum at night with a suspect individual."

"I was just interested in visiting the dodo, sir. I don't think that quite fits the description of cavorting."

"Are you romantically attached to Maria Altamira?"

Henri was surprised into a laugh at the delicate phrasing, then saw that the question was quite serious. He sobered. "No, sir." What could he say that would clear them both? "We've only just met. She's nice enough I suppose, but she's a maid, I'm a scholar. We come from different worlds. All we share is curiosity – about dodos."

"You wouldn't be the first scholar to get a maid in trouble, I promise you." Schmidt gathered up the statements. "Stay here. Inspector Gideon will want to question you."

Half an hour later, Schmidt returned with his superior.

"Volp, I want you to show us how you got out of your room undetected last night," said Gideon.

"Yes, sir." Betraying the scholars' plank was a small consideration compared to the charge of murder. Henri followed the two policemen out of the room, expecting to see Ree in the corridor. "Where's Ree?"

"We've moved her to the lockups while we check your story," said Schmidt.

Anger swelled in his chest. They had done that because they could get away with treating a maid like she was nothing. "It doesn't seem fair, sir. We are trying to do the right thing by reporting the crime but you're punishing her."

"No, we are just being cautious," countered Gideon. "You both were out last night against the rules, remember, even if you were nothing to do with the crime that was committed."

Henri felt very conscious of wearing the orange garb as he walked through the scholars' wing. Zena dared anyone to make a remark, shrieking if they came too close. His classmates couldn't help but look shocked, except for Spurzheim who met this development with delight.

"Lock him up and throw away the key, officer!" he crowed. "He's had it coming for a long time."

Zena emitted a series of threatening cries, fur stiff as a clothes brush.

Gideon gave the boy a quelling look. Spurzheim backed down and scuttled into a classroom.

"What's all that about?" he asked Henri.

"He hates my guts because I'm from Algeria."

"And because you're cleverer than him. Yes, I've read your file, Master Volp. Jealousy is a powerful force. But justice is blind to such things as the country you come from."

But not to class and gender, as it was Ree sitting in a cell, not him, thought Henri.

Henri led them up to the attic and wedged open the window. Climbing on a chair, he pulled himself up and waited for the two men to join him. The first thing he noticed was that the plank had been pulled back and was lying innocently in the gutter. Had one of his friends tried to cover his tracks for him? The second was that there was a truly beautiful sunrise in progress, red and gold flushing the horizon.

"Tell us about this secret route," ordered the inspector.

Henri explained how Ree was able to jump across from the maids' tower, join him here, and then use the plank to cross the gap between the buildings. Fortunately, neither Gideon nor Schmidt remarked on the fact that the bridge had been drawn back.

"It's been like this for decades," admitted Henri.

"So some of the professors would know about it?" asked Gideon.

Henri frowned, thinking. "I suppose they would. It's a tradition."

"One that will have to end. With murderers on the loose, as well as a chalk writer, no one should be wandering at night."

Henri was beginning to see that the inspector was a more approachable character than Schmidt. Gideon would not judge them guilty without more proof.

"You don't think it's us, do you?"

Gideon turned to look at him with his shrewd grey eyes. "The evidence is not pointing that way. I cannot see any motive for you, and the idea that a five-foot-nothing maid like Maria Altamira was able to wield a stone axe against a grown man strikes me as absurd. No, I think you were probably guilty of nothing more than going to visit a dodo when you should've been obeying the curfew. As far as offences go, this is not one that should be a matter for the police."

"So you'll release Ree?"

"We'll see. There's still the matter of the chalk writer."

"Could the murderer and the writer be one and the same? Maybe the acting chancellor surprised him in the middle of making another message?" Henri found it hard to rein in his detecting instincts. He hoped he wasn't perceived as overstepping the mark.

Gideon clapped Henri on the shoulder in a comradely gesture. "I like your reasoning. That had occurred to me too. It's going to come down to who had the biggest axe to grind against the chancellor – I don't think the odd choice of murder weapon was an accident. But I suggest you take yourself off and get changed. No doubt we'll need to speak again later. You are the closest thing we have to a witness."

"But Ree?"

Gideon gestured to Schmidt to follow him back down. "Don't worry about her. She's none of your concern."

But she is, thought Henri fiercely, watching as the sun edged over the horizon, staining the museum with a blood-red dawn.

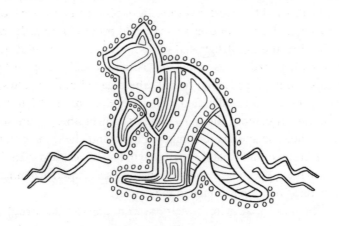

Chapter 13

Dreamtime

Ree was getting used to being in the lockups but that did not make it any more comfortable. Phil had not been allowed to accompany her, and from the yells she heard earlier he had made his displeasure known with application of beak to police buttock. That noise had died down, so she had to hope he'd scuttled off somewhere to wait. Policemen would occasionally come to check on their prisoner and have a brief word with the warden at his desk in the corridor but not talk to her. By chance they had put her in the same cell as had held her father. She had searched the graffiti on the wall for his initials, but he appeared to have not left his trace – was that all part of his insistence that he should be forgotten in the old world? What would he be thinking now if he saw her?

Lying on the thin mattress, she stared up at the ceiling, then grinned with delight. She had been wrong: he had left his mark, but not with anything as boring as his name. Up in the corner he had carved the most beautiful face. She fetched her candle and dragged the stool over so she could see it close up. It was only when the candlelight fell full on it that she realized it was her mother, made so as to look down on him while he spent the hours waiting for his ship to sail. She recalled how Da always said people never really died while they lived on in the hearts of those left behind. Her ma – and her baby brother – were still here while she and Da remembered them and could carve their faces in stone. But what if she started to forget? She had to find a way to bring Da home – and soon, before her memories dimmed to nothing more than a face in the dark.

The rattle of keys in the corridor alerted her to the arrival of yet more policemen. Ree jumped down from the stool. If she didn't think they would purposely send her to a different camp in the New World, she would've welcomed a charge that got her transported to join her father. Not murder though: the penalty for that was death.

Sitting back on her mattress, she watched two officers escorting a prisoner into the cell next to hers. It was Mr Billibellary. He also was wearing prison orange.

The warden opened the cell, pushed him inside, and locked it behind the zookeeper.

"Inspector Gideon will be back to interrogate you after we've completed the search of your quarters. If you've anything to confess it will go better for you if you do it now," warned Schmidt.

The zookeeper didn't say anything, merely moved around the cell clearing a space in the centre.

Ree clung to the bars. "Why have you arrested him?" The policemen left without replying. "Mr Billibellary, are you all right?"

"No worries, Ree. But you'll see my animals get their tucker, won't you?" said the keeper. "Make sure Humboldt is doing his job. The boy means well but without me there..." He sat down cross-legged on the floor, not bothering with the mattress.

"But I'm stuck in here too."

"They think it was me. They have to release you now." His eyes were closed; he appeared to be meditating.

If that was true, of course she'd see that the animals were looked after. "I'll go to the menagerie first thing if they let me go."

"That's all I can ask."

"Why do they think it's you?"

He opened his eyes. "And you don't?"

"Of course not!"

"I'm a black fella. Black fellas are always the first to be blamed."

"That's not fair!"

"They said one of the displays had been raided in the archaeology room – some flints and an axe taken. The flints were found in my wheelbarrow; the axe was found in that man's head."

"Someone is trying to frame you."

He nodded.

"So what are you going to do?"

"Go on walkabout." He tapped his head. "Speak to my ancestors from the Dreamtime and see what they know."

Familiar with his ways, Ree respected his belief in his spirit world but thought he could do with help that might stand up in court. "I'll be quiet then."

He began a low hum that turned into a crooning song. She didn't understand the words, but from his expression she could tell that he was walking a landscape far removed from the stone box that contained them both. Finally, the singing stopped and he sat silently, absorbed in a dreamworld that she could not access.

"Miss Altamira, you're free to go." Schmidt had returned.

Ree wanted to shush him but didn't think that would go well. Instead, she said nothing and let the warden open the door for her.

"You're to report to the housekeeper. Keep yourself available for further questioning."

"Yes, officer."

No one followed her as she exited the police station. She fully intended to report to Mrs Mantell but Schmidt had not said she had to do so immediately. There was something else she should do first. Ree set off for the menagerie, ignoring the surprised looks of the servants and scholars on seeing a girl in prison orange out in daylight. The museum was shut in honour of the former chancellor – both of them, she supposed – so there were no school parties to point at her, something that she counted a bonus. She reached the menagerie and found the main gate open. The police were searching Mr Billibellary's house, which was over to the west side of the zoo. As long as she kept to the eastern paths, she should be able to retrieve her map and key, as well as ensure that Humboldt was doing his job.

There was no sign of Phil. After greeting the ostrich and rhea, she scrambled over the wall on the opposite side from where the body had been found. Her map was where she had left it, and she used a stick to drag the key clear of the dung heap. Grimacing, she wiped it off on the hem of her skirt. Now for the part where she was most in danger of being spotted. Tucking her items into her bodice, she quickly checked all was clear before using the crates to drop to the ground. She darted behind the elephant house and out of sight. No sound of anyone raising the alarm. Good.

Glancing up at the roofs of the museum, Ree sought out a clock tower to find out the time. Just as she shifted to bring one into her eyeline, Old Saul began striking. She counted his strokes: ten o'clock. If Humboldt was doing his job, then that meant it was time to feed the penguins. This was good news, as their pool was in the north-east corner in the coolest spot of the menagerie, far away from the police. As hoped, she found Humboldt miserably chucking handfuls of herring to the birds, who also seemed downcast, barely bothering to peck up the meal they normally rushed to eat. She didn't really believe in magic, but the menagerie had certainly lost its sparkle now Mr Billibellary was no longer in his post.

"Mr Humboldt?"

The young man put down his bucket. A gentle giant, he was known not to be the most intelligent person in the zoo but undoubtedly devoted to his animal charges.

"Oh, hello, Ree. You heard what happened then?"

"I did. Mr Billibellary wants to know if you are keeping up with the feeding?"

Humboldt nodded and pulled out a schedule. "Look, I made a plan for myself. With all the creatures back, there's so much to do and I had to make a new one. One of the gardeners said they'd help me later."

Following orders, Humboldt had written "Tucker Times" across the top. Ree ran her finger down the list, checking he'd not forgotten any creature. It was indeed a lot of work for one man. "That's really good. I'll send a message that he's not to worry."

"But it's not right, Ree. None of them should be locked up, especially not Mr Billibellary."

"I know, Humboldt. I can't see anyone stopping you letting them go now – that was all the new chancellor's idea."

The zookeeper put the now empty bucket in his wheelbarrow. "I might just do that. But as for Mr Billibellary, it can't have been him. He was too busy."

"What do you mean?"

"The police don't believe me but go ask the gardeners. They know."

After checking that Ziggy was taking her daytime sleep, Ree hesitated at the gate of the menagerie. Surely yet another delay in reporting to Mrs Mantell was excusable, as she had to apologize to Mr Olmsted for not coming to work that morning? Lifting her skirt out of the dirt, she ran to the botanical gardens, which shared a boundary with the zoo. At the entrance, she found Henri and Zena waiting for her. He had had time to change back into ordinary clothes.

"Ree, they let you go!" Henri hugged her, Zena chattering enthusiastically on his shoulder.

"Eventually. And you?"

"Earlier this morning. I went back to the station as soon as I could, but they said you'd already left to report for duty. You said you were working here this week."

"You remembered that?" It was nice to hear that he cared enough to check that she was all right. "I was. I'm not that sure I still have a job."

"And I'm not sure I still have my assistant curatorship. I've been summoned to see Professor Gall, the new acting chancellor, at midday."

"Oh rats." That really didn't sound promising. "Did you know they arrested Mr Billibellary?"

"Yes, it's all over the academy. An anonymous tip-off. I don't know him as well as you, but he gave me Zena when I felt homesick; I owe him so much. And the tip-off? That's too… neat."

"Exactly. He's being set up to take the blame. He didn't do it – wouldn't do it. He's a peaceful man. That's why I'm here: his assistant said the gardeners would be able to say why he couldn't be our murderer."

Henri glanced over her head at the glistening glass dome. "You're investigating? Is that a good idea for you?"

"Probably not. But they'll keep on jumping to the wrong conclusions if we don't find out the facts."

"We?"

"Don't you want to find out the truth?" asked Ree.

"Yes, always. That's what I like doing: detecting."

"And if you've lost your curatorship anyway, what have you got to lose?"

He gave a grim laugh. "Plainly put. I agree. It appears the police lack the necessary curiosity to find out who really did this. It's going to take two people who can't help asking questions to solve the murder."

"You and me?"

"That's right." He took her arm, walking slowly into the botanical gardens. "A detective duo."

Zena transferred to Ree's shoulder. "I think she wants us to say trio – or whatever the word is for five, when Ziggy and Phil join us."

"A quintet then. But first, can we do something about that orange outfit you are wearing? Everyone can see you coming a mile off."

Ree dipped into the gardeners' potting shed and borrowed another uniform.

Henri handed her an apron from the peg by the door. "Put this on too. It's almost like a skirt from the front and will stop people staring."

Bundling her prison clothes into a sack to be collected later, Ree joined him at the door. "Right, let's begin our investigation."

"Where do we start?"

"With Mr Olmsted. He usually knows everything that goes on in here."

They found the head gardener in the palm house, butterflies garlanding his head and alighting on his shoulders as he fed them sugar water.

"Mr Olmsted?" said Ree.

He put the bowl down, losing half his garland as he did so as they migrated to the food source. "Ah, Maria, I wasn't expecting to see you again."

"I'm sorry I'm so late."

He dug his hands into his grey jacket pockets. They bulged like the growths on the trunk of an old beech, misshapen from carrying twine, secateurs, and gloves. "I know you couldn't help it, lass."

"Did you know they arrested Mr Billibellary?"

"Aye, it's hard to credit he'd do such a thing." He fumbled for a clay pipe and set it between his teeth, sucking on the mouthpiece.

"He didn't. Humboldt said the gardeners would know what he was really doing last night."

"He said that?" Mr Olmsted filled the bowl with some shreds of tobacco from an old leather pouch, tamping it down with an equally leathery fingertip. "But I was at home with the wife."

"Oh." Ree wondered what Humboldt had meant.

Henri, meanwhile, had been admiring the butterflies clustered around the sugar water. "Amazing. I've never seen so many on one place."

"Aye, lad. They love it here. As do the parakeets."

Then Ree realized what she was missing. "Mr Olmsted, what happened to the monkeys?"

The old gardener scratched his head, staring up into the canopy. "Oh, they should be here somewhere." He caught Ree's thought. "You think…? Let me ask Fred. Fred?" he called.

The under-gardener emerged from the bushes, a parakeet on his shoulder like a pirate in the jungle. "Yes, sir."

"Where are those dratted black and white monkeys?"

"Mr Billibellary came and fetched them last night. He said they'd be easier to take while they were asleep and he was right. We put a little something in their feed and they slept like babies through the whole thing."

"So you were with him the whole time?" asked Henri.

"Well, we were both in here but not together, as you might say. He was up one tree, I another."

"But you would've noticed if he'd gone out?"

"He did go out, but only to take the monkeys back."

"And when was that?"

Fred scanned the roof, thinking. "It was close to dawn as I said that saying about red sky at night."

"Shepherd's delight," continued Henri.

"Red sky in the morning, shepherd's warning," finished Ree. It certainly had been a danger signal for all of them.

"Well then, lad, you must get yourself off to the police station and tell them what you know," said Mr Olmsted.

"What? Why?" asked Fred.

"Haven't you heard?" asked Mr Olmsted.

"Heard what? I've only just come on duty, having had a kip by the lily pond since we finished with the monkeys."

"Acting Chancellor Shelley was murdered last night and they are accusing Mr Billibellary of the crime," explained Henri.

"Never!" Fred brushed off the parakeet and pulled on his jacket. "Right, I'll go straight to the station." He hurried out.

Mr Olmsted took a puff of his pipe. "Well done, you two. You might've saved Mr Billibellary some hours in the lockup."

"Do you want me to stay now and do the window cleaning?" Ree tried to hide her yawn.

He shuffled his feet awkwardly. "No, lass. You'd better go and talk to Mrs Mantell. She wants to have a word with you."

Dread settled on Ree's shoulders, far heavier than the butterflies resting on Mr Olmsted's. "All right. Thank you for yesterday. I enjoyed working here."

"Best of luck, lass. If ever you want to come and visit us, you'll always have free entry – you and your friend." He nodded to Henri.

"Goodbye, sir." Ree turned on her heel and left the warmth of the glasshouse for the chilly morning outside. She was pleased that Henri didn't say anything. "I'd better go and see what the housekeeper has to say to me."

Henri bumped her elbow with his. "I have my meeting with the acting chancellor too. Do you want to meet up afterwards?"

"Where? They might tell me to get out." She was fairly certain that was the message she had waiting for her.

"Fiftieth Hall?"

"Yes, I suppose that'll do. Will you find the way?"

"Show me the map again. You do have the map?"

Ree nodded and pulled it out of her shirt. "I hid it in Phil's nest."

"Good thinking." Henri studied the passages between the Fortieth and Fiftieth halls, trying to visualize the route. There were so many little twists and turns that he was worried he wouldn't be able to keep it all in his head. "I'll lay a trail with thread. If I go wrong, at least you'll be able to find me."

They parted by the door leading back into the museum. Henri and Zena headed off to the scholars' wing, Ree to the housekeeper's room. She knocked on the door, wondering if Mrs Mantell would still be on duty. Normally by now all the maids and their manager would be asleep.

"Come in."

She wasn't going to get a reprieve. She sidled around the door. "You wanted to see me."

"Sit down, Maria." Mrs Mantell moved from her armchair by the fire to her desk. Ree took the upright seat in front of it.

Best to meet this head on. "You're going to dismiss me, aren't you?"

Mrs Mantell looked down at the letter on the desk. "I have no choice. You've disobeyed direct orders more than once and last night you were in a place you had no right to be, in the company of one of the students. I can't save you this time. Our new acting chancellor has demanded your dismissal. You have until nightfall to leave the island."

Ree swallowed against the lump in her throat. "The police told me I was to keep myself available for further questions."

"Then you should leave the address where you will be staying."

"I don't have an address, Mrs Mantell. I don't have any family off the island – and my friends don't really have room for me."

She couldn't bear the idea of going back to the Simplon family having failed again.

The housekeeper pulled a piece of paper out of a drawer. "I thought that might be the case so I took the liberty of writing down the addresses of some orphanages in the city. And the workhouse. That will take you if the orphanages are full."

The workhouse had a dire reputation, worse than a prison, as the unofficial sentence there was death by starvation or hard labour. The politicians thought they were discouraging people from being poor if they made conditions worse than living in the most abject slum. Ree took the paper, vowing she wouldn't let it come to that.

"There are employment agencies also. I can provide you with a reference. We needn't mention your..." – Mrs Mantell sought for an appropriate word – "...lapses. You work hard and I'm sure you'll be good from now on, won't you?"

"I'll try my best but it never seems good enough, does it?"

"Well now, you let me know when you're settled and I'll send that reference. Here's your wages for the last week and a little extra." She handed over a suspiciously heavy bag. "Be careful out there, Maria. The world isn't kind to a girl on her own."

Ree knew that already, which was why she was determined not to find herself alone.

First stop was her room to pack her few belongings. Beata and Mary were asleep but woke when they heard Ree moving around, packing everything into a canvas bag that had once held her tools. Mary, long brown hair in two plaits, sat up in bed and hugged her knees.

"Is it true you found the body, Ree?" she asked.

"Yes." Ree decided she didn't want the mob caps. She'd never liked wearing them. "Here, you two can have these."

"You're leaving?" said Beata, rubbing the sleep from her eyes.

"Yes."

Her friends leaped out of bed, Beata's hair bouncing in corkscrew curls.

"But that's not fair!" exclaimed Beata. "I thought with Mr Shelley dead our jobs were safe!"

"I was out of bounds when I found him. There was nothing Mrs Mantell could do to save me."

"Where are you going to go?" Mary had realized quicker than Beata that protest was pointless.

"I'll stay with friends for the moment. Don't worry about me. Maybe it's for the best. I didn't really fit in here, did I?"

Mary hugged her. "No, but then none of us do."

Ree squeezed her back. "Be careful: there's a murderer on the loose. They haven't got the right man in the lockups and you all being out at night puts you at most risk."

"We will – and we'll tell the others what you said. But I think I should say the same to you." Beata examined the contents of the bundle that Ree was packing: paper, pencils, a key, and the map. "I'm good at arithmetic and this doesn't add up. You're not really leaving, are you?" She opened the folded map as Ree snatched it back.

"Sorry, best you don't know about that." Ree blushed. It was awkward having secrets from her friends.

"We wondered what you were doing every night when you requested all the solitary tasks." Beata nodded to Mary. "She thought you were making new designs for more stonework and I thought you were teaching yourself science like we do, but you were exploring, weren't you?"

"You are too clever for me. Look, I have secrets that aren't mine to share, but if you need me, give Phil a message – tie it on his leg. He'll find me."

"We will. Likewise, if you need us, leave a message with Ingrid in the kitchens. She can be trusted and she likes you," said Mary.

Bidding her friends farewell, Ree slipped out of her room, wondering if it would be the last time she was in the maids' tower. It had been a home when no other was available and she had good friends. She would miss them.

When she reached the kitchen courtyard, Phil and Ziggy joined her. Phil she was not surprised to see, but she was pleased someone had moved so quickly to let the other animals loose.

"So Humboldt let you out?" she murmured, scratching her between the ears. "Or does it mean Mr Billibellary is free already? That would be nice."

It was unsettling to realize how many people were privately quite happy that the acting chancellor was out of the way: the zookeepers, the women employed in the museum, even Professor Gall. It gave too many a motive for murder.

But not everyone would then frame Mr Billibellary. That had to be significant and certainly cleared Humboldt of any suspicion in Ree's mind. Without a doubt, the assistant zookeeper was strong enough to do the deed and would have been on site as he lived next door to Mr Billibellary, but he would never have let his mentor be blamed. He would confess first rather than plant evidence in the keeper's wheelbarrow.

Unless he panicked? Ree tested that idea. No, Humboldt had not shown anything but shock and outrage that Mr Billibellary had been arrested. He was not the kind of man to be able to play-act innocence. She could take him off her long list of suspects.

The clocks began striking midday. Ree's thoughts went to Henri facing his interview with Professor Gall. She couldn't help him, so the best thing she could do was say her goodbyes to her friends in the kitchen, get something to eat, then disappear down in the labyrinth so she would be there to meet him when Henri came looking for her.

Slinging her bundle over her shoulder, she walked into Ingrid's domain.

Chapter 14

Seeking Sanctuary

Waiting outside the chancellor's study, which was in the tower of Old Saul at the heart of the museum, Henri heard the clock strike midday. No one came to summon him. From behind the door came the sound of an argument: Professor Gall was talking loudly, shouting in fact, so Henri could not help hearing.

"I will not have that man lying in state next to Chancellor Grassmann! Holding the position for one day does not match decades of service."

The man who responded, Lord John, Henri guessed, was quieter but Henri caught snippets such as "tradition" and "what would people think?".

"They will think nothing of it because there is nothing *to* think. In any case, the police require the body to be kept on ice in the refrigeration chamber as evidence while they investigate the crime. We'll bury it only when we've caught this murderer.

Chancellor Grassmann's funeral goes ahead as planned tonight."

Someone murmured something else. Henri thought he heard "disrespect" among the terms used.

"I have every respect for my predecessor in this post but that doesn't mean I think he should be accorded the same honours. No, we will proceed with Chancellor Grassmann's funeral. I will, of course, make mention of the unfortunate Shelley, but his fate shouldn't overshadow the solemnities."

The meeting broke up soon after that, with Lord John leaving the room in a hurry, followed more slowly by a gaggle of professors and doctors. Henri was shocked at how much the nobleman appeared to have aged. His hair seemed to have gathered some grey and lay lank against his brow. But the greatest change was that there was no bounce or arrogance in his step. Lord John's spirit appeared cowed, if not broken. Did he have something to regret?

The clock chimed the quarter. Left alone in the antechamber, Henri gazed down at his shoes, realizing they were still covered with mud and scuffs from his adventures of the night before.

"He'll see you now, Volp."

On hearing the familiar sneer, Henri looked up, braced for an unpleasant surprise. Gone was fussy Secretary Morley, the old guardian of the office, and in his place was Kurt Spurzheim. He stood in the doorway, wearing crisp black robes; his shoes were polished to a shine to rival the scrolled mirror on the wall.

"What are you looking at, Volp?"

Henri knew better than to rise to any bait cast by his enemy. He stood up and made a move toward the door.

Spurzheim caught his arm above the elbow. "Just so you know who you're dealing with, I'm the chancellor's private secretary now."

"*Acting* chancellor," murmured Henri as he walked past his old classmate. In his mind, the door to his curatorship slammed shut: no way would he be allowed to stay on at the museum if

Spurzheim had anything to do with it.

In past times the chancellor's study had been an inspiring place to visit, covered skirting board to ceiling with books and paintings reflecting the taste of the occupant, manuscripts, and images of Indian temples. The floor retained the intricate rug from Afghanistan, curling flowers woven in jewel-bright colours, and the tiger skin in front of the fire. The walls, however, were bare but for empty picture hooks and there was a stack of frames in one corner. Professor Gall was installed behind a large mahogany desk, surface piled with papers, quills lined up ready to be cut. He was well known to prefer the old method of writing, rather than modern fountain pens. He was losing no time in putting his own stamp on the place and he showed every sign of preparing for a long stay. Henri wondered if Gall was the least bit worried for his own safety, with his predecessor dying within a few hours of appointment. There was no evidence of it here.

There wouldn't be – not if he did it. Henri found himself very interested in the whereabouts of Professor Gall the night before. As an angry man with his professional reputation at stake, Gall had plenty of reasons to bash his rival over the head with an axe, and, what was more, Henri could imagine him doing it.

Unsettled by that thought, Henri cleared his throat. He knew Professor Gall was aware he was standing there but the acting chancellor was pretending to be too busy to notice.

With a world-weary sigh, Gall threw aside his quill. "Ah, Volp. Sad business."

"Yes, sir."

"It must have been quite a shock to find the body as you did?"

The suggestion that Gall might be sympathetic took Henri by surprise. "Yes, it was."

"Not that you saw anything – or so the police tell me. Is that correct?"

"Yes, sir. We arrived too late."

"*However*," the professor shifted to reprimand, "you would not have found the victim at all if you had been where you should have been."

"Indeed, sir."

"Nor have you explained adequately what you were doing out at night in the company of a known troublemaker."

"We were worried about the dodo, sir."

Gall waved away that explanation. "That girl has an enlarged area of the front temple indicating recklessness and stubbornness. I do not see the same in you, so I assume that you were led astray. Your scalp indicates lack of leadership, a servile quality common to those of your country."

Professor Gall was back to his old tricks. Henri knew now that Gall made up his bumps and depressions to fit what he wanted. Henri wasn't in a position to object so all he could say was: "Sir?"

"In part you can't help it, so I had to bear that in mind when deciding your punishment. However, it is clear that you aren't the sort we want for our curators. For the flagrant breach of our rules, you will leave at the end of the academic year and not return. Do I make myself clear?"

Considering his outstanding results automatically qualified him for a post, Henri doubted the new chancellor had the power to do this under museum statutes, not without a full meeting of the trustees, but there was nothing to be gained by raising this objection now. Henri had to find himself allies outside this room. "Very clear, sir."

"Inform your family to expect you in June. You are dismissed."

"Sir."

Henri walked out, head held high. He wasn't as devastated as he once might have been. When he'd won the scholarship, imagining his future, it had always been the museum at the centre of everything. Now his dreams were changing. The events of the night put everything in perspective. The pursuit of science was not worth taking a man's life. Henri himself had nothing to be ashamed of because he had done the right thing in reporting the death immediately. Either he got the decision to expel him overturned or he would take it as the final sign that the museum was no longer worthy of its reputation as the pre-eminent seat of learning. If it was going to let a phrenologist call the tune, Henri would go study elsewhere. More pressing was solving the murder. What happened to him after that could be dealt with once that mystery was explained. And if Gall was the killer, then his decisions would all be voided.

After collecting Zena from his room, Henri's route to his rendezvous with Ree took him through the main halls, as he didn't want to risk the labyrinth beneath without the map. He had momentarily forgotten that Grassmann was lying in state in a chamber off the Twentieth Hall until he saw the line of people waiting to sign the condolence book. Near the back of the queue, Maxwell spotted him and waved him over.

"Henri! I've been so worried about you."

"I'm fine, Maxwell."

"But that lump of mould Spurzheim said they were getting rid of you?"

A tall man two places forward turned around and shushed them. "Have you no respect?"

As the dead couldn't hear, Henri didn't think Grassmann would mind them talking. He did, however, lower his voice. "They are. Or at least trying to." Henri shrugged. "I can try to stop them but maybe I'd be better off elsewhere."

"But you can't let them win." The hiss of anger in Maxwell's tone took Henri back. "Cousin John – you know who I mean by that, don't you? – says that the museum is falling apart with the wrong people in charge."

Henri really didn't want to risk this conversation being overheard by anyone else, particularly not the man in front who was shooting them severe looks. He tugged Maxwell from the queue and took him into a high-ceilinged room devoted to hieroglyphs and pyramids. "When did he say that?"

"Yesterday, before Shelley was killed." Maxwell ran his hand over the curled horns of an Egyptian ram, guardian of a tomb. The statue was something of a favourite with the younger boys because it looked so friendly. "But he won't be any happier today. He's not a fan of Professor Gall, but no one else wanted the position."

"But I thought he sponsored Shelley for the top job? He pretended to be happy with the appointment."

As there was no guide on duty to stop him, Maxwell jumped up to ride the ram. "Can I tell you a secret, Henri? You won't tell anyone else?"

Henri thought of Ree and their investigation. "I won't tell another man, I promise."

"Shelley forced our cousin to give him the position."

"But how?" Henri thought he could guess: it had to be blackmail. But what damaging secret did the nobleman have to hide? He had always seemed above reproach and lived life in the public eye, his activities well reported in the press.

Maxwell pulled a face. "It's to do with another relative of ours, Uncle Luc. He's a cousin of Lord John, like my mother."

"The one in the camps?"

"How do you know that?"

"Your mother mentioned him. Is he in the civil service or military and wants to get out?"

"No, no, nothing like that." Maxwell patted the ram. "Look, Henri, I'm trusting you with a secret that could bring our family down. He's a prisoner. He was transported for staging a Theophilus protest here a couple of years ago. He cut ties with our family, knowing he could only do us harm, but Shelley found out that we were related."

"But it's not a crime to be a cousin of a criminal."

"But the fact that Lord John hid the connection looks suspicious; you have to see that. It would damage his standing in society, put us all under a cloud. My sisters would never make good marriages and I'd probably lose my place here. Cousin John has been trading promotions for keeping all of this under wraps. In my family, we hated Shelley but we also needed him kept happy."

This sounded like yet more motives for murder. Henri could rule out Maxwell, mother, and sisters as axe murderers, but Lord John could easily have lured Shelley to the remote spot of the dodo cage and killed him. The question was whether the nobleman had it in him.

Maxwell looked down at Henri in misery. "It sounds bad, doesn't it? I've thought about it and there's a reason why none of us would want him dead. Last we heard, Uncle Luc is really ill. He refused to stop preaching so he's been given harsh treatment in the camp and that broke his health. We think he has consumption. Shelley agreed to act on Luc's behalf to get him moved to a hospital on the coast if Cousin John made sure he became acting chancellor. My cousin wouldn't kill him, would he, if Shelley hadn't yet had a chance to complete his part of the bargain?"

Henri wasn't as trusting in Lord John's good nature as Maxwell. Perhaps the pressure on him had got too much to bear? Perhaps Shelley had gone back on his word once he got what he wanted and the nobleman had snapped at the betrayal? "Do you think Lord John would speak to me about this? If you tell him you've taken me into your confidence and I'm trying to find out who did it, do you think he'd talk?"

Maxwell bit his lower lip, his face anxious. "I'm not sure. I guess he would like the chance to discuss it with someone else. It's eating away at him, anyone can see that. But you're just a student."

"I was there when the body was discovered and I'm good at detecting crimes. The police keep blaming the wrong people, so I've decided to find out the truth."

"You're investigating?"

"With a friend. You can tell your cousin to prepare himself. It's likely that his relationship to Luc is going to come out, especially if Shelley left any record of what was really going on. Lord John might have to choose between talking to me and my partner now so we can find out the truth, or to the police later – and by then he will be under a cloud of suspicion."

Maxwell thought about this for a moment. "You know, he might talk to you if I tell him I think you have a good chance of solving it. I'll ask him."

"Thanks, Maxwell. Why don't you suggest that he meets us here after Grassmann's funeral tonight?" Henri thought that would be the most convenient time, as there would be crowds and nobody would have time to watch what was going on at the margins.

"I will. And, Henri, I'd like to help too. Who's the other boy anyway? Not Ramon? He couldn't keep a secret to save his life." His friend sounded a little jealous.

"You're already helping, Maxwell, and it's not Ramon. In fact, it's not a boy."

Maxwell grinned. "I should've guessed: Maria Altamira – the girl you were caught with!"

"Yes."

"What can she do to help?" Maxwell slid off his ram and dusted off the seat of his trousers.

"You'd be surprised. Remember your sisters? Well, Ree is like them but ten times more so."

Maxwell sucked in a breath then patted Henri on the arm. "Poor you."

Leaving Maxwell to sign the condolence book as ordered by his tutor, Henri and Zena carried on through the Thirtieth and Fortieth halls. It was hard to imagine them as they had been on his last visit at night, lit only by soft gaslights and his lantern. Having seen Ree's map, he now understood the basic idea behind the museum's arrangement of rooms. The large halls were hubs around which the many antechambers and the antechambers to those antechambers spread, sometimes upwards to new floors, sometimes outwards until reaching the edge of the island. New rooms had been added as scientists made discoveries in each subject area. The entrance, or First Hall, and connected rooms were dedicated to evolution and life sciences, displaying the most up-to-date findings in fossil hunting and zoology. The Tenth Hall celebrated mathematics and its achievements, such as calculating the circumference of the Earth. The Twentieth Hall was devoted to archaeology, as well as the study of human cultures and languages. The Thirtieth was Henri's personal favourite, for that was centred on the great scientists of the seventeenth century and the instruments they made to look near and far, optics, and thermodynamics, as well as the equipment to carry out laboratory experiments. The rooms around this hall were given over to chemistry and physics. On the floors above were astronomical displays going all the way up to the turret observatory that housed the most advanced telescope of the day.

The much-mocked Fortieth Hall, however, was something of a hotchpotch, the odds and ends of scientific theory that seemed to lead nowhere. Mesmerism resided here, though Henri thought it unfair to have the new area of electricity bundled along with the more dubious theory of animal magnetism. It was time these two strands were unravelled.

But not today and not by him. His task lay beyond the exhibit of the galvanized frog. Taking the ball of thread out of his pocket, he went through the door Ree had pointed out on her map and continued underground. He tied the twine to the bannister at the bottom of the steps and began the riskier part of his journey. During the day some light entered through the floor vents from rooms above. As his eyes adjusted he realized he wouldn't need the lantern he'd brought with him. He took the turns in the order he had memorized. Water seeped down the wall at one point, leaving chalky traces that, left long enough, would turn into stalactites.

Seeing the white stain reminded him of the chalk message writer. It made sense to think that the writer had used the underground passages to escape detection. Ree had been lucky not to have run into them. But was that person the same as the murderer? They were very different crimes. Henri went back to wondering if the writer hadn't come from among the renegade scientists. By the sounds of it, some of them were fanatics and it would take someone with extreme foolhardy courage to take the chance.

Once he crossed the bridge, Henri came to a stop, realizing his thoughts had taken him away from concentrating on finding the right path. He was faced with two passages, one on the right and one half-right. Straight in front was a little grotto decorated with shells, a half-man half-seahorse creature rearing from the scalloped basin: the god Neptune, he thought, remembering the classical stories his father had read him. He didn't remember the map showing this. Had he gone wrong already? Sniffing down the far right one he thought he smelled drains, which suggested long neglect and possible roof falls, so he took the other. It wound around the foundations of a keyhole-shaped chamber. That didn't match any room he had seen above. Peeking up through the floor vent, he could see a dimly lit room of marble statues, some caught mid attitude, arm out-thrust to emphasize a point, others gazing downwards in contemplation. It looked like a wizard had passed through the chamber, turning the men to stone. It was big enough to constitute a major hall of its own, which suggested he had gone off track by some margin.

"Blast!" Henri kicked the wall, then regretted that when it released a trickle of crumbly stone. He retreated, winding up his thread as he went. He would have to start over again or wait for Ree to rescue him.

Ree found Henri and Zena sitting at the bottom of the steps, a thick ball of twine in hand.

"Sorry I took so long. The cook insisted on feeding me. So you waited for me?" she asked as Phil and Ziggy brushed past Henri. Zena jumped onto Ziggy's back and interestingly the wolf made no protest.

"No. I tried three times and got lost on every attempt. I'm convinced this place is meant to confuse you. That's the only logical explanation."

Henri wasn't fooled by her murmur of sympathy: Ree was hiding a smile. But at least she didn't suggest the other possibility, which was that he had a poor sense of direction.

"No need to panic now." She patted his shoulder. "I've got my map and I know how to use it."

Henri sighed and shook his legs out to get the circulation going again after sitting still for so long on a cold step. "I'm going to have to make a copy of that."

"Come on then. Keep up." Ree headed off on the right track.

"Do you want me to carry your bag?"

"I'm fine. It's not heavy." She paused at the trickiest intersection and checked her plan. "Most people would think to go half-right here but in fact it's the right. It switches direction a little way on. Shame it smells of drains though."

Henri tossed a coin in Neptune's fountain, where it joined pennies left there many centuries ago.

"Did you just make a wish?" she teased. "How illogical of the logical scholar!"

"Yes, I did. Not to get so blasted lost next time."

She chuckled at his chagrinned expression. "I'll let you copy the map."

Both had been avoiding the main subject. He gestured to the bag. "I take it that you've lost your job? I'm sorry."

"Not your fault. And you, how did your interview with Professor Gall go?"

"He wants me on the first train home in June."

"Oh, Henri, that's so unfair!"

"He would've found a way to get rid of me. If it wasn't last night as an excuse, it would be something else later. He's appointed my enemy, Kurt Spurzheim, to run his office."

"Kurt Spurzheim? Who's that?"

"A boy in my year, seventeen, about so high. Fair hair, blue eyes. Always looks angry or mean. It says everything you need to understand about him that his research project is measuring the heads of the prisoners in the city jails. That's his idea of fun."

Ree took the stairs upwards and brought them out into the Hall of the Four Humours. "You don't sound as upset about losing your curatorship as I thought you might."

"That's because I decided that this place doesn't deserve me if the others go along with Professor Gall. I also wondered if Gall might not be our murderer. If he is, no decision by him will stand."

"He certainly has the temper, and the grudge." Ree hurried them through the hall and portrait gallery.

"But will the police dare to question him? He's put himself above their touch by assuming the top job."

"Then the evidence against him will have to be convincing."

Ziggy, Zena, and Phil were waiting for them outside the room Hypatia and Hamid had shared. Getting no answer to her knock, Ree eased open the door but they had already moved out.

"Welcome to my new home," she announced, dumping her bundle in the chair by the fire.

Henri looked around the little room. It wasn't so bad a refuge. He particularly liked the chained books. Zena liked them too, as they gave her something from which to swing. "You've nowhere else to go?"

"Not while I'm investigating this crime. After that I'll have to see about getting another job." She checked the coal scuttle and found enough to start a fire. "Can you see if there's anything to boil water in?"

Henri went back out into the corridor and opened doors until he found one that belonged to an old alchemist's laboratory. Cobwebs festooned the apparatus, but there was a little cauldron that didn't look as if it had been used for anything too toxic. There was also a working tap over a little sink so he gave it a thorough cleaning and took it back to Ree.

"Not only do I have a kind of kettle for you, but fresh water." He placed it on the hotplate. "What now?"

Meanwhile, Ree had found some chipped cups at the back of a cupboard. "I'm going to send Ziggy with a message to Hypatia. She should be able to sniff her out and that's safer than venturing into areas I haven't yet mapped."

"Good idea."

Ree began unpacking a little stock of supplies, including tea and biscuits.

"Where did you get those?"

"The cook in the third kitchen is a friend."

"What? Ingrid the Terrible?"

"She's not so terrible – at least not to me." Ree scribbled a note and tied it to Ziggy's neck with a little of Henri's twine.

"You're not putting it in the pouch? I would've thought that a perfect carrier."

"And have Hypatia have her hand bitten off trying to retrieve it?"

"True." Henri eyed Ziggy, who stared back at him with her merciless gaze. They had a truce between them but he was not harbouring any illusions. If Ree wasn't here, the wolf would happily chew on his ankles.

Shooing Ziggy out of the door, Ree then made a space on Hamid's old desk for their tea. Phil settled down on the hearthrug.

"Right, let's work out what we know and what we need to find out."

Henri took on the task of writing. "Mr Billibellary, most likely innocent as he was collecting drugged monkeys." He lifted his pencil. "Do you know how strange it is to live in a place where that is a normal sentence?"

Ree raised a brow, urging him to get on with it.

"Humboldt, also on site." Henri scratched the name down below the zookeeper.

"It's not him. For one, he just doesn't have it in him, and, secondly, he would never try to make Mr Billibellary look guilty. He's devoted to him," said Ree.

"I don't know Humboldt as well as you but I think you've made a good a point. And besides, would Shelley agree to meet a lowly assistant zookeeper in the middle of the night? I'd say not."

"You think Shelley went there by appointment?" Ree gave the coals in the fire a poke.

"It seems likely. He never showed much interest in the menagerie before so why suddenly go there for a midnight walk?"

"Yes, that would be out of character. Unless he wanted to check his orders had been carried out and the cages were locked?"

"True." Henri drew a dotted line through Humboldt's name, his code for unlikely but possible. He moved his pen to his next name. "Professor Gall. Definitely worth looking into."

"He's my prime suspect."

"I have another." Writing down Lord John's name, Henri hoped he wasn't betraying Maxwell's confidence as he explained the connection. He hadn't promised not to tell a girl.

"That Uncle Luc knows my father. They're friends in the camp. Da said he was ill." She closed her eyes briefly. Henri could tell she was battling back her worries for her father. Her desire to see him freed still tugged underneath everything she did or said like a hidden current. "I don't blame them for doing everything they can to help him. I feel the same way."

Henri nodded, understanding how desperate she must feel.

He was grateful his father was safe from scientific politics in his post in the colonial government in Algiers. "So I can't rule out the possibility of Lord John lashing out to get rid of his blackmailer."

"But the axe and the flints – that suggests he came prepared."

"Premeditation? You're right. That does seem cold, and Lord John has always struck me as a warm-hearted person, even if he is often very annoying. Still, if he was really at his wits' end, he could change."

"And put the blame on Mr Billibellary?" Ree finished the thought.

"Maybe he panicked and dumped the other things, not realizing what would happen?"

"It wouldn't be the first time he did something and left others to clear up his mistake." Ree explained about his disastrous attempts at bricklaying.

Her story made Henri smile. "So, who else do we have for our list?"

Ree yawned. "All the female employees, anyone he has recently dismissed or put under pressure, one of the renegade scientists who finally cracked. It could be the chalk writer, caught in the act, or maybe deciding to ramp up what he was doing."

"Going from scrawling messages to killing someone is a bit of a leap, don't you think?"

"Just saying it's possible."

"There's just too many who had a grudge against Shelley to see clearly." Her yawns were catching. Neither of them had had much sleep. Henri pushed the list to one side. "I don't know about you, but I need a nap if I'm going to have my wits about me for our meeting with Lord John."

Ree dragged a footstool over so they could both sit in armchairs and put up their feet. "Well, we've done everything we need for now: found a body, been interrogated, lost our jobs, lost our way…"

"That was me."

"I'm speaking on behalf of the quintet. Lost our way, found it again, and now reached sanctuary. I'd say we've earned a few hours' sleep." She threw off her boots and put her soles to face the flames. Henri matched her, amused by the hole at the end of her stockings where her big toe peeped through.

He linked his hands across his stomach. "You really are quite a remarkable girl."

"Thank you. And you're not bad for a scholarship boy."

Exchanging a companionable smile, they nibbled on biscuits, sipped tea, and when that was finished, dropped off to sleep, toes warmed by a cheerful coal fire.

Chapter 15
Funeral Rites

Hidden in scholar's robes borrowed from Maxwell, Ree lurked with Henri and his friends at the back of the chamber in which the ceremony was being held. Since Theophilus talk had been banned, funerals had become odd affairs. Many of the old religious ways remained – solemn processions, eulogies over the dead, flowers on the coffin – but there were no prayers, nor any comfort to be had unless you liked the idea that you were joining the elements for recycling. Ree was no longer sure what she thought. Separated from her father, she couldn't bear the idea of never seeing him again, if death took one of them before they could be reunited, not to mention her lost mother and baby brother. Might it not be better to hope that something remained once the body was gone? Did she not feel more than that, like music when played was far more than the score that held the notes?

That's just wishful thinking, Ree scolded herself. Life is miraculous enough without adding the fairy tale hopes.

Up on the hastily erected stage, the trustees took it in turns to praise the deceased. A poem was read out in one of the dead languages he so loved, intelligible to only one or two people in the room; everyone else listened in polite incomprehension. Last to take the podium was Professor Gall. After repeating the praise already made of the former chancellor, he went on to address the crisis facing the museum.

"The events of the past few days have shocked us all to the core. I am here to reassure you that we will not let this stop our great work. Science marches on. Justice will be done, the killer found, and punished, according to the law."

The reporters present for the occasion scribbled down every word for their front pages.

"Simplicius Shelley only occupied his position for a brief few hours. I have no wish to speak ill of the dead – "

"But he's going to anyway," murmured Henri in Ree's ear.

"But some of the changes he introduced were precipitate."

"He rushed into things," glossed Henri.

"I'm stopping any further reforms until we have dealt with our immediate problems. And I'm sure Chancellor Grassmann will not mind me taking this opportunity while we are gathered to stress that anyone in possession of information touching this crime should come forward and speak to Inspector Gideon of the museum police." He let a heavy silence fall, sweeping the gathering with his dark eyes. Ree lowered her face, glad the funeral dress required the boys to wear the fur-trimmed hood of their best robes over their heads.

The acting chancellor gave a signal and the museum orchestra began a dirge. The carriers shouldered the coffin and headed through the double doors at the far end of the chamber to the museum burial ground. Grassmann's old secretary, Morley, followed as chief mourner, dabbing his eyes with his white handkerchief. The congregation began to disperse.

"Time for our meeting," whispered Henri.

Ree entered the Egyptian chamber on Henri's heels. Lord John hadn't yet arrived. She'd cleaned in here many times and was particularly fond of the bronze hippos on display in a glass case. She wandered over to say hello. She then became aware that Maxwell was beside her. Only an inch or two shorter, he was gazing at her as if she was at least as interesting as the hippos.

"Yes?" Ree raised a a questioning brow.

"You are..." Maxwell faltered.

"I am what? Come on, you can't stop there like the message writer does. I'm what?"

He gulped. "Very impressive. Not like I thought you would be."

Was that all? Absurdly touched by the younger boy's praise, she smiled and rubbed her knuckles lightly on his head. "And you are a noodle."

He nodded enthusiastically. "I know. My sisters think so too. Henri says you need a new job?"

"I will do."

"I could ask my mother if she'll take you in as a maid. I think she'd like you."

"Oh, Maxwell, that's very sweet of you." Not that Ree wanted a life of cleaning, but it was better than the streets.

The boy blushed. "It's nothing."

"And I might take you up on that offer, but first we need to solve this mystery."

Lord John slipped into the room and closed the doors behind him, dropping the bar across the entrance. "Maxwell?"

"Here, cousin." Maxwell pulled Ree with him as he went forward to greet the nobleman. "This is Maria and this is Henri." He gestured to his friends. Henri bowed. Ree hesitated and bobbed a shallow curtsey.

Lord John perched on the ram's plinth. "I must need my head

examining to agree to this meeting," he murmured, mainly to himself. "But Maxwell said you were investigating?"

"Yes, sir." Henri pulled out a notebook in which he had begun to make jottings about each of their suspects. "And I promise we won't keep you long. As you might know, Maria and I were the first to be interrogated as we found the body. Coming close to being accused, we decided we needed to investigate the murder ourselves in case suspicion swung back to us or another innocent person."

"And you're sure it was murder?" Lord John scrubbed his hand over his face like someone driving off a bad dream.

"Yes, sir. No one puts a stone axe in their own head."

"He couldn't have, oh I don't know, tripped and fallen on it?"

Ree thought it odd that Lord John was so desperate to find some accidental cause.

"No, it didn't look that way," said Henri firmly.

"Sir, why don't you want to think it was murder?" asked Ree.

Lord John shuddered. "Because murder is so ugly, an offence against…" – he waved at the ceiling where once God would've been thought to be watching them – "against everything. If we don't cherish life, what are we? Nothing but brutes."

Henri turned to a fresh page in his notebook. "Do you mind telling me, sir, when you last saw Mr Shelley?"

"Last night, but it was in his office, I swear to you." Lord John's eyes went to his young cousin. "Maxwell, did you explain about Luc?"

"Yes, Cousin John."

"Well then, you'll understand that I went to ask when I could expect Shelley to send the letter recommending Luc be transferred to the hospital. I wanted it dispatched government express, which shaves months off the passage, and could be the difference between life and death for Luc. A letter from the chancellor of the museum, even an acting one, is as good as an order to the authorities in the prison camps."

Ree sensed there was more. "And what did he reply?"

"He... he laughed. He said that Luc had a death sentence from nature and that he wouldn't live long enough to be transferred – that it would be a waste of his influence to write such a letter."

"And what did you do, sir?" asked Henri.

Lord John looked over their heads, seeming to find some comfort in the benign expression on the ram's face. "To my eternal regret, I threatened him. I said if he hadn't written the letter by the end of tomorrow – which is now today – I would report his blackmail to the sponsors and hang the consequences."

"And how did he respond to that?"

"He didn't believe me. We had a frightful quarrel, him cold and controlled, me raging, until finally I stormed out. I was going to go back and plead the case again this morning but... well, he was dead."

"What did you think when you heard Mr Shelley had been killed?" asked Ree.

"Think? I didn't know what to think. My first thought was to go to his office and see if he had made a start on the letter despite our quarrel, but his desk was clear."

"Really?" Ree suspected Lord John had gone to remove any incriminating documents.

"Not a scrap on it. Come to think of it, that does seem wrong. It was covered in papers yesterday."

"And is today," confirmed Henri. "I had a meeting with Professor Gall."

"I'd guess that someone got in there before you did and took everything," said Ree.

"But I was one of the first among the senior officials to hear and I went straight there," stated Lord John.

"You might've been first to hear, but the murderer would've known many hours beforehand, wouldn't he?"

"By Newton, you're right." Lord John looked at Ree in admiration. "I should've thought of that."

"Did you see anyone?" asked Henri.

"Not a soul." Lord John blushed. "Not that we have souls, of course. Figure of speech."

Ree suspected that Lord John was far more sympathetic to Theophilus beliefs than he pretended. "If Mr Shelley had got papers on his desk concerning your conversation with him, it's possible someone else might try to blackmail you."

Lord John groaned. "Oh Lord, I thought all that was over, that at least I'd be free of it."

"No, no, it's good. Because if they do, then we know it's the killer and we can set a trap!"

The nobleman stared at her. "I see I've been quite wrong about you. You really are the most nerveless individual I've ever met, Maria Altamira. You want me to welcome a new attempt at blackmail?"

"Oh yes," said Ree. "Very much."

"Then I'll let you know if anyone does contact me. But really, I hope you solve this without having to resort to such tactics."

"So do we, sir," said Henri. "Thank you for your time."

The nobleman was taken back by the clear note of dismissal in Henri's voice. "Well then, carry on, carry on. Keep me informed of your progress."

As Maxwell showed Lord John out, Ree borrowed Henri's notebook to remind herself of the many lines of enquiry they were pursuing.

"What do you think we should do next?" she asked.

"I'd like a look at the display that the axe was taken from. I want to test it for fingerprints – I've been working on a fine powder that should stick to the traces left behind by a human touch. If we capture the prints, they might tell us something about the murderer and what drew him to choose that as his weapon."

Maxwell returned to their side. "I'm sorry I can't stay but they'll notice I'm not there for the curfew if I don't leave now."

Henri patted his shoulder. "You've been an enormous help. I'll come and find you tomorrow."

"What about you? You're not coming back to your rooms?"

"Not yet. I've too much to do – and they've expelled me already so I'm hardly worried about my absence being noticed."

Maxwell wasn't as happy about that state of affairs as Henri. "But won't they think that you're…"

"I'm what?" asked Henri when the younger boy's voice trailed off.

"Up to no good?"

Ree laughed. "Oh I do hope so."

Henri smiled. "But oddly I'd be up to the very best, wouldn't I? Trying to find out the truth. Isn't that what the museum is all about?"

After walking most of the way back with Maxwell, Henri and Ree diverted to the halls displaying the tools from the Stone Age. This chamber was on every school tour, as the new scientific philosophy rested on Darwin's discovery that humans had descended from earlier species. This story was shown in the case of skulls, starting with apes, then going to close relatives, Neanderthal and Cro-Magnon man, and then all the way up to modern examples with smoother brow and smaller skull. Images of the cave art of these first people and examples of their tools accompanied the central display of bones.

"The weapon and flints must've been taken from here," said Ree, pointing to a wall display sectioned off with police tape. "It looks like the lock was forced." She peered a little closer, noticing the scratches on the wood. "I'd say they used a chisel; the marks are distinctive."

"A chisel? Like stonemasons use?" asked Henri.

"Yes, but that doesn't mean it's one of them." Ree felt very protective of her old friends. "Chisels are easy to come by."

"Absolutely, but I did notice that the scaffolding had been moved to the hall just outside and they are working on a mural over the door."

Ree had seen that too as she walked in. "All right. I'll ask them when they arrive for work. But it's more likely someone left their chisel behind by mistake and that is what the murderer used."

"But that raises another question, doesn't it? If you already have a chisel, why kill someone with a blunt instrument? Our murderer could've just stabbed Shelley and been more certain of causing death." Henri drew out a fine brush and box of powder from his detective kit.

"Unless the choice of weapon means something to the murderer?"

Henri dusted around the lock. "There are an awful lot of skulls in here. I bet a phrenologist would love to examine them in great detail."

"Back to Gall again?"

"Yes, back to our least favourite professor. Look, Ree, it works!"

"What works?"

"My fingerprint dust. I've never had a chance to field test it. There are clear prints here and on the shelf from which the flints were taken."

"How do you know they belong to our killer?"

"I don't – but they might. Hang on a moment." Henri flipped through the pages of his notebook to the earliest entries. He compared the prints he had revealed to a piece of paper with a brown stain. "Oh my goodness! I wish I had a camera to capture this. Look, they're the same." He showed her the marks on the paper and the shelf. "See the ridge pattern? They're a match."

"So you know who took the axe?"

"No, but I know what else this killer has done and that he's been living here for at least two years. This person decapitated several pets belonging to my friends back at the time of your trial. He even had a go at Zena until she drove him off. He left behind bloody prints in my study, which I've been saving all this time. Now he's struck again – but this time it's a human he's attacked."

"Killed pets? But why?"

"I thought it was to punish boys he didn't like, but now I think it's more significant that he always took the heads and discarded the bodies. What if he wanted the skulls for his research? What if he read character from bumps and wanted to see if animals also showed the same patterns?"

"So it *is* Professor Gall?"

"I'd say he's mad enough if he thinks nothing of killing off his rival with an axe. But how to get a fingerprint from him to compare?"

"Break into his office?"

Henri nodded. "We'll have to wait until it's clear, but yes. This will need careful planning. I'll find out when it's likely to be empty and meet you later. You talk to your friends about the chisel, all right?"

Ree decided to wait on the scaffolding, hoping to catch the stonemasons when they arrived shortly after dawn and then slip away into the labyrinth. Henri fetched her some food from the kitchens and they picnicked in the Stone Age chamber. They could almost have been in a cave themselves, with only the flickering light of their lanterns to illuminate the paintings on the wall. The drawings were more effective by candlelight, seeming to run and leap. These were no crude production of a childlike brain but clever images that caught the spirit of the animals.

"Why do you think people started painting? I mean, you don't see apes making pictures," mused Ree.

"True. I suppose they must have developed the idea of a symbol."

"You mean, 'Look, Ug, here's the mighty ox, let's go hunt it? Or worship it?'"

"Who knows what messages Ug took from the pictures, but basically you're talking about a kind of language. Just as well they did or we wouldn't be able to do maths or design a building."

"Not to mention compose poetry, stories, and music. In fact, we wouldn't be human. So which skull holds the brain that made that leap?" She walked over to the skulls. "*Ip, dip, sky blue, who's it? Not you.*"

"It's a fascinating question, but maybe your methods of elimination aren't the most scientific." Henri packed up the basket he had brought from Ingrid. "Do you need me to stay?"

"No. I'll be fine. I'll hide up on the scaffolding platform to avoid any patrols."

"Then I'll return to the scholars' wing and ask around if anyone saw Professor Gall on the night of the attack."

"I'll meet you by the stairs from the Froggy Fortieth Hall at ten in the morning then?"

"Sounds good to me. I'll smuggle out some breakfast."

Left alone in the quiet of the night, Ree bedded down on some old sheets used to protect the cases from dust. They made her sneeze at first but the scent was so familiar, it was more of a comfort than an annoyance. She soon fell asleep, drifting off into dreams. Images flitted through her brain – skulls and axes, chisels and carvings, Shelley stretched out on the path by the dodo pen, reaching for something that he would never quite grasp.

She woke up, heart racing, her dream having dipped into nightmarish territory. She found she wasn't alone. Phil roosted beside her and Ziggy was crouched at her feet, on guard.

"How did you both get up here?" The mystery of how the animals found their way around the museum was one she didn't think she'd ever solve, but she was pleased they were with her.

She then noticed that Ziggy had a message tied around her neck. Had she not found Hypatia or was it a reply? She tugged the paper free, discovering it was indeed an answer.

Dear Mapmaker

We are sorry to hear of your problems. You are welcome to stay among us as long as you need. To aid your investigation, we've called a meeting of our Sisters and Brothers in the Hundredth Hall tomorrow at midday so you and Henri can tell us what is going on. If one of our number knows anything, they will be given the chance to speak then. Keep safe.

Dr Hypatia

Good. It was vital they spoke to the many potential witnesses among the renegades.

Ree was well awake now, though she felt sure there were still many hours to go until dawn. Then it struck her. There had been no sound of any patrol while she and Henri were having their picnic nor now in these quiet hours of early morning. She waited, listening, but could only hear Phil's snuffly sleep noises and the occasional mew from Zag buried deep in Ziggy's pouch. Had Professor Gall ordered the patrols to cease? Did that mean he no longer feared the chalk writer would strike again? She hoped Henri would find out because it just felt a little odd. They should be more worried, not less anxious, after a murder, surely?

She lit her lamp, not liking to sit in the dark with thoughts of violence to keep her company. Ziggy would give her plenty of warning if anyone approached, giving time to extinguish it. The light brightened the area of stone the craftsmen were working. Even after all this time, she recognized Paul's handiwork. He was making the entrance into a series of hunting scenes, echoing the cave drawings.

Ree ran her finger over one antelope. "Oh, Paul, you twit: you don't understand the cave artist, do you?" He was making them too crude, falling into the idea that the drawings of the first men had to be primitive, like something a clumsy child might sketch. She took up the pencil that had been left on the designs he had had approved by – she noticed from the stamp in the corner – Simplicius Shelley. Turning the paper over she began to draw. She entered the space in her brain where she didn't even notice the passage of time, so caught up was she in the beauty of creation. She felt powerful. A kingly bison, a leaping antelope, a man, part stag, in pursuit with his spear held overhead.

"What!" The burst of outrage, quickly suppressed, recalled Ree to her position. Her guard had now changed: Phil was on duty and Ziggy asleep but no alarm had been raised, as it was Paul who climbed up to his platform. Phil considered him a friend. "Ree? What are you…? No, that doesn't matter. Are you all right? We heard that you had been thrown out." Paul grabbed her shoulders, ignoring the sleepy growl from Ziggy. He gave her a quick inspection, then pulled her to his chest for a brief hug. "Ma and Da will be so relieved I've seen you."

"Paul. It's lovely to see you too." Ree grinned. Her friend looked so grown up since she'd last spent time with him, quite a young man rather than a boy, hair a little longer than it used to be.

"What are you doing here, other than messing with my design?" He took the paper from her and studied her sketch. "Blast. You are good, aren't you?"

"Missed me?"

"We all have. But I won't be able to do it like this. It's been approved, see?" He pointed to the stamp.

"By a dead man. Do you really think they'll care now if you go a little away from your design?"

"Not now." Paul scratched the back of his neck, smiling at her. "And why not? But I don't think you're here to discuss cave paintings with me, are you? Do you need somewhere to live? Ma and Da were expecting you last night. You didn't have to wait here to ask if it was all right to come."

"Thank you, Paul, and thank them too. I'm fine for the moment. I'm staying with some other friends." She made a vague gesture to the depths of the museum, but Paul would assume she meant elsewhere in the city. "I stayed because I wanted to ask you about the break-in."

Paul began unpacking his tools. "What's it to do with you?"

"You know I found the body?"

"With a boy, one of the scholars. I heard about that." He took out a mallet and gave a chisel a practice tap on the plank.

Was that a note of jealousy? Ridiculous. "He's just a friend. We were visiting Phil. Anyway, that isn't relevant. The police had me down as a suspect so I decided to investigate. I noticed that the weapon display case was broken into with a chisel. Do you know anything about it?"

Lowering his tools, Paul turned on her angrily. "You suspect me?"

"No, of course not!" Why had he leaped to that conclusion?

"The police have questioned me already. It wasn't my fault."

"What do you mean?"

"That morning two days ago when they announced Professor Grassmann had died, we were summoned to a meeting and told to leave off work for the day. None of us were allowed to fetch our tools. Mine were sitting here, exactly where you see them. I didn't discover until yesterday that a chisel was missing. The police haven't found it."

"So are you saying that anyone could've climbed up here and taken it?"

"Everyone in the museum except us stonemasons. It's really annoying: it was my good chisel too."

"But that's very helpful: it means the thief took it on impulse." Ree reconstructed the crime in her head. "He was furious, wanted the axe, and found the tools to open the case waiting for him as if it was a sign that he should go ahead."

"Go ahead and what?"

"Kill the acting chancellor."

"Sounds like a madman."

"Maybe, or just someone who is very, very angry."

Paul leaned forward and brushed the dust from her cheek. "That makes him dangerous, Ree. Don't do this. Don't stick your nose into such business. Come and stay with us. We'll look after you."

"Oh Paul." Ree didn't want to put into words what he was really saying. "I need to do this."

"He might strike again." Paul sat back on his heels, a little embarrassed now that he had revealed so much.

She laid her hand over his. "I know. Be careful."

He turned his palm to hold her hand. "I'd say the same to you but I know you won't listen."

"I'll come find you again later, when this is all over."

He gave a long look then released her. "At least come and see what I've done with your design even if you're not coming for me."

"Goodbye, Paul."

"Goodbye, Ree." He picked up his chisel, resuming his usual teasing expression. "But don't take too many risks. You're in danger of believing you've godlike powers, thinking to solve this yourself."

She began climbing down the ladder. "A girl has to aim high."

Paul chuckled and began tapping at the uncut stone.

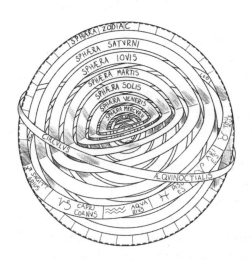

Chapter 16

Renegades

Henri found Ree in a thoughtful mood when they met by the stairs from the Fortieth Hall. His heart did a little stutter: his friend looked so sad, sitting in the dark waiting for him with only her animals for company. Ziggy snoozed at her feet, while Phil rooted through some leaf litter piled in one corner hoping for something to eat. Ree smiled brightly when she saw him, but he felt she was making a conscious effort to turn on the sunshine.

Zena gave her a chattering welcome.

"Nice to see you too, Zena. Let's go. We've a meeting with the renegades," she explained, showing Henri the note.

"You look a little sad, Ree. What's happened?" he asked as he followed her through the passages. Knowing she couldn't always be there to guide him, he tried to anticipate her choices and was almost confident he now knew the way himself. He nodded to the Neptune in passing, having grown quite fond of that little corner where yesterday he'd kept going wrong.

"I was just thinking about Paul, my friend from among the stonemasons." Her tone was wistful. "We're all growing up so fast – at least he is."

Henri wasn't sure what she meant by that and decided that maybe he didn't want to know. Best to stick to practical matters. "Did Paul know anything?"

"Oh yes." Ree quickly filled him in on the events of the day after Grassmann's death. "So it was probably a crime of opportunity: grab the chisel and use it to get the weapons."

"But choosing the stone weapons was premeditated. The murder didn't take place there."

"Yes, I know. The theft must've happened after dark as a break in would've been noticed during the day," said Ree.

"With the patrols, I would guess in the middle of the night."

"I'm not liking the feeling I'm getting about this thief. He feels like a monster waiting to pounce on you out of the dark," added Ree with a shiver.

"That's because we can't put a name or face to him yet. His motives will become clear when we find out who he is and then he'll stop being so frightening."

"That's a bit like a fairy tale: name the monster to break its power over you." She glanced over her shoulder at him, blue eyes lit up by a shaft of light from one of the grills in the floor above. She seemed almost unearthly, as if she'd vanish though a doorway like one of the fairy folk of the stories she mentioned.

Henri caught up with her and took her hand, partly to remind himself that she was real. "I'm a great believer in fairy tales. They often tell us a truth about ourselves and the world that we can't get in a textbook. There are monsters but they can be defeated."

Ree squeezed his hand back.

Hamid was waiting for them in Ree's library refuge. He had a pot of tea on the warming plate.

"Ah, our intrepid detectives!" He offered them both one of his flourishing bows, which they returned. "You must be ready for some refreshments."

They made a picnic on the desk with the rolls and butter Henri had brought from Ingrid and the tea Hamid had prepared. Hamid muttered a little blessing before eating his share.

"I think it wise always to be alert to the good things by which we are surrounded," said Hamid, noticing that they were both watching him. "You may be interested to know that I number you both among my blessings. I believe in patterns."

"You're a mathematician, sir, so of course you do," said Henri.

"But I believe you've been put here at this time to solve this. You are going to be our equals sign resolving the formula – two straight dashes leading to the answer."

"It's a pretty picture," said Henri, "but I think we're still a long way off, lost in the workings of this sum."

"We have an hour until the meeting and I'm rather happy to have the excuse to let Hypatia do the task of rounding up our Sisters and Brothers. Tell me what you know."

Henri ran through the evidence they had gathered so far, explaining the hidden connections between some of the suspects and those whom they had been able to clear of suspicion.

"But there's one trailing end that worries us," Henri concluded.

"The chalk writer?" said Ree, showing her mind was in tune with Henri's. "Yes, where does he fit in to the picture? If we could find out if he was one of your renegades, then that would snip off that loose end."

"Then I'd better take you to see them, but I feel I must apologize in advance. Some of them take a lot of work." Hamid took out a notebook from a little bag hanging from his belt. "My version of your map, Ree. Nowhere near as elegant, but even after all this time down here I still get lost. We'd better hurry as it's almost noon. My brethren have a tendency to wander off once gathered. It's like trying to herd frogs on to the same lily pad. Hypatia's the animal trapper – I left it to her to catch them all." Hamid led them further on than they had yet gone, into the forgotten depths of the museum.

"Why can't we go through the halls above?" asked Henri. The pathways were easier to find on the surface compared to this honeycomb below.

Hamid paused at a crossroads to consult his book. "I'm afraid many of those rooms are deathtraps – ceilings on the point of coming down, or filled with dangerous substances that need careful removal. They really should've spring-cleaned the old halls before going on to build the new ones, but the authorities were in too much of a hurry to make progress. There are some places where it is still safe to emerge but we haven't time for a tour today. Maybe on another occasion."

Henri wondered if he would ever get to see the hall of statues and asked if Hamid knew it.

"Oh yes, the Philosophers' Gallery. Roof's down in one corner and the leaves are piling up. I've not dared a visit for years."

Ree's stonemason sensibilities were clearly offended by the idea that the building was just being left to rot. "We should be doing something about that. It'll undermine the whole place if they let it go to rack and ruin."

"I'm quite of your mind, Ree. Still, let's fight one battle at a time, yes?" Hamid tucked his reading glasses back in his pocket and strode off in what they all hoped was the right direction. Henri took heart from the fact that the animals seemed quite happy to follow him.

Hamid brought them to a flight of steps leading up to what he said he thought would prove to be the Hundredth Hall. He didn't sound very sure. Henri went first and opened the door on to the largest chamber he had seen yet. It was a huge room arranged in circles, climbing like a tiered wedding cake stood on its head. People sat in the circular balconies, gathered in little groups.

"Congratulations, Dr Al-Ghazali, you've brought us to the right place," said Henri.

"Welcome to Aristotle's view of the universe," said Hamid. "Down here, we are standing on Earth in what they called the sublunary sphere, which means everything between us and the moon."

"That's clever: use the room as a teaching aid," murmured Ree, standing in the very centre of the Earth to look up.

"Around us," said Hamid, "represented in those balconies with their plasterwork, are the orbits for the moon and known planets."

Henri could make out godlike figures in the classical mode: Mercury, Venus, Mars, and Saturn. A sun god was positioned on the row between Venus and Mars, the brightest but treated as just another planet. Zena leaped from his shoulder and hung from a spur-like candle bracket on Mercury's heel.

"After them come the fixed stars, or constellations, called that because they do not move in relation to each other." Hamid pointed to the golden stars set out in the patterns that had once been so important to astrologers: Pisces, Gemini, and the rest.

"What's that in the roof?" asked Ree.

"Sorely in need of cleaning but that is a glass dome, as large as they could build it then, to show that beyond the tenth or outer rim is the realm of the First Mover. The only image for this they could agree was the sky itself."

Henri was annoyed by what he considered the illogical position of the sun, bundled up with the other planets. "Surely they had to have known the sun was different?"

"Only in degree. If you think about it, Henri, would you know the Earth was spinning on its own axis, let alone orbiting the sun, unless astronomers had told you? The ground feels solid enough; things seem to move around us, not us around them. There were a few clever Greeks before Copernicus, who suggested the Earth was in orbit, but usually the person of intelligence then would say that, of course, the Earth was at the centre."

"But this is wrong?" said Ree, waving at the rows of balconies.

"It's more a working theory that had to be discarded when something better came along. That's what science does: it adjusts our eyesight like a good pair of spectacles and makes us see differently. It just takes some people longer to accept than others, as each advance, particularly the big ones, involves a revolution in all we think we know. That's uncomfortable. Some prefer to stick to the slightly out-of-focus spectacles that they've grown used to." Hamid raised his hand to Hypatia, who had just entered on the far side of the chamber. "People like me would claim that Theophilus ideas do the same, but in a different area of human experience – that of spirit, heart, and soul. They are both forms of seeing."

Hypatia approached across the tiles that made up the Earth. She was followed by a group of women in academic dress. None of them were as tall as her. Quickly noting the faces, Henri saw that some were old, some quite young, in appearance taken from all different countries – yet more evidence that scientists did not come in one size, as Professor Gall would have it.

"Welcome to our assembly, Mapmaker, Scholar," said Hypatia, her voice carrying to the people in the galleries, a signal that the meeting was beginning. They seemed more intent on their own conversations. Rolling her eyes at Hamid, Hypatia took her pistol and fired a blank (or at least Henri hoped it was) to catch everyone's attention. Ziggy howled and Phil gave an alarmed squawk. Silence rapidly fell after that.

"Sorry, pal," said Hypatia, patting the dodo's head. "Right, now we can begin. We'd be grateful if you could start by telling us all what is happening out there in the first rooms of the museum."

A man with a long white beard and black robe, embroidered rather impressively with gilt stars, thumped his walking stick on the wooden railing of the Mars balcony.

"Dr Paracelsus," said Hamid, "an alchemist."

The star-clad man rapped again. "Hold on a minute, Dr Hypatia. Before you let these youngsters into our secret council, how are we to know that we can trust them? Has their worth been proved?"

The little gaggle of his fellow alchemists nodded their heads sagely and muttered some "hear, hears" and "quite sos".

Hamid gave Hypatia an "I'll take this" look. He swept a bow to Paracelsus.

"Learned doctor, I can attest myself to their worth. They have passed through the fire and emerged as gold."

"What fire was that, pray?" asked the alchemist dubiously.

"When they found the body of the acting chancellor, they did not run. They stood their ground, even though it would have gone much easier for them if they had pretended ignorance."

An approving murmur ran around the chamber. These exiles for their various faiths and theories agreed on one thing: the value of courage.

Or maybe not. A man right at the top of the room, sitting on his own in the balcony for the last ring of fixed stars, shot to his feet.

"I won't believe a word they say! All of you are mad!" he screeched.

"One of our Flat Earthers, and unfortunately the most outspoken of them," murmured Hamid. "The others are a cheerful enough bunch but he likes to disagree with everyone about everything. He's managed to fall out with his own group over which way around the world is. He says north is really south, and south north."

"Why do you let him in here?" wondered Henri.

"Who are we to decide who gets entry to a room of renegades? Thought is free."

Seeing Hamid was leaving this one to her, Hypatia fixed the wild Flat Earther with her gaze. "Brother Eric, we do not require you to believe; we require you to listen and offer any information that might help them."

The man sat down, mumbling fiercely to himself.

"So, if we have no more objections, we'll hear what these young people have to tell us," declared Hypatia.

"Do you want to speak first?" Henri asked Ree.

"All right. I'll tell them what we've found out; you can ask the questions." Ree smoothed her rumpled gardener's shirt nervously, then took a step to stand on the centre of the tiled Earth.

Henri sat with Hamid among the Sisters of Science as everyone paid respectful attention to Ree's account. She had a natural storyteller's flare, bringing the scenes in and around the museum to vivid life. He appreciated that she didn't divulge the reasons behind Shelley's blackmail of Lord John, leaving it as unspecified pressure. Although she wasn't bound by a promise, he had told Maxwell they'd keep it a secret.

When Ree finished, she looked to Henri to continue.

He got up and took out his notebook, feeling better for having a prop in his hand. "We have questions connected to this case to which some of you might have answers. I suppose the first question is more of a plea: if you are the chalk message writer, please tell us now. It is muddling up our investigation as we wonder if we are after one or two people. No one will take your confession and use it against you: you have my word."

Henri let the silence stretch. No one raised a hand or said a word.

"Right, then I hope we are correct in eliminating you all from our list of suspects for that minor crime."

"It's not a crime," announced the lady sitting to his left. "The writer should be allowed to point out the truth: God is."

"No, he's not! It's all poppycock!" bellowed a man up on the balcony belonging to Venus.

"Yes, he is!" countered another, sitting in the sun's ring. "He created everything, even cretins like you!"

"Gentlemen, ladies!" called Hamid, stepping forward to break up the brewing row. "We have our next symposium on Sunday; let's not rehearse our arguments here. What will our guests think of us?"

Henri grinned. "That you are just like every scientist I've ever met: quarrelsome and sure you're right."

"That's people, Henri, not just scientists." Hamid gestured to Henri's notebook. "Please, may we return to business? You have more questions, I think?"

"Yes. The most important one involves the man who is our chief suspect. Please, don't get me wrong, we have no proof, but this person stood to gain most from the acting chancellor's death so has the strongest motive. We'd like either to prove he had the opportunity or that he is innocent." Henri took a breath. It was all right to bandy around theories with Ree, but to make a public announcement was a far more daunting step. "We are trying to trace the movements of the phrenologist, Professor Gall, the same man who is now acting chancellor. We want to know what he's been doing the last few days, and, in particular, at the time of the murder. That's the night before last. Were any of you in the halls then?"

A shy-looking lady at the back of the group of sisters raised a hand. "I think I saw him keeping vigil for Chancellor Grassmann. The senior staff were taking it in turns and his period of duty was in the small hours, between twelve and two. I checked the roster on the door to the chamber where the body lay in state to make sure they would not be changing over when I returned with our provisions."

That was around the time of the murder, or a little before, so not decisive.

"He was inside?" asked Henri.

"What I saw was a dark-clad man of the right stature with his back to me, head bowed as he stood by the coffin. I took it to be Professor Gall." Her answer was scientifically accurate but not quite the decisive alibi Henri was searching for: the door was still open to doubt and gave no answer to the question of whether Gall had gone on from there to the menagerie.

But would he have had time to raid the axe chamber as well? The window of opportunity was narrowed by this witness.

Dr Paracelsus tapped his stick, drawing everyone's eyes upwards to where he sat. "I didn't see him that night, as I was keeping well away from the outer halls. But I did see that Gall fellow on previous nights shadowing the police patrols. I assumed he was making sure they were doing their job."

"That's true. I saw him too, last Wednesday." This came from the man who had called his opponent a cretin. "I remarked to my brethren that Professor Gall must've been frustrated by the lack of police progress on the case and was mounting his own search."

Brother Eric spluttered up in his lonely gallery. "You fools! You can't see the obvious!"

"Oh, put a sock in it, you miserable old coot," called one of the Scholastics.

"Perhaps you can enlighten us then, Brother Eric," said Hamid with admirable patience.

Eric hung over the balcony, looking wild-eyed and shaggy, like he had been living with wolves for the past few years, not hiding out in the depths of the museum.

Though it wasn't unthinkable; there could be a wolf pack here somewhere, thought Henri.

"I've seen that man on many occasions recently. He walks the halls as if the museum is his own palace." Eric clenched his bony fist. "*He* is the chalk writer. It's as plain as the nose on my face." As he had quite a prominent one, this was no small claim.

Henri's hand hovered. He had been making notes but surely there was no point writing down such mad ramblings?

"Did you see him writing the messages? Stoop with chalk in his hand to scrawl words so against his known beliefs?" asked Hamid.

Brother Eric spat on the balcony beneath. Fortunately there was no one sitting there. "Of course not; he's too clever to be caught."

"Then why, Brother Eric, would an opponent of Theophilus beliefs deface the museum that you claim he regards as his own domain?" asked Hypatia. "It makes no sense!"

"No, wait!" Ree stood up. "I think I know what Brother Eric is claiming. You say the museum was defaced, but it was only chalk, easily removed. I've washed some of it away myself – it doesn't leave a trace. If he had wanted to make a real protest, he would've used paint."

"Or carved it on the walls," murmured Henri.

Ree flushed. "Well, yes, he would, wouldn't he? As for what he wrote, who knows best how a real Theophilus follower thinks than someone who has made it his life's work to hound them? He knew the kind of message that would seem to be genuinely their work. In fact, it's a very clever bluff."

Henri was fast catching up with Ree's thought. "Then he did it to undermine Shelley?"

"Yes, he was afraid his subject was going to be relegated to an obscure place in the museum, so he was trying to prove Simplicius Shelley was not up to the job of curator in charge of displays."

Henri remembered the morning of Shelley's promotion. "And he made it the test of Shelley's leadership. If the murder hadn't intervened, I would wager more messages would have cropped up after Professor Gall made one of his nightly patrols."

"That's why I heard no police patrols last night. He knows there will be no more messages as he won't be writing them."

Brother Eric sat down. "At least there's some brains in the younger generation, not like you lot. Of course, the Earth isn't shaped like an orange: we'd all fall off."

The meeting broke up into a twitter of arguments between the rival groups. Hamid this time made no effort to rein them back in. Pleased with their progress, Henri turned to Hamid. "I take it this isn't the moment for a lecture on gravity?"

Hamid stroked his neat beard. "No, Brother Eric is a lost cause: he likes to believe something no one else does just to be contrary. But I think he's been of great help in this, hasn't he? It makes sense, unlike the rest of his convictions."

"Did you find out when Professor Gall's office will be empty?" asked Ree, drawing Henri to one side.

"In the small hours. Word is that Gall and his new private secretary have been working late into the night since he was appointed to catch up with the paperwork, so I think it will only be safe at around two or three."

Ree smiled ruefully. "Brother Eric is right about one thing. We have to be mad to do this."

Chapter 17

Poisoned Pen

They rested awhile on the benches in a quiet balcony of Aristotle's universe, then dined with the Sisters of Science. When the moment came to venture out they persuaded Phil, Ziggy, and Zena to stay with Hamid and Hypatia, but only after numerous bribes. Phil was most definitely not impressed, turning his tail feathers on Ree with a disgusted huff.

"Sorry, Phil, but if they see you with me, it's like a fingerprint – a dead giveaway to my identity."

Henri was a little jealous to leave Zena with her tail wrapped around Hypatia's neck. His astute pet knew the best punishment was to pretend she didn't mind.

Their guide back through the underground passages was the shy lady who had spoken during the debate. Her name, she told them, was Ada, an engineer, and a relative of Mildred, cook in the second kitchen, which was why she was so often sent to fetch the supplies.

"What do you do when someone sees you?" asked Ree, thinking that she surely must've been caught if her visits were so frequent.

"Pretend I'm a maid." She showed Ree that below her cloak she was wearing the standard maid garb. "The police don't really notice the female servants so they've never questioned my claim."

"You're lucky not to have bumped into Mrs Mantell. She'd certainly notice."

Ada pulled a face like she'd just bitten into a sour apple.

"You have? Oh, how did that go?"

"She thought I was the sweetheart of one of the museum workers sneaking in so she handed me a mop and told me to clean the corridor. She then said if she ever saw me again, she'd report me. I've made sure to avoid her since."

Ree could just imagine Mrs Mantell handling it that way.

They parted in the cellars below the tower of Old Saul, Ree and Henri beginning the long climb up as Ada went on to the kitchens.

"Are you sure no one will be there? What time does Professor Gall normally go to bed? And what about that enemy of yours – Spurzheim?" asked Ree.

"I was told around twelve. It's gone two now and surely neither of them sleeps in the study when they've comfortable apartments that go with the job? What about the maids?"

"There's a special cleaning crew that does the lower floors at night, and the chancellor has a manservant to clean his private quarters during the day. At least, that was the arrangement under Chancellor Grassmann."

"But it's a reminder to be quiet."

"Don't worry. Most of them are my friends. If they see us, they'll turn a blind eye."

"Even so, we should get off the stairs if we hear anyone."

They got as far as the fifth floor when they heard footsteps running down the steps – heavy boots, not the light tread of a maid. Henri opened the nearest door, found a walk-in cupboard, and pulled Ree in after him. It was pitch dark inside, the air filled with the dry smell of paper, ink, dust, and sealing wax. The footsteps carried on and went past. Ree made to move but Henri kept hold of her elbow and shook his head. They waited to make sure no one else was following.

Having decided it was clear, Henri nudged open the door, letting the light spill in.

"Sorry for grabbing you."

"It's fine. You thought quickly – well done." Ree brushed white dust from her grey cloak, a garment she had borrowed from the Sisters. She lifted her hand and stared at the pale tips. Following her thought, Henri opened the door wide. On the shelf against which she had leaned was a row of neatly laid out chalks.

"Well, we are in a place of learning," he said. "Not surprising to find a store of chalks here."

"But the chalk in all the other areas has been locked up, hasn't it, used only during teaching and then returned?"

"No one is going to lock up the chancellor's private supply, are they?" Henri's tone was ironic. "He's above suspicion."

"Which means that anyone who knew it was here could help themselves."

"And the people who would know are the senior staff." Henri brushed off the back of her cloak, then started up the stairs again. "Let's go."

They arrived in the waiting area outside the chancellor's grand study. The only downside, thought Ree, was living directly under a striking clock.

Henri lay on his belly to peek under the door. "I can't see a light on the desk – just a dying fire."

"Try the handle," whispered Ree. "Maybe he's so confident no one will search his room, he doesn't lock it."

Henri turned the knob and the door opened smoothly.

The room was a mess, turned upside down, with papers scattered across the floor.

"Looks like someone got here first. It's going to be difficult getting fingerprints from this. We'll have to find something only he would've touched and get away quickly before we get the blame for this." Ree took two steps in before Henri held her back.

"Don't," he said.

Looking down, Ree saw a hand half-buried beneath a layer of academic journals. "Oh no, not again."

Henri took a breath through his nostrils, calming himself when really he wanted to yell. This was a nightmare, to be on site for a second time at the discovery of a body.

"Is he quite dead?" asked Ree.

She was right. Henri had assumed they were looking at a murder victim, but maybe he had just passed out; maybe there was something they could do to save him? Sharing the same thought, they both moved toward the body.

Ree kneeled down and felt for a pulse. "I… I think he's dead. He's not cold though."

Recently killed then. By the owner of the footsteps on the stairs? wondered Henri.

"It's Professor Gall, isn't it?" said Ree. They couldn't see his face, as it was buried as if he'd pulled the contents of the bookshelf down as he crashed against it. Or had someone thrown them over him in a clumsy search over his dead body?

Before Henri could draw any conclusions, they heard murmuring of people approaching. He could make out the clear tones of Inspector Gideon bellowing about securing the area. The police knew something was up, which meant the person they heard on the stairs must have been the first to discover the body and had run off to find help.

"What do we do?" asked Ree, running to the window. But

they were many floors above the ground, ruling out that as an exit option.

"We can't get past them. If they find us hiding, it would be worse. As the body has already been discovered by someone else, they can't blame us." At least Henri hoped not.

"They'll find a way." Ree scrabbled in her pocket. "Quick: we need to get rid of the map and your notebook." She took it from him, went to the stack of Grassmann's paintings that had not yet been removed, and slipped them between the frames. "That'll have to do."

"Our excuse for being here?" Henri recalled the questioning of the previous murder. Their stories had to match.

"To plead against our dismissal."

"At two in the morning? Well, it's not as if we have much choice. Now run out and scream."

Correctly guessing his intention, Ree dashed out of the room and released an almighty screech. "Oh help! Help! He's dead! Help!"

Henri joined her. He could hear the thunder of feet much closer now. "Please, someone, come quickly! Help!"

Inspector Gideon, accompanied by Kurt Spurzheim, as well as a full police patrol, turned the last corner of the stairs. "You! What are you two doing here?"

"Please, sir, come quickly," said Ree. She grabbed the sleeve of Gideon's jacket, drawing him toward the door. "We came to appeal to the chancellor but he's… he's…"

Deciding that a dead body came before enquiries, Gideon pushed her to one side. "Stay out here. Schmidt, secure the pair of them." He strode into the room. "Doctor?"

A senior member of the medical faculty hurried inside, followed by Spurzheim. Henri realized that his classmate must've been the one to fetch the police. Henri and Ree waited in tense silence, eavesdropping on everything that was being said in the study.

"No visible blows," said the doctor. "From the rigidity of the body and the blueness around the lips, I'd say it was poison."

"What kind?" asked the inspector.

"If pushed, I'd say he has the classic signs of strychnine ingestion."

"Ingestion. He's eaten or drunk it?"

"It takes a surprisingly small amount, but yes, while there are other ways to be contaminated, I'd say he unwittingly consumed it."

Through the crack where the door stood ajar, Henri could see the inspector carefully examining the desk, his hands protected by leather gloves. "There's no sign of a recent meal or drink. Spurzheim, at what time did the professor last eat anything?"

"In hall with everyone else, sir. That was around eight o'clock." Considering he had just lost his master, Spurzheim was holding up well. "I didn't see him after that until I came to take the last post from him."

"After midnight?" queried Gideon.

"It's been a busy time with all the death notices to write. He asked me to work late. I came just before two."

"And what did you see?"

"Just what you saw when you came in: the professor stretched out on the floor, the place in a m… mess." The little break was the only hint Spurzheim gave that he was affected more than his stoic bearing suggested.

"The final convulsions of strychnine poisoning are acutely painful," said the doctor. "It is entirely possible that in his desperation, the professor made this disorder himself."

"I thought that he might've been looking for an antidote when he realized what was happening," said Spurzheim. "I noticed he'd pulled the books off the shelf."

"Then he was wasting his time. Unfortunately there is no antidote yet known to science."

Zena hopped up the stairs and jumped on Henri's back. Her

stream of chatter was clearly full of monkey questions.

Henri had one of his own. "What are you doing here, menace? You were supposed to stay safely out of the way."

Zena leaped down again and bounded into the room to the desk.

The doctor sat back on his heels. "I'm sorry, Inspector, but I must protest that we have yet another unsolved murder. I like to heal people, not pronounce their cause of death. Is anyone safe?"

"I understand, Doctor, believe me, and I'm going to catch the one responsible and make them regret the day they were born," said Gideon.

Henri's gaze followed Zena. "Get back here!" he hissed. "I'm in enough trouble already."

She was tossing the evidence on the desk with her usual curiosity. She loved nothing better than to shred candle spills or quills.

Quills. Strychnine.

"Stop the monkey!" shouted Henri, lunging for his pet. "Zena, no!"

The macaque had her hand poised over the row of white feathers, Gall's favourite quills ready for cutting. Officer Schmidt misunderstood Henri's intent, thinking he was making a run for it, and tackled him to the floor, but fortunately Gideon was quicker on the uptake. He took the brutal method of throwing a book at Zena, scaring her away from the desk. She ran to Ree and hid quivering under her robe.

There was a pause, then Gideon asked: "Was your master in the habit of writing with a quill, Spurzheim?"

"Yes, sir, it was one of his odd ways. He liked the traditional touch and was proud of cutting his own pens."

Allowed back up, Henri watched as Gideon inspected the crushed quill lying on an unfinished letter, ink splattered on the surface.

"And was he in the habit of wetting the nib before dipping it in the ink as I've seen some scholars do?"

"Yes sir. And he would occasionally brush the end against his lips. It helped him concentrate, he claimed." Spurzheim took a shocked breath. "You aren't thinking...?"

"I'm afraid I am. We'll be taking this ink and all his pens for analysis. If someone knew his ways they could have dipped his quills into the poison, or dribbled it into the ink, and then just waited for a time when he had a lot of correspondence to deal with."

Spurzheim shuddered. "And I missed the signs! When I left this evening, he was complaining of a stiff jaw, muscle spasms, and a strange taste in his mouth. When I asked if I could fetch him anything, he said it was probably just a migraine – he suffered from them once every few months."

"It was no headache, boy, but poisoning," grumbled the doctor. "If you had fetched me then I could've done something. Maybe stopped him before it was too late!"

"I'm so sorry, sir, but I was only following orders."

Henri closed his eyes briefly. Zena had had the narrowest of escapes. "Zena?" he whispered.

She peeked out from under Ree's hem and then ran and jumped into his arms.

"You could've been killed, you reckless creature."

"I find it somewhat ironic you of all people are calling the monkey 'reckless', Master Volp," said Gideon wryly. "Master Spurzheim, you've been most helpful and I'm sorry for your loss. I know you admired the professor." Gideon beckoned to one of his officers. "Please take the lad to the station and get a statement. Then he may return to bed."

The doctor was perhaps regretting that he had implied Spurzheim was to blame for not acting more quickly. "I can send you a sleeping draft if that would help, young man."

"Thank you but no. I don't think I could sleep tonight."

Spurzheim sounded genuinely shaken. He had been devoted to Gall. Despite disliking him, Henri found he pitied his classmate: he'd lost his sponsor and mentor in this murder.

"I'd appreciate it if you kept this news to yourself, Master Spurzheim. I need to think what to do next," said Gideon. "This murderer is clearly more dangerous than we knew. First a savage blow and now acting by stealth: he's going to be very difficult to catch."

"Maybe not, sir." The tone of Kurt's voice hardened. "What about Henri and the girl? Why are they here? The professor dismissed both of them yesterday."

Henri's sympathy ebbed somewhat to find himself accused so readily.

"Don't worry, I'll deal with them," said Gideon.

Spurzheim left under escort; he sent Henri a bitter look as he passed him in the doorway. Gideon followed him out a moment later.

"Schmidt, take over in there. Get the team started on evidence collection. Make sure everyone wears protective gloves. Doctor, if you could take charge of the body, please?"

The medical man sighed. "I'm running out of space in my cold room."

"I'm sorry to inconvenience you – and I'm sure Professor Gall is even sorrier to be a burden."

"Yes, well." Shamefaced, the doctor returned to the study.

Gideon clicked his fingers. "You two: explain why I'm finding you on the scene of another murder?"

Henri cleared his throat. "Well, sir, we had both lost our positions. We came to appeal to the chancellor."

Gideon shook his head, arms folded. "No, I'm not buying that. Tell the truth."

"Like that's always served us well in the past," muttered Ree.

"It might be all that can save you now. Tell me why I shouldn't just charge you with murder on two counts? You've had opportunity, possibly motive too, on both occasions, as I know you had plenty of reasons to dislike Professor Gall and may not have been straight with me about your feelings toward Mr Shelley. As for means, strychnine is used as a rat poison. I imagine two enterprising young people could find that either in the housekeeper's stores or with the gardeners."

Ree shook with anger. "Why shouldn't you charge us? Because we didn't do it, you... you stupid man! You've got a murderer on the loose who likes killing off anyone who gets to be chancellor."

"What's that got to do with it?" snapped Gideon.

"Think, inspector! Are you sure now that Grassmann died a *natural* death?"

"What? Are you saying the former chancellor was murdered too?"

"I don't know: I'm not the police. But I'd certainly be looking into the possibility, seeing how his successors haven't managed to hold the post for even a day before someone killed them!"

"Ree," said Henri. The inspector's temper was rising to match hers and the two of them looked close to flying at each other.

"But that's – " said Gideon.

"That's what?" snapped Ree. "Evil? Yes, exactly! But someone has done it so don't come accusing Henri and me when all we did is find the body before you!"

"You, girl, have no respect for the law!" Gideon crowded Ree so she had to take a step back.

Her chin was up. "I'll respect it when it earns it!"

Zena shrieked.

"Right, I'm arresting you – and you. Constable, hold the boy." Gideon seized Ree's arm, practically lifting her off her feet as she resisted.

"Stop it! This is not getting us any closer to solving this!" said Henri. "Ree, we've got to tell him why we came here."

"Don't bother. He's not interested in listening to a thing we say." She squawked as Gideon turned her roughly to handcuff her hands behind her back.

"Sir, Inspector, just stop, please, I beg you. There's more going on here than you know," pleaded Henri.

"Oh, a confession, is this, sonny?" Having secured Ree, Gideon shoved her toward a waiting policeman and turned to deal with Henri.

"We came to collect the professor's fingerprints, to compare them to the ones in the axe display case. And we found out that he was the one writing the chalk messages." Henri knew as soon as he said it that he'd made a serious mistake. Gideon's anger hardened into something much more deadly.

"Throwing around accusations while the man lies murdered not feet from us is the action of a scoundrel." He used a second pair of handcuffs on Henri. "Take these two down to the interrogation room. I'll be there as soon as I can."

Henri and Ree were bundled down the stairs with little ceremony, Zena running behind trying to trip their guards. At the bottom they met with a cluster of maids. Henri thought he saw Ada among them.

"Ree, what's wrong?" called one girl.

"Mary, they're arresting us – but they've got the wrong people," Ree replied before the officer told her to "shut it".

"Arresting you for what?" To Henri's surprise, the maids didn't make way. A dodo beak appeared among their skirts, clacking ominously. Led by Mary and Phil, they blocked the corridor, determined to get an answer to their question. "Officers, why have you arrested Ree?" Mary asked.

"Because they think we murdered the chancellor – both of them," Henri managed to get out before a policeman wrapped his palm over Henri's mouth. Henri didn't care if that meant he would be punished. Word had to get out to their friends or the policemen were likely to lock them up and pretend it was a job well done. A sacked maid and a dismissed scholar made excellent scapegoats.

The patrol raised their batons to clear a path through the maids and irate dodo. Phil escaped the scuffle and scurried after them. Ziggy slunk in from a side corridor and stood in their path, growling.

"Call off that dog or I'll shoot it!" warned Schmidt, drawing a pistol.

"She's a wolf!" said Ree. "Ziggy, stand down."

Ziggy didn't quite obey. She pushed her way between Ree and her guard, walking alongside her so that no one could manhandle her as they were escorted to the police station. They weren't imprisoned in the lockups but taken directly to the interrogation room. After a brief pat-down search, during which their handcuffs were removed, they were told to wait. The constables left, slamming the door behind them.

Ree wrapped her arms around Phil and Ziggy, shivering. Now the fear was setting in, after the shock and the fury. "Why have they left us together?"

Henri had a theory but he couldn't blurt it out. "I don't know."

He sat down at the table, burying his head in his hands. Zena ruffled his hair lovingly.

Ree bent closer. "Don't worry, Henri. We didn't do it so they can't find proof against us."

Now she was close enough to hear a whisper, he muttered: "I think we're being watched."

Ree's breath hitched, indicating she'd heard him. She spoke a little louder for the benefit of anyone observing them. "They'll find evidence of who did it if they look hard enough. I mean, it isn't everyone who can plant poisoned quills in the chancellor's study, is it? It has to narrow down the list of suspects."

Henri sat up, letting his hands fall to the table top. "If it was the quills."

"Inspector Gideon seemed quite sure. Then again, Inspector Gideon is an ass, so who knows what he will say next?"

On that choice insult, the door banged open. The inspector marched in, accompanied by Schmidt.

"Does this look like a zoo, officer?" he barked at Schmidt.

"No, sir, but I didn't think you'd want me to shoot them."

"I suppose not – just think of the paperwork. Right, you two, explain this." He slapped Henri's notebook on the table. "And this." He shook out the map so they could all see Ree's careful annotations.

Henri's spirits sank further. They had hoped the police would be careless, but it appeared they were better at searching a study than they had been a dodo pen.

Henri opened the notebook to the first page where he had written his name, as he did in all his books. "This is mine."

"So I managed to work out for myself, even if I am a lowly ass. What was it doing hidden between paintings?"

Ree glanced at Henri. "That was me. I tried to hide it when we heard you coming. We knew we'd be searched and those things are private."

"A private notebook and a private… what is this?" Gideon poked at the map.

"Architectural drawings of the museum. I've been making a study to keep up my skills."

"But they show passages even I didn't know existed, and rooms that are no longer open to the public."

"I'm curious. It's not a crime."

"Maybe that is exactly what curiosity is when it comes to you two." Gideon turned back to the notebook. "You've been investigating the first murder." It was a statement.

"Yes, sir," admitted Henri. "That's what I study: the science of detection."

"So I've heard. One of the few names I don't see here is mine."

"We could add it if you like," said Ree with a humourless smile. She was not making friends here with her sassy responses. Ziggy growled, neck fur sticking up on end.

"Your name isn't there because you're not a suspect," Henri said quickly.

"But Professor Gall was. He is named as your chief suspect?"

"Yes, sir."

Gideon hooked his thumbs in his belt. "Schmidt, leave us. Clear out anyone left in the observation room."

Giving his superior an odd look, the junior officer left the chamber. Gideon waited until the door was shut, and then added a few more seconds to give time for the second part of his instructions to be carried out. The silence seemed to stretch forever. Zena jumped on his shoulder and pulled fluff from his beard. Gideon didn't brush her off.

"I lost my temper with you and was too rough. I apologize. That was unprofessional," said the inspector. He took a seat opposite them. "I don't suspect you of murder."

"So you're on our side?" asked Ree.

"No, I'm on the side of the truth. I said that because I need the real perpetrator to think he's got away with it. Hopefully by now news of your arrests and Professor Gall's death has got out. If he thinks he's clear, he's more likely to make a mistake."

"But you told Spurzheim not to tell anyone," said Henri.

"And when has that stopped the spread of gossip in this place? If he doesn't say anything, the maids surely will."

"I see."

Ree rubbed her wrists fretfully, not ready to forgive her rough handling.

Gideon sat back in his chair. "But what are you doing interfering with my crime scene? Your presence muddles things. I have to explain you away before I can move on."

"It really was just chance that we were there. We had nothing to do with either murder." Henri decided it was safer if he answered for them, as Ree and the inspector acted like oil and a lit match when they talked together.

"I doubt it was chance in either case. There are patterns behind any crime that only become clear when you have the solution." The inspector was talking now rather like Hamid.

"Shall we tell you again what we know, but this time can it end without handcuffs?" Henri asked.

Gideon gave a huff that might have been a laugh. "All right. This time I'm listening." He scooped Zena off his shoulder and nudged her across the table to Henri.

Settling the macaque on his lap, Henri looked at Ree. "Do you want me to tell him?"

Ree gave the inspector a hard smile. "You'd better or he'll probably end up strangling me."

"Yes, you do seem to have that effect on my temper. Maybe because we're too much alike?" suggested the inspector.

"Never," she muttered.

Gideon tapped his fingers on the table, marking out his points. "Quick tempered? Don't suffer fools easily? Convinced we can change the world for the better if only people will do what we say?"

"He does have a point," said Henri.

"Traitor," said Ree. "Go on: tell the inspector what we found."

"Inspector, Professor Gall was seen following the patrols on the nights the messages appeared. We think he wrote them himself to undermine Shelley, who was in charge of the displays at the time. As a senior member of staff, Professor Gall would've had easy access to chalk. We found an unlocked store in the tower of Old Saul. There might be others that were forgotten when all the chalk was confiscated from the academy. He called off the patrols once he became chancellor. Why would he do that unless he knew no more messages were going to appear?"

This time Gideon didn't explode in fury at the accusation. "What did he hope to achieve with the messages?"

"To weaken respect for Shelley so his plan to move the professor's phrenological display didn't go ahead," said Ree.

"So this is all about an academic dispute? Why would anyone kill for that?"

"The messages are. We're not yet sure about the murders. We thought Professor Gall had killed Shelley, but if he did, who then murdered him?" asked Ree.

"And with him dead, we'll never know if he was guilty of either crime," said Gideon.

"So you believe us?"

"I believe you have a working theory. I had begun to look closely at the staff when the messages carried on despite the curfews on students and changed work practices of the maids. Finding out that you are able to come and go as you wished across that plank bridge muddied those waters for a while, as I had to ask if others could not also move undetected."

Henri thought of all the renegades moving about the museum like an army of grey ghosts. "There might be others, but I think the professor's motive in this case is the strongest. We thought that a real Theophilus protestor would have attempted to make his mark in something more permanent than chalk."

"Very true. That did bother me too. I had it down as a schoolboy prank to start with, but I was beginning to think I wasn't seeing everything. Your theory is plausible. But as for Gall also being a murderer, I don't believe it. I think he would've preferred to vanquish his enemy publicly, humiliate him before his peers, not do away with him in the dark."

"If it were him, and he feared he was about to be found out, maybe he committed suicide?" suggested Ree.

"Does he strike you as a man who would kill himself? And if he did, why choose a particularly painful way to die? There are other, more gentle poisons and quicker means by which he could have done it."

Henri's respect for the inspector was growing. "I think Inspector

Gideon is right, Ree. He wouldn't do it that way and, besides, as far as we know, we were the only ones to suspect him. He didn't know I'd perfected my method of collecting fingerprints and was coming for his. There was no cause for desperation."

"Unless someone found out his secret and was blackmailing him?" said Ree.

The three let that suggestion hover in the air between them.

"I think we need to talk to Kurt Spurzheim. He would know what was going on in the professor's mind tonight if anyone does," said Henri.

Before anyone could comment, there came a knock at the door.

"Sir, you have some people here to see you," said Schmidt. "A very odd set of someones, sir."

"Can't you see I'm busy?" said the inspector.

"But they said they could prove that our two suspects are innocent and insist on seeing you."

"Then you'd better show them in." Inspector Gideon stood and straightened his uniform jacket. "Do you know anything about this?"

Henri shook his head.

The door opened a second time and an eight-strong delegation of the renegades swept in, led by Hamid and Dr Hypatia.

"Inspector, you have arrested the wrong people," said Hypatia, an impressive figure in her boots and wide-brimmed hat. "They have been with us since noon and had no time or inclination to go around poisoning people."

"You must release them at once," concluded Hamid, appearing quite formidable unlike his normal friendly manner, "or you will have us to answer to."

"Will I indeed? And just who the devil *are* you?" asked the inspector.

Chapter 18
Flame Out

With so many renegades to accommodate, the interrogation had to move to a new venue. Inspector Gideon had already sent runners with news of the second murder to wake the senior members of staff. Arriving in dressing gowns, eyes still heavy with sleep, they could not be dismissed back to their beds, not when they were calling for enquiries and action with the urgency of the clueless. There was no choice but to add them to the meeting. Gideon decided to convene it in the shell chamber – this was on Ree's prompting. She suggested it on the grounds that a circular room would put everyone on equal footing, a consideration when old enemies were gathering for the first time in an age. It was no small thing the renegades had done for her and Henri, tearing the veil that had hidden them from the eyes of the authorities and risking their futures to save them.

Lord John arrived last as he had to be summoned from his

mansion across the park. He joined fossil hunter Joseph Anning, old botanist Dr Erasmus, and zoology expert Professor André. Lord John faltered in the doorway on seeing the renegades seated in their segment of the round table. They took up a good third of the space.

"Good grief, where did you spring from?" exclaimed the nobleman.

Ree tensed, holding herself ready to leap to the rescue should he order her friends' arrest. She need not have feared; once recovered from his shock, Lord John actually looked relieved to see them. He strode towards Hamid. "Dr Al-Ghazali, I thought you returned to Egypt when they... you know?"

"When they booted out all us Theophilus followers? They didn't boot me that far." Hamid smiled at his old student.

Lord John shook the man's hand vigorously. "I enjoyed your lessons even though I was an appalling student. And Dr Hypatia, charmed to see you, charmed." He bent over and kissed the back of her hand, a bravely gallant gesture. "I have you to thank for my love of nature."

"Then I succeeded with one pupil at least," she said graciously.

Inspector Gideon cleared his throat. "I'm sorry to interrupt the reunion, Lord John, but as the most senior person of the surviving board members, I must ask you to chair this meeting. You have heard the terrible news?"

Lord John took his seat, only now noticing that Henri, Ree, and their animal companions were sitting beside the inspector. "Indeed, my chauffeur brought the news. I can hardly credit it. Our murderer has struck again?"

"Yes, this time using poison."

"You don't think these two had anything to do with it?" Lord John gestured to Ree and Henri. "They were trying to investigate the first murder when I last met them. I doubt they harboured any deadly intentions toward the professor."

"They are guilty only of being annoyingly persistent and getting underfoot."

Ree took that as praise rather than criticism.

"Please, Lord John," continued the inspector, "with your permission, I think you all need to be brought up to date with tonight's events."

"Carry on, carry on."

Gideon then gave his audience a succinct summary of what had been discovered and the new theory that Gall himself might've been behind the chalk messages and was a suspect in Shelley's murder too.

"The young scholar here can match the fingerprints at the axe display case with our suspect's. We should be able to prove if the late chancellor was our first murderer or not."

"Do you think, Inspector, that the one who killed Gall might've discovered what he had done?" asked Hypatia.

"You mean that someone took the law into his own hands and pronounced a death sentence? It is indeed one of the scenarios with which I am working."

"Excuse me a moment," said Professor André, monocle firmly in eye socket as he glared at Hypatia. He had succeeded her as head of the biology faculty, Ree surmised, from the fact that it was his name rather than Hypatia's listed on the brass plate in the academy. "I want to know what these... these..."

"Our preferred term is renegades," said Hypatia smoothly.

"These outlaws are doing here?"

"Outlaws? That works too," commented Hamid.

"They are here on my invitation," said Inspector Gideon. "They came to offer Henri Volp and Maria Altamira an alibi. It appears they've been living in the museum under our noses and the young persons were with them this afternoon and evening until the time they came upon the body."

"We've not been doing anyone any harm, merely carrying on with our work in the shadows," said Hypatia. "The Madagascan specimens that informed your recent article on mammalian evolution were provided by me, André, or did you not stop to ask from where Mr Billibellary continued to get his creatures? You left us little choice."

"We got rid of you for a reason!" protested Professor André.

"That reason being fear and bigotry, neither of which have a place in science."

Gideon held up a hand. "Please, my lady, Professor, this is hardly the moment to settle your differences. The important thing to focus on is that you and your colleagues in the shadows were able to clear these two young people of suspicion, and that in turn helps me move on to the rest of the investigation. We have two leading scenarios: that Professor Gall was murdered as revenge for his own acts, or he was innocent of wrongdoing and killed by the same hand. If the latter is true, then anyone who takes the position of chancellor would be at risk. Who is going to take charge now?"

It wasn't the most attractive job description, thought Ree. Become head of the museum and die.

Lord John cleared his throat. "I suggest we leave the position free. As chair of the trustees and representative of the sponsors, I will take control of museum business until such time as it is safe to appoint a new chancellor."

Gideon nodded. "Then, with your permission, sir, I would like to question all those who have access to the chancellor's study. I believe the poison was delivered to the mouth on the tips of the quills he so favoured – a clever mechanism as it meant only the one who was the target was likely to touch them."

"Of course, of course, take any and all steps you think necessary."

Further discussion was interrupted when the door banged open. Hans and Maxwell appeared in the entrance, dressed in their nightshirts, hands and faces streaked with black.

"Sir, the museum is on fire!" cried Maxwell.

The room echoed with the screeches of chairs being pushed back.

"What? Where?" asked Lord John, grabbing his cousin.

"It started in the roof of the academy," Maxwell blurted out.

"But not just there," continued Hans, gecko peeking out from his breast pocket. "The kitchen, the first hall, the tower of Old Saul – a lot of places – someone did it on purpose. Master Ricardo sent us to tell you that we need to evacuate."

"Evacuate *and* save the museum!" Lord John cast around the room, looking for someone to take charge, emergencies not being his strong point.

"Has anyone organized the boys to leave their wing?" asked Gideon, stepping up to the role.

"Yes, we're doing that now," said Maxwell.

"What about the maids?" asked Ree. It was nearly dawn so many of them would be just going to bed.

"Oh, I don't know." Maxwell looked flustered. "I'm not sure Master Ricardo will think of them."

There was no time for fury over that oversight. "We'll go and alert Mrs Mantell and the girls." Ree stood up, pulling Henri with her.

"And we'll warn the others who live in our part of the building," said Hypatia, gesturing to the other renegades.

"We need to alert Mr Billibellary and the gardeners," said Hamid. "Professor André?"

He nodded and hastened out.

"We'll use the menagerie as our evacuation area," said Inspector Gideon. "I'll telegraph for help. If the staff will make sure all areas are cleared, my officers and I will do what we can to control the blaze before the city fire brigade can reach us."

"I think we can help with that," said Hamid. "There's a few of us with water engineering experience."

"You're with me then."

Everyone rushed off to their appointed tasks. Ree and Henri ran to the maids' tower, followed by Ziggy, Phil, and Zena. They alerted anyone they passed. Many of them already knew that something was amiss as the menagerie animals that roamed the corridors at night were fast making their escape, an invaluable early warning system that would no doubt save many lives. Ziggy dived into the third kitchen and towed an indignant Ingrid out by the hem of her skirt.

"Can't you control your wretched wolf, Ree! She won't let go!" the cook shouted.

"There's a fire, Ingrid. You need to get out!" Ree called back.

"We'll see to the maids," Henri added. "Do what you can to stop it spreading here."

The cook stopped resisting and ran into the kitchen courtyard. The next thing they heard was the clanging of the fire bell. The other cooks and their helpers poured out of the second and first kitchens to help. The laundresses appeared, rolling up sleeves on muscled arms. Buckets of water were drawn up from the well and passed to a chain of volunteers.

Crossing the courtyard to the entrance to the maids' tower, Ree smelled her first smoke. Looking up, she could see darker billows against the predawn sky.

"Looks like it's coming from the scholars' wing. I hope they've all got out," she said.

"They were the first to raise the alarm so I imagine they've had time," said Henri. He banged on the next door they passed. "Fire! Get out of the building now!"

From the screams issuing from inside, that had worked.

Not sure her own voice would carry, Ree turned the handle and shouted in to the next room. "Leave now! Fire!"

Mrs Mantell was asleep by her fireplace, head lolling to one side of her winged armchair. She had slept through the bell and the shouts. Zena jumped on her shoulder and gave her hair a hard yank to wake her.

"Mrs Mantell, the museum is on fire!" called Ree. "We'll send the girls out to you."

"Oh my!" Grabbing a shawl, Mrs Mantell hurried out to take a roll call while they continued on up.

The last room in the tower was Ree's old chamber. Beata and Mary weren't there, but, as they had been the first to hear of the professor's death, they probably had never gone to bed. Just to be sure, Ree went to the window. There was a slight chance they might have panicked and tried to escape that way, though they had never approved of her ledge-walking antics. As she opened the shutters, a billow of smoke entered.

"Are they out there?" asked Henri.

Ree turned her face to the side, coughing. "No." She was about to close the shutters when she spotted someone moving on the rooftop opposite. "Henri, someone's trapped on the scholars' wing. I can see them on the tiles. They must've expected the plank to still be there, not knowing the police moved it."

Henri joined her at the window. "The whole building is ablaze. He'll never get down now." He cupped his hands to his mouth. "Hey! You there! You'll have to jump across. We'll help you!"

"He can't hear us," said Ree. "The noise of the fire is too loud."

Henri swung his leg over the sill. Ree caught the back of his jacket. "But you're scared of heights."

"Right now, I'm more scared of watching someone die. We have to go out there and get his attention."

Ree had a bad feeling about this, but, of course, she followed him on to the ledge. The wind was gusting between the buildings, whipped by the currents of hot air from the areas in which the fires had already got hold. Sparks flew up, then turned direction viciously, stinging faces and hands as they edged along the narrow parapet. Henri had a white-knuckled grip on the ivy that clothed the stonework of the maids' tower. Little black house martins screeched and flashed their white bellies as they fled the mud nests under the eaves, abandoning their fledglings. Henri and Ree edged to the point where she normally jumped, the place where the gap was at its narrowest.

"Hey, you there!" shouted Henri.

"Can you see who it is?" Ree rubbed smoke-stung eyes.

"I think… yes, it's Kurt Spurzheim."

What on earth was he doing up here? "On the count of three, we'll shout his name together." She gave the count. "Spurzheim!"

This time their voices rose over the roar of the flames. He turned and stumbled across the roof toward them, his face blistered by the heat, hands raw.

"Jump! We'll catch you!" called Ree, holding out her palm.

"It's no use – no good! I can't make it."

"I'm going over there," said Ree.

"I knew you'd say that." Henri didn't wait but pushed himself off the ledge and jumped the gap. He landed with inches to spare, then waited to catch her if she slipped. She landed safely, Zena nimbly following. Henri set off in pursuit of Spurzheim, who had stumbled to the place where the plank should've been. Flames were licking at the attic window. It wouldn't be long before the timbers holding the roof collapsed. They would all be plunged into the inferno beneath.

"Kurt, please: come with me," Henri begged. "We've another way out."

Spurzheim loped to and fro like the old dancing bear Ree had once seen in the market, tormented beyond the limits of endurance. "It should be here. I pulled it back. It should be here!"

He was talking about the plank. Did that mean that he had been out on the night Shelley was murdered?

"The police took it," Henri explained. "The only way out is to jump, like we did. The maids' tower isn't yet on fire. Come."

Spurzheim shook off Henri's touch on his arm. "Not you. I'm not going with you. You have no head for intelligence or leadership – he told me."

Ree really did not want to give her life to have some stupid discussion about phrenology while the ground was literally burning beneath them. "Spurzheim, if you want to live, you've got to do what we tell you even if our skulls are all wrong by your standards!"

Spurzheim sank to his knees, holding his head in his hands, rocking to and fro. "But mine is all wrong – I'm all wrong." He looked up, blackened face streaked with tears. "Was it all a lie? Did I do it all for nothing?"

"Do what?" Henri danced away from a hot patch on the tiles. "Actually, never mind that now; this roof won't hold much longer. Let's talk when we're safe."

Spurzheim wasn't listening. "I don't know what happened. I tested the theory out on those animals. I measured the heads of the convicts. My readings were exact." He took something from an inside pocket and held up a page of what looked like meticulous notes. With a sob he threw them up, letting them drift on the wind and catch fire. "There's a bump right here," he pointed to the area above the ear, "that shows a man's animal destructiveness and a dip here," he pointed to another zone further forward, "that shows lack of morality. I found them in the prisoners, but I also found them in myself. I was always destined to be criminal."

Ree wanted to shake him, tell him it was a load of hogwash, but the boy was not listening. She feared he'd lost his sanity when he lost hope for himself.

"Did you kill Simplicius Shelley?" asked Henri, seeing the end of the story a fraction before Ree did.

"Yes, yes I did." Spurzheim raised his chin defiantly. "He'd insulted our science – undermined the professor. Oh, how Professor Gall raged to me about the man. And then I saw it – like a sign from the fates."

"Saw what?" asked Ree. Even though they could not linger, they were held trapped by their desire to hear this confession.

"The tools just lying there, and the axe untended. A man so keen on stones should be killed with the tools of his trade, don't you think? Poetic justice and all that?"

The piece they had been missing dropped into place. Ree hardly had time to feel the shock. Right idea but wrong culprit. It had been the disciple that killed, not the teacher.

Spurzheim wrapped his arms around himself, his rocking continuing. "I sent an anonymous note to meet me at the menagerie, claiming I had proof the keeper wasn't doing his job properly. He came like a lamb to the slaughter. But he deserved it. Shelley had done his best to ruin a great man. The professor was a great man, wasn't he?" For the first time, Spurzheim sounded doubtful.

"Professor Gall?" said Henri. "He was certainly well respected." He found better words than Ree could've managed. "Come, Kurt: we'll carry on with this when you're safe. You can ask all the questions you want."

"You don't understand," Spurzheim screamed at Henri. "I did it for the professor; I did it because I was doomed by this," he pulled at his scalp, "but he was great. He has to be worth it. I don't believe in hell, but I feel like I'm in it now because I no longer believe in him. I can't bear it."

Ree then knew what had happened that night. "Kurt, did you poison your master?"

He shuddered, eyes closed.

"But why? You were loyal to him," said Henri.

"He changed his mind," whispered Spurzheim. "I saw his new article. He changed his mind."

"About what?"

"Where destructiveness lies. He moved it back. I don't have a pronounced area there. According to his new scheme, I should be one of the most peaceful people alive. But I'd already killed for him! I hate him, I hate this place! I'm pleased I set it on fire. It should be destroyed."

Ree reached out to take Henri's hand to pull him away. The boy was maddened by his loss of faith in the science that had sustained him, driven to murderous extremes by a professor who had been oblivious to the crisis his most loyal follower was undergoing. By one stroke of the pen on a chart, he had destroyed Spurzheim's faith and been killed for it. "Henri, we've really got to go or we'll die."

He nodded. "Kurt, please: you need help. If you just come with us now..."

Spurzheim sagged forward, almost like he was praying, then he straightened his spine. "You're right. I can't stay here." He pulled himself up by the parapet wall. "You know I also have a bump denoting courage?" He tapped his head in the appointed spot.

"Good, that's right. You're brave," said Ree coaxingly. She didn't like the way he was talking; it was like he was very tired, or confused. Had the smoke got to him already? "So you'll follow us? It's a bit of a jump, but you'll manage."

"If I can do it, you certainly can," said Henri.

Finding some strength, Spurzheim followed them over the tiles to the jumping off point. Zena leaped the gap easily and shrieked her encouragement from the ledge.

Ree turned to face him. "Do you think you can manage?"

The smile he gave her was odd, an arrangement of features in an upward curve but with no humour. "Show me how."

"All right." Ree took a little run and sprang across the distance. She grabbed hold of the ivy, alarmed to feel it shift under her grip. It was beginning to protest at being used so many times as a lifeline. She gulped and schooled her expression into positive encouragement. There was no room for doubts once you'd committed to the leap. "See? Easy."

Henri pressed Spurzheim's shoulder in an encouraging gesture. "Let's jump together, agreed? I'll count to three."

A crack came from the roof behind them and the section over the attic window collapsed, sending up a fountain of sparks.

"Henri!" shouted Ree. "You've got to hurry."

Zena wailed.

"Come on, Kurt. We take a few steps back to give us some room. Ready?"

Spurzheim nodded but he seemed in a daze. "Fine. Run up then jump."

Henri gave him an anxious look. "Right. On my mark: one, two, three!" On three, Henri leaped, clearing the distance. His fingers looped into the ivy but it came away. Prepared for this, Ree had laced her hands in another patch and grabbed his shirt, pulling him toward her. He landed awkwardly but safely, one knee on the ledge, one leg dangling. He scrambled to his feet with her help.

"Kurt, why didn't you jump? Come on, you can still make it!" Henri shouted desperately.

Spurzheim was watching them with his odd empty smile. He had given up, Ree realized.

Coaxing had failed. Perhaps jeering would work?

"Kurt, you don't want two unpromising specimens like us to best you! Surely you've a bump on your head somewhere that tells you that you have to survive?"

Spurzheim gave what sounded like a genuine laugh. "Good try. But you see, it's too late for me."

"It's not," shouted Henri. "Take a run up and jump. Everything else can be dealt with later."

"Please don't make us watch you die!" begged Ree.

Kurt glanced behind him, seeing the flames only feet from him now, the heat beating on his back. He took a couple of paces. Had he finally listened?

"For you then. It's not your fault, if I don't make it. Remember that." Spurzheim bent forward and rocked on his heels like an athlete beginning the long jump. As he made to run, the beams gave way beneath him. To their horror, Spurzheim vanished, along with the rest of the roof.

"No!" shouted Henri. He made a move as if he was going back over.

"It really is too late now," said Ree, gripping her friend's arm in case he had any mad ideas about going back to see if Spurzheim had survived his fall. "There's nothing we can do from here. I don't think he really wanted to survive. He was only trying for our sakes."

Henri nodded and wiped a hand over his face. "Let's get back inside."

Ree could see curls of smoke rising from the roof of the maids' tower where the wind had driven sparks across. She edged along the parapet, annoyed that her arms were trembling, a poisonous combination of horror and exhaustion. It was hard to believe she'd just watch someone die. It didn't feel real. Climbing back into her old room, half hauled by Ziggy and Phil, she helped Henri over the ledge. Finding patches on the back of his jacket smouldering, she emptied a water jug over him with no warning.

That stirred him out of his shock. "What was that for?"

"You were on fire."

"Oh. Thanks."

"No problem. What are friends for?"

Henri opened the door into the tower staircase. Ziggy streaked ahead, a good indication that it was safe to go down. "She thinks it's all clear. Let's go."

Chapter 19

Hands Carved in Stone

Taking shelter against the wall of Phil's pen, the dodo snuggled against her, Ree hugged the blanket closer to her shoulders. On arriving at the evacuation area in the menagerie, they had told Inspector Gideon what Spurzheim had confessed. With a grim nod, he had thanked them and said he considered the case closed.

"Do you think Kurt was going to jump or had he given up?" Ree asked Henri.

He sipped the cup of hot chocolate Ingrid had pressed in his hand a few minutes before. "I don't know. And I don't know if he knew."

That agreed with Ree's impression. "He was so lost."

"He'd lost his faith in phrenology but was still holding on to it because without it he was just a foolish killer. That's the danger when you treat science like it has the answers to everything."

"He didn't believe in anything in the end, did he?"

"Not really. I wish he could've spent some time talking to people like Hamid. He might've been able to convince him that we need more than just scientific facts to decide such things."

Ree swirled her hot chocolate, still finding it hard to believe what had happened on the roof. Someone had just died – someone who had killed. She didn't feel like drinking the chocolate anymore so put it aside. "Kurt couldn't just say it was wrong to kill because it is against the law, or God, or human standards of good behaviour. He had to have a lump on his skull before he was allowed to think. I feel sorry for him."

"So do I. But he did kill two people," said Henri.

Ree groomed Phil's tail feathers, clearing out the ash that had got lodged between the quills. "Maybe it was better that he went the way he did? They would only have tried him and sentenced him to death or to life in a mental asylum. He was right in a way that it was all over for him."

Ziggy padded over with a string of burned sausages in her mouth and settled down to breakfast. Someone always benefitted from any disaster. Zag emerged from the pouch, blinking, and made her first unsteady steps to share in the feast.

"Aw, look: she's walking!" crooned Ree. "About time too! I've thought for months that she's been stalling. Ziggy is really an old softie letting her get away with all those free rides."

Henri tipped his head back and smiled.

The sun was climbing above the clouds of smoke still belching from the museum. Ree wondered if she'd ever get rid of the smell from her clothes and hair. Most of the fires had been extinguished through the combined efforts of the kitchen team, the police, and the city fire service. At one point the blaze looked as though it was going to take hold in the labyrinth and then the whole building would've been lost. Fortunately, the renegades had acted swiftly. With the help of

Hamid and Ada, who had studied the hydraulic engineering of the ancient Egyptians, they diverted the river that bisected the museum between the Fortieth and Fiftieth halls, flooding the foundations. The fires were extinguished and now they had reversed the flow and the water levels were receding. Hamid was now explaining what they had done to Lord John, Inspector Gideon, and the surviving trustees, Ada standing beside him.

"Do we know how much has been lost?" asked Ree.

"No lives other than Kurt but large parts of the building are smouldering ruins: the scholars' wing, the tower of Old Saul, much of the First, Tenth, Twentieth, and Thirtieth halls, and the rooms around them. The roof of the maids' tower is gone but the rest of the kitchen quarter escaped."

"Are you telling me that we lost most of the good stuff in the displays but that the giant frog survived?"

Henri joined in her hollow laughter. "Yes, ironic, isn't it?"

"Is this the end for the museum, do you think?" Ree had both loved and hated the place but she knew she would feel a great loss if they gave up on it.

Henri shook his head. "No, not that. We'll still want to do science, even if it is housed in temporary buildings for a while. Besides, it gives us a chance to build it bigger and better next time, doesn't it?"

"You're staying?"

Henri closed his eyes for a moment, letting the early sun warm his forehead and cheeks, Zena asleep on his lap. "Yes, I think I will. Professor Gall and Kurt were the only ones who wanted me gone, and I want to stay to shape the future of the museum. It's going to be very different. You can tell that already." He nodded to where Hypatia was helping Mr Billibellary and Humboldt tend the minor injuries on animal and human patients alike. The medical doctors, both men and women, were dealing with the more serious casualties. The injuries had come mostly from smoke inhalation, so they were being treated over in the glasshouses, patients lying on camp beds among the butterflies and parakeets.

Boots crunched on the gravel, and Ree looked up to see Lord John and Inspector Gideon standing over them. Henri jumped to his feet and offered his hand to Ree. It was a sign of how tired she was that she took it.

"I hear you two solved the mystery," said Lord John.

"But we couldn't save Spurzheim," replied Henri. "I'm sorry."

"Not your fault, lad," said the inspector. "It would've been an ugly business, prosecuting a young man for two brutal murders. Maybe things worked out for the best."

"So now we know the truth," said Lord John. "Inspector Gideon has ruled that Professor Gall wrote the messages for his own reasons and his follower killed Shelley in the muddle-headed belief he was doing it for him. Spurzheim then turned on Gall when he felt betrayed. Do we think the professor knew what Spurzheim had done?"

Ree had wondered that too. "I don't believe so. I think he would've hated what had been done for him as it was so... so..."

"Unscientific?" suggested Henri.

"Yes, exactly."

"That's true. He was a proud scientist even if few respected his area of study."

Lord John folded his arms. "So I expect you'll want a reward for uncovering the truth?"

Ree knew at once what she wanted.

"Sir, we didn't do it for a reward," said Henri.

"But we don't mind getting one," Ree added quickly.

"Oh yes? And what would that be?" asked Lord John.

"As temporary stand-in for the chancellor, would you please write to the authorities in the camp where my father is held, giving him a pardon and saying he can come back?"

Lord John rubbed the side of his nose. "I see. And what about you, Henri – what do you want?"

Ree expected Henri to say he wanted funding for his experiment but he surprised her. "I want the same thing as Ree, though I'd like the pardon extended to all other Theophilus protestors."

Yes, of course, that was a much better request than even hers!

"You're suggesting we change our most fundamental rule?" asked Lord John, but his tone was encouragingly warm.

"Absolutely, sir. Many of us would've been burned to a crisp and the museum lost if it hadn't been for the renegades," Henri said bluntly. "The museum needs them. You can't work with Theophilus followers only when it suits you; that's neither fair nor logical."

"Nor women neither," added Ree. "Dr Hypatia, Ada the engineer, Ingrid, the washerwomen, and all the others: they've proved their worth tonight, saving the day in the kitchens and diverting the river."

"And solving the crime," added Inspector Gideon, smiling at her.

"Yes, that too." Ree kept her chin up, refusing this time to pretend to be anything she wasn't.

"All right. I'll see what I can do," said Lord John.

Ree squeaked with excitement, grabbed Henri, and danced him in a circle, Zena uttering shrill cries as she clung on. "Thank you! Thank you! Thank you!"

Phil clacked his beak as Ziggy tweaked his tail.

"I'd better go and see if any paper survived the fire," said Lord John, walking away. "Oh, and by the way, I think there's going to be lots of work for stonemasons, male *and* female ones, after tonight, don't you, Miss Altamira?"

Eight months later

Ree put the final touches to the carved archway over the new entrance to the museum. She had done a portrait of Phil, but imagining him in his native land among lush fruit trees and sandy coves. Below him, a tiger wound through a Javan forest, a macaque grinning in the leaf canopy. On the opposite side, a Tasmanian wolf nursed her young in the grasslands of her home. A python formed the scrolled edge of the archway, head on the right plinth, tail tip on the left.

The ladder creaked. Someone was coming up to see her work, though she would have liked it to remain hidden until the grand opening at the weekend. Henri had sneaked up a couple of times when he could spare a few hours from his laboratory. He was always welcome and they spent most of their spare time together. As her fellow apprentice, Paul had offered a few grudging compliments and teasing remarks. Maxwell had come bearing chocolates from his sisters and mother, so earned entry through shameless bribery. No one else had been allowed to see.

She stood, hiding as much of the carving as she could behind her back. "Who is it? What do you want?"

"I was just coming to see how your project is getting along, Ree," a familiar voice rumbled.

"Da! Oh Da! It really is you!"

Her father climbed on to the scaffolding platform. She flew to him, tools discarded with a bounce and a clatter. His strong arms surrounded her. "My darling girl. You did it. You earned my freedom."

Ree let loose the great heaving sobs she had kept locked inside ever since he was exiled. All she could say was his name. He smelled the same, looked almost the same, apart from the gathering of white at his temples and the long beard he had grown on his sea voyage. "You're here."

"Yes, I'm here. I told you to forget me and you didn't. I told you not to write any more letters and you ignored me. I told you not to hope that you could change the world, but you did so anyway. From now on, Ree, I expect you not to take the slightest notice of my wishes, as that is all better for the both of us."

She laughed and cried at that description of her behaviour. "I'm so pleased you're back, Da. I've so much to tell you."

"I can see. You're up here, working openly without disguise. I want to know how that came about."

She sniffed and wiped her eyes on her sleeve. "It helps if the head of the museum is now on your side. Lord John has been confirmed as chancellor. Everyone else was too scared to take the position, fearing it was jinxed."

Her father chuckled. "And I thought those scientific chaps were supposed to be logical."

"He has welcomed the renegades that I wrote to you about back to their old positions – well, most of them. There are still a few, like the Flat Earthers and the Phlogistonites, clinging on to opposition over in the Hundred and Twenty-Second Hall, but they are happy there and he makes sure they get fed. Dr Hypatia has been reinstated as a fellow in the biology department, soon to head up an expedition to look for a female dodo for Phil. She's asked me and Henri if we want to go with her. And Dr Hamid is teaching mathematics again, much to Maxwell's delight, as he is a wonderful tutor. And I've been living with Hypatia and Hamid until your return."

"So you knew I was coming?"

"No, I knew the letter had been sent," she corrected him. "The rest was just hope. Is anyone with you? What about your friend, Luc?"

Her father sighed. "I'm afraid he didn't make it. But he died peacefully in the camp shortly after we got our pardon, 'At peace with man and God,' he said."

Ree hugged him hard. "I'm sorry. Maxwell, Lord John, and their family will be so sad."

"Luc was a great man. He knew what he was living for and death was no end for him. Don't be too angry, Ree, but thanks to him, I've become a Theophilus follower myself."

She rubbed her cheek against his chest, right over his heart. "Don't be silly, I'm not angry. My friends have taught me that there are patterns to things when you look deeply, and some say that's because there's a God, and some can't see it that way. Not everything we're curious about has a straightforward answer. People should be allowed to believe what they want, even my da."

He chuckled. "When did you get so wise?"

"Spend more than five minutes with me and you'll want to take that back. I've not changed so much."

He shifted so that one arm was looped around her shoulders, but he could see her carving. "All right, apprentice stonemason, show me what you've been working on."

Ree reached up and pulled down the last sheet that hid the apex of the arch. Over the door to the museum was a pair of cupped hands holding a dividing cell, or, if you liked to interpret it another way, a star. From the very small to the very big, that was what the museum was about. "The hand of the creator, or the hand of Stonemason Ree: take your pick."

Her father beamed at her. "You just don't give up, do you?"

"Never," she agreed.

Behind the Scenes of
A Curious Crime:
An Interview with
Julia Golding

Was the world really like this in the nineteenth century? If not, what was it like, and what inspired you to write about a society where "why" questions were not allowed?

No, it wasn't like this, though there are plenty of similarities. I thought of the book as an alternative history. Imagine two doors in front of you in about 1850: our world went through one; the society in my book took another.

Why did I write it? When I watch television or read certain books, sometimes I get the impression that the programme makers and writers think everyone shares their view that science and faith are completely separate things – even at odds. However, I know lots of scientists who also have a deep religious faith so I know this can't be true. Ruling out someone with a belief in God from the laboratory is as silly as handing it over to theologians who wouldn't have a clue how to conduct an experiment! We've seen in history what happens when religion gets in the way of science, but what about when scientific people turn their back on the wisdom of other viewpoints? What then guides their behaviour? In Ree and Henri's world, they aren't allowed "why" questions because the scientific leaders are afraid of the answers; they are only allowed to investigate the mechanisms, or the how of things. It's like being allowed to look at the engine and not ask who might be driving the car – or maybe wonder if it is self-driving, self-replicating... The story invites everyone of all faiths and no faiths to wander in the science museum because that diversity enriches our understanding.

At one point in the story, it looks as though phrenology might become the forefront of scientific thinking. Was phrenology real, and if so, why do we not learn about it in school today?

Ah, phrenology! Maybe you've seen pictures of a human head sectioned into little blocks with labels like cautiousness and self-esteem, like in the picture at the start of Chapter 3? This was a pseudo-science (that means it's not a real one) and was amazingly popular in the nineteenth and early twentieth centuries. Some people even used it to justify racial and gender prejudices. I thought it an interesting case of what happens when some bad scientific thinkers head off (pun intended!) in a wrong direction without any moral or ethical boundaries. We don't learn about it in science lessons at school because it doesn't have a foundation in fact. You might hear about it in History though!

What are your favourite "debunked" scientific ideas from history?

There are lots of wonderfully wrong ideas. My favourite is the four elements, first dreamed up by the Greek thinker Empedocles (c.490–c.430 BC). I like it because it is so poetic. He thought that the basic building blocks of life were earth, air, fire, and water. Unfortunately, it led to some very bad medical practices, as doctors tried to get your humours (the elements) back in balance by bleeding or purging you. Another favourite idea that hung around until the late eighteenth century was phlogiston. This was the idea that phlogiston was present in anything that burned and was released by fire. It doesn't exist, but it does have a lovely sounding name.

Why do areas of science get "debunked"? Does that mean the people who came up with the ideas were stupid or bad at science?

The science we have today can be described as the best picture the experts can come up with to explain how the universe works. Ask any professor working in science and she or he will accept, and even welcome, the idea that tomorrow some of what they think might be proved wrong, or not be the best description. But you can only come up with something better if you have the picture in the first place. The scientists of the past weren't stupid. They were often very clever people making their best guesses about things. As Isaac Newton wrote: "If I have seen further, it is by standing upon the shoulders of giants."

Dr Hypatia and Dr Hamid are a very interesting couple. What do you think we could learn from them?

They are very different people. Dr Hypatia is an explorer and a naturalist who likes nothing better than going on expeditions up the Amazon to see the wonders of the world for herself. Dr Hamid prefers to stay at his desk and travel the mathematical universe in his brain. They also have different views on religion: Hamid believes in God and Hypatia doesn't. The important thing to learn from them is that they appreciate each other's differences and will fight to protect the other's right to freedom to think and speak. In short, they love each other.

Why do you think a world with only "how" questions doesn't work? What do you think is so important about "why" questions?

A world that only allows us to ask "how" doesn't allow us to be fully human. We start as a young child with "why" questions. Why is the sky blue? Why does two and two equal four and not five? Why are we here? Why is really important as that is how we learn. If we just accept things without asking these deeper "why" questions, all spiritual, ethical, and moral ground disappears from underneath us. Society is in free fall.

What do you think Henri has learned from Ree by the end of the story?

It's not one way: they both learn from each other! They come to appreciate skills other than his or her own. We can't all be brilliant scientists; we also need artists, builders, laundry workers, cooks, gardeners, zookeepers, and so on! Henri and Ree also learn the value of a good friend.

Where do you see Ree, Henri, and the museum headed in the future?

Where do readers think Henri and Ree will end up? My first thought is that they go with Hypatia on one of her expeditions and maybe find a mate for Philoponus… As for the museum, it's much bigger now. There are rooms for Einstein's theory of relativity, quantum mechanics, DNA, space travel, artificial intelligence…

Which of the animals in the menagerie is your favourite, and why?

The dodo, of course, because Philoponus is full of mischief – but I have a soft spot for Ziggy, the Tasmanian wolf, as she has a fierce dignity. Almost all the animals mentioned in the menagerie are sadly extinct, which is why I brought them back to life in my book. I hate to think of what we have lost through human actions. I hope we can make them the last casualties of the human race – but that's another story!

About The Faraday Institute

The Curious Crime has been produced with the support of

The Faraday Institute is an interdisciplinary research enterprise based at Westminster College, Cambridge. Our Youth and Schools Team are committed to providing high-quality events and resources that encourage young people of all backgrounds to explore the interactions of science and religious faith in exciting and engaging ways. We think it's really important that all young people are able to search for answers to any and all of their questions.

If Ree and Henri's adventure has captured your curiosity, head to **www.faradayteens.com** for the chance to explore all sorts of interesting questions about science, faith, and what it means to be human. You can also find out more about our other books, apps, and videos, and to share your experience of reading this book with us! If you're a parent or teacher, check out **www. faradayeducators.com** for more information about our other resources and events.

www.faradayteens.com

www.faradayeducators.com

This project and publication was made possible through the support of a grant from the John Templeton Foundation. The opinions expressed in this publication are those of the author and do not necessarily reflect the views of the John Templeton Foundation.